A Crack in the Ice (RED FILES SERIES BOOK 2)

Copyright © Tom Watts 2016

All rights reserved. This is a work of fiction. Names, characters, places and incidents used are entirely fictitious. Any resemblance to actual events or persons, living or dead, is coincidental. All rights reserved. No part of this publication may be reproduced, or transmitted in any forms or by any means, electronic or otherwise, without written permission from the author.

Edited: Jessie Sanders
Cover Art: Linda Braine

Authors Note 1: While Seattle is the main setting for this novel, there are inconsistencies present mainly due to my overactive imagination. To the fine people of Seattle, please do not be too hard on me. If you like this work, please take a trip over to https://tomwatts.net. Sign up for a bunch of free content! Without the continued support of my family and my readers I wouldn't be able to keep doing what I'm doing and I thank you from the bottom of my heart.

Authors Note 2: Post Traumatic Stress Disorder is no joke and it features heavily in the following work. I'll talk about policing as it's in my wheelhouse, but this could extend to all my brothers and sisters in emergency services (military, paramedics, firefighters, etc). Most suffer in silence, though this should not be the way. If you are one of the nameless few, suffering from PTSD, please know that you're not alone. Help is out there.

ALSO BY TOM WATTS

RED FILES SERIES

Silent Witness

A Crack in the Ice

Writing is, by and large, a one-person act, but I'd be a fool if I didn't acknowledge some of the people who helped put this book together. To my faithful "first readers" who gave me the straight goods when it came to the nuts and bolts of this story, Holly Kehler Klaassen and James Watts, I salute you. To Dr. Derrick Klaassen and some of his insights into the mind. To Doyle Klaassen, proof-reader extrodenair…extroordinarrie…extradonair…you get the idea. Finally, to my wife Denise, for being my greatest defender.

For my mother, who never stops fighting.

TW

One

The city streets were dark except for two light sources casting uneven shadows through the towering maple trees which lined the roadway. The street lamps were one such source. Their dim yellow light hardly penetrated the deep gloom that had fallen like oilcloth over the wet roads. Incongruently, the Christmas lights from nearby houses were the second source, and the festive red and green bulbs made the raindrops that fell from an inky black sky flash like fireflies before they were gobbled up by the slick pavement. The rain collected in the gutters and splashed outward as the large front tires of the dark sedan pulled up to the curb, the worn brakes from the '88 New Yorker squealing in protest as the wide vehicle came to a stop.

The lone occupant inside slid the vehicle into park and settled back into the seat. He would have preferred a different vehicle, but as always he sought to blend in. In this neighborhood a high-end car like a BMW or Audi stood out like a beacon, whereas the rusted-out heap he had stolen from the airport parking lot looked like it belonged. Any passerby wouldn't give it a second glance. He had taken the extra step of switching the plates out with a similar-looking car, throwing the original tags into the cavernous trunk, where he had stashed all the other provisions he'd need for the week ahead.

He leaned sideways and peered through the rain-splattered window to the street beyond. The hour was late, approaching midnight, and most of the houses were dark, though a few still had their Christmas lights plugged in, the twinkling red and green reflecting off puddles in the pavement. He was pleased to see that there was hardly any traffic, with only the intermittent set of headlights rumbling past. He leaned over in the seat, the faded leather upholstery creaking under his body, and reached into the glove compartment, pulling out a tablet, turning the small, 8-inch device on with a press of his finger. He entered in a four-digit code and the main screen came on. Navigating through the icons he pulled up a folder and bent down in his seat to review the information.

Bryce Turner 1973-10-19

2547 Oak Street

Along with this tombstone data - an interesting phrase, all things considered - was a picture of a middle-aged man wearing a cheap suit, sporting an even cheaper haircut. He studied the photograph for a stretch of time before switching the tablet off and returning it to the glove box. Peering back through the window he saw the house three doors down. It looked the same as it had the two other times he had driven by, except now the living room light was on and he spotted figures moving past the drawn curtains.

He waited until a car had driven past and out of sight. Taking a deep breath he stepped out, closing the door quietly behind him. His black boots splashed against the rain-soaked pavement and he strode casually across the street and to the sidewalk, looking slowly left and right, seemingly at ease. This was key, he found. Pretending that you belonged. Act like you were meant to be there and, more often than not, people would stare right through you.

In the inside pocket of his jacket he had a wallet filled with three hundred dollars in cash, a driver's licence, a healthcare card, and two credit cards. These were in the name of Richard Kincaid, which listed his primary address as being in Florida. This was not his real name, merely one of many identities he had adopted over the years. If pressed, the man would have had difficulty remembering his real name, but for now the name in his wallet was as good as any other.

Kincaid walked up three short cement steps to the door and paused. From his car, he had seen two shadows moving in the living room. Kincaid's file told him that Turner lived with a woman whose last name was Beasley. Now, standing on the front patio, a wooden pergola blocking the rain, he could hear movement from inside in the residence. The voices were muffled and raised in a heated argument.

The man, whom he assumed was Turner, was yelling obscenities. The woman, likely Beasley, was pleading for him to stop, to calm down. Her plaintive cries were followed by a sharp crack, the unmistakable sound of flesh on flesh, and then breaking glass and a cry of pain.

Once again, Kincaid surveyed his surroundings. He was sure that the loud altercation could easily be heard by the neighbors, but there were no sirens of attending police, no furtive glances through curtains to see what the problem might be. This was a situation long ignored, and like good neighbors, they kept out of each other's business.

Raising a fist, Kincaid knocked loudly and the noises inside the house abruptly stopped. He knocked again, twice, and heavy footsteps approached the door. The curtains beside the door were parted and a man's head peeked through, regarded Kincaid for a moment, and disappeared. A dead bolt was disengaged and the door slowly opened with the face of Bryce Turner peering through the crack.

Once the man saw that it wasn't the police, he opened the door fully and stared at Kincaid. He looked much like his photograph, with short-cropped brown hair and close-set blue eyes that were glazed over and waxy, three days' growth of stubble on a square chin. Incredibly, the man wore a white muscle shirt – a wife beater, no less - and Kincaid could see by his build that he had probably been an athlete in his younger days. His biceps were hard and tense, his chest covered with a thick matt of black hair, but the midsection had given away to a considerable amount of flab.

Turner was angry, the jaw set, as if expecting a confrontation. He wobbled, swaying side-to-side, and Kincaid picked up the stench of beer, mixed with the putrid odor of sweat. With his arms at his sides Kincaid could see that the man's knuckles were bruised and bloodied. He looked past Turner to see the woman, Beasley, sitting on a couch in the living room, legs pressed together, fearful like a spooked rabbit. Her right eye was partially closed, the skin beginning to swell shut from where Turner had struck her, and a trail of blood ran from the side of her mouth down to her chin. Her white housecoat was dotted with blood and the collar twisted out from where Turner had grasped it as he struck her in the face. Turner turned his head slowly and looked back at Beasley, and Kincaid picked up on the unspoken command: *Don't say anything.*

Turner swung his head lazily back to Kincaid, and he could tell that the man was absolutely gunned. This was confirmed when Turner spoke, the words tumbling together in an almost incoherent string. "Whad the fug do you want?"

Kincaid smiled, savoring the moment. This was an important time, and he could feel the weight of it in the air, an almost tangible presence that hung in the atmosphere. The very moment between life and death when time seemed to slow, and the very fabric of his existence took on an entirely new meaning.

Confused by the warm smile that danced on Kincaid's face, Turner repeated his earlier question, though with more force, growing more confident with this sudden interloper who had interrupted his Monday evening wife beating session. Turner's confusion intensified, even under the influence of his heavy intoxication, as Kincaid smoothly removed a Beretta PX4 Storm from a concealed holster and leveled it at the man's face.

The sound of the gunfire was deafening as the .45 calibre round tore into Turner's face between the eyes. An explosion of brains and blood ejected from the back of the man's scull and painted the wall behind him as the round penetrated the drywall like a missile. Turner, already dead, collapsed to the ground in a heap, arms and legs flopping woodenly on the floor. He twitched once, the brain still firing with residual impulses, and then was still.

Beasley, still sitting on the couch, began screaming wildly and brought her hands up to her face, eyes alight with terror. Calmly Kincaid brought the pistol to bear on her, pointing the barrel directly at her face, a wisp of smoke trailing from the tip of the handgun.

"Quiet," he said, in a tone so calm it was almost cold. He had to raise his voice before she finally settled down, dialing her hysterics down to a low whimper. She had her face buried into her hands and was curled on the couch, trying to make as small of a target as possible, thinking that would somehow save her. "Look at me," he ordered, keeping his voice calm and still, and after a few moments she did as was told and dragged her fearful eyes to his own.

They held each other's gaze for a moment, and then he tucked the pistol back in his holster and said, "Merry Christmas." Kincaid, feeling very satisfied about the night's events, turned around and walked out, turning his collar up to guard against the rain.

Two

A pain blossoms in his chest like a hot poker. Bright and sharp, a crushing pressure seizes him, and every breath he takes plunges him deeper into a well of torment. Two sounds, like the muffled bark of a thunderclap, slice through his misery and bring him to consciousness. Feeling muddled, he struggles to open his eyes, his eyelids heavy.

His head is to the side, the bedcovers soft against his cheek, and he opens his eyes to find his wife, Laura, facing him. She is motionless, and her mouth is open in a wide O. Her eyes are closed. She could very well be sleeping, but in his heart he knows that this is something else.

He knows that she is dead, and he reaches out a weak hand to touch her cheek. Her skin is cold, the flesh hard. Her mouth twitches, begins to close. She lets out a long breath and then her eyes, milky white, snap open and settle on his own. "Don't go," she breathes. "Don't go..."

Jack Peterson shot up in bed, clutching his chest where the phantom pain still sank its icy fingers into his skin. He was out of breath and sweating, his lungs working in great heaving gasps that sent him into a coughing fit. He barked into his left hand while his right hand braced himself in bed, the hacking increasing to such a fervor that he began to gag. After what felt like an eternity, the coughing abated and he put a hand to his forehead, nausea rolling through him like a wave.

Peterson kicked back the bedcovers that were soaked with sweat and settled his feet on the cold wood floor. He placed his forearms on his knees and bent forward, hands clasped, and focused on slowing his heart rate, on getting his breathing under control. His heart beat like a jackhammer against his ribcage, black spots swimming across his vision, the afterimages of the frequent dream flashing in his mind like grainy photographs.

He was on the bottom level of his house in the Green Lakes district of Seattle, staying in one of the spare bedrooms that was on the main floor, between one of the bathrooms and the laundry room. As his eyes adjusted to the gloom and his heart resumed a steadier rhythm, he looked at the bedside clock reflexively. 3:20 a.m.

Peterson stood up and scratched the scar on his chest. Below his sternum, the white discolored tissue was shaped like a rose petal, and it hurt to the touch. His ribs were like speed bumps under his fingers—no fat, just flesh stretched over bone. The other scar, above his eyebrows and just under his hairline, was less noticeable and would be difficult to see if one didn't already know it was there. Peterson saw it, every time he looked in the mirror, and it served as a constant reminder of how close he had been to death.

Peterson left the bedroom and headed to the kitchen, where he retrieved a glass from the cupboard and filled it with water. He didn't bother with the lights and stood in the kitchen bathed in darkness, wearing only a pair of boxer shorts and a white t-shirt. The house was cool, quiet, and had the unmistakable feeling of being empty. Empty house. Empty life.

Draining the glass, he placed it in the sink and padded back to the bedroom. Leaving the kitchen, he passed near the stairway that led to the upstairs part of the house. He stopped and looked up. The only light visible spilled through an upper hallway window, barely penetrating the gloom. Even at the foot of the stairs panic crawled over his skin like marching ants as the memories came flooding back.

Six months earlier his wife and unborn child had been killed. He himself had been seriously wounded. After returning from the hospital, Peterson had tried to survey the damage that had occurred in the bedroom where he had spent almost every evening with his wife. His colleague, Charles Denly, had informed him that they had brought in a company which specialized in crime scene cleanups. The walls had been scrubbed, the carpet replaced, and the bed removed.

He had been curious to know what the room looked like, but halfway up the stairs he had collapsed and passed out. Twenty minutes later or so he had come to at the bottom of the stairs, a golf-ball-sized contusion on his forehead from where he had struck the tiled floor. He had not made the attempt again.

Bringing his eyes back down, Peterson continued past the stairs and toward his new bedroom, the sweat on the back of his neck cooling his skin, a chill running down his spine. He returned to the bedroom and saw that it was now almost four. In less than four hours he would be back at work, back at the Seattle Police Department, back at the Red Files. His first shift back after almost six months away. Sighing, he laid back down on the bed and stared up at the ceiling. Usually the dream didn't come a second time in one night. Usually.

His eyes drifted shut, and he settled into an uneasy sleep.

It was 4:20 a.m. when his cell phone rang, the Blackberry buzzing on the bedside table. Feeling sick to his stomach with exhaustion, he rolled on to his side and flipped open the phone.

"Peterson," he said, mouth thick with sleep.

"Jack, it's Charles," the other end said. Charles Denly's southern drawl poured through the speaker like molasses. "Sorry to wake you, but we got a scene out here that you need to take a look at."

Peterson flicked on the bedside lamp and grabbed a pen, writing the details on his hand.

He told Denly he would be there as soon as possible and he ended the call, swinging his feet back out of bed and putting his head in his hands.

"Welcome back," he said to no one in particular.

Three

By any standard Oak Street was a narrow roadway, a newer development where the planners had attempted to capitalize on making as many homes as possible by narrowing the lanes. With the crush of humanity at the Turner scene, reporters and police alike, Peterson had to park three blocks away and hoof it to the house, weaving through reporters and onlookers who cast him sideways glances as he pushed past. Once he reached the relative safety of the yellow police tape, ducking under it after flashing his badge at a member, he heard two reporters call him by name, one turning to her partner and swearing under her breath. "That's Jack Peterson." He had no idea he was still a hot topic in the city. If it bleeds, it leads. Sometimes for longer than expected.

  The rain was coming down in sheets, soaking his clothing, his bones. Anywhere else and it would be snow, but in this part of the world it came down wet and generally stayed wet. It was six a.m. and the sky was still pitch black, no promise of anything but another gray day.

  He found Charles Denly standing with his hands in his pockets under an awning that had been extended from a CSI mobile command station. The vehicle was a fourteen-foot Mercedes Bluetec van, white in color, with a large SPD logo stamped on the sides. The awning had two metal arms that kept the heavy plastic sheet in place, which rocked in the pressing wind. Denly nodded at Peterson as he hurried underneath the awning to join him and extended his hand in greeting.

  "Coming down like cats and dogs," the Southerner drawled, releasing Peterson's hand and shoving both fists back into his oversized coat. In his mid-thirties, Denly's blonde hair was ghostly pale under the white lights of the CSI van. A slight smell of bourbon trailed from the man, and his eyes were red and bloodshot. Peterson wondered if it was from the lack of sleep or the booze.

"How long you been out here?" he asked, slipping his own hands into his pockets, shivering with a slight chill.

"Only got here about an hour ago myself," Denly said, his breath puffing out in a haze. At least his voice wasn't slurred, Peterson thought. He knew Denly sometimes hit the bottle, perhaps harder than he should, but he didn't want to say anything. At least, not on this morning. Denly continued, "They originally thought it was a straight up domestic and it was nearly a blue file, but forensics thought otherwise."

Peterson nodded. Last year, under his guidance, the SPD had begun a pilot project that was designed to distinguish the types of calls that they encountered. Easy solves, labeled blue files, were handled by standard investigators, who scoured the scenes quickly and efficiently. These files were no brainers and could generally be solved within forty-eight hours. By contrast, the red files were more complicated and required more resources.

Peterson felt the younger detective inspecting him and, raising an eyebrow, he inquired, "What is it?"

Denly rubbed the back of his neck and looked uncomfortable. "How are you doing with things?" he asked. "First day back and all…"

Peterson looked out toward the house and collected his thoughts before answering. A uniformed officer stood guard outside the front door, which was opened a crack to let a sliver of light through. From the drawn curtains he could see the flashbulbs of the working identification officers, who were trolling around the interior, taking photographs and probably marking evidence. "Oh, doing okay. Coping, y'know," he said, clapping the younger man on the shoulder. "I'm doing okay, thanks for asking."

This statement had been well crafted from the numerous times that question, or a vaguely similar one, had been asked of him. "How are things?" "You doing okay?" "Such a terrible shame, how you holding up?" "Things happen for a reason," etc., etc. Empty platitudes not worthy of responses. "Why don't we take a look inside?" Peterson offered. Denly nodded and although he looked ill at ease he followed Peterson toward the house without another word. A cement walkway led to the front door, and the pair stopped in front of the SPD officer who was acting as scene security.

"Sorry, guys," the officer said, taking their names down in a notebook which he held close to his body to avoid getting it wet. He hooked a thumb toward the door, and Peterson could see a man's shoe just beyond the threshold, a small pool of blood near the heel before the rest of the body was blocked by the doorway. "Can't go in that way. Vic's blood blocks this door. Have to go around back."

They thanked the officer and hurried back through the rain, passing on the left side of the house and through a wooden gate that creaked loudly as they pushed it open, climbing up a set of wooden steps that were badly in need of a paint job, and through a covered patio that was in an equal state of disrepair, before finally slipping into the house through the rear door.

They found themselves in the kitchen, and they were not alone. Another SPD officer, a big guy named Barnes, was standing in the threshold that led from the kitchen to the living room. He had his arms crossed over a thick chest, and he nodded a greeting to Denly and Peterson as they shook water off their coats. A woman sitting at a straw-colored kitchen table was smoking a cigarette with shaky fingers. The tip of the cigarette bounced like a red firelight as she took a deep drag. If she noticed their arrival she didn't show it and she sat with her back against the wall staring past the officer and through to the living room, thoughts apparently occupied with the dead body on the foyer floor.

The kitchen was roughly L-shaped, and the tan-colored cabinets met a white fridge and a chrome stove. In the kitchen sink, stuffed next to some dirty dishes that had probably been used for dinner, were six empty beer cans. Peterson wouldn't be surprised to find more alcohol in the fridge. Maybe in the cupboard too. The house had the smell of stale alcohol, an essence of whisky and beer that rode along the cigarette smoke like an unwanted house guest.

Peterson pulled up a chair and sat across from the woman. She blinked once, bringing her eyes slowly to his and regarding him through a haze of smoke. Denly took a chair on his left and settled in, flipping open a notebook, pen poised to take notes. This hadn't been discussed but had been a frequent practice of theirs in the past, and Peterson was pleased to at least feel the same rhythm as before.

"Mrs. Turner," he began. "I wanted to tell you how sorry I am-"

"Beasley," she said, her voice like sandpaper. "My name is Lindsay Beasley. We weren't married, just common-law."

Lindsay Beasley had at one point in her life been pretty, Peterson could see that. Maybe still could be. She had a round face with sandy blonde hair, striking blue eyes that seemed drained of any emotion. Her white housecoat was speckled with blood, the collar and cuffs torn. All visible skin had a patchwork of bruises and scars, some old, most new. Her one eye was nearly swollen shut, the skin waxy and stretched. She moved slowly as though manoeuvring in a fog and she looked back and forth between the two detectives.

"I know this is difficult," Peterson continued. "But we need to ask you about what happened here tonight."

"They think I did it."

"Who?"

She nodded towards the officer in the hallway, Barnes, who pretended not to hear.

"They did at first," Peterson responded.

"But not now?"

"No."

"Why not?" she said, her lip quivering. "I could have. I should have. He beat me almost every night, you know that?" She took a long drag on her cigarette, the grey ashes on the tip curling as gravity dragged them towards the floor. "Of course, you know that, you're the damn cops after all. Not that you ever cared before. No one cared."

With her free hand, she wiped her nose, smearing blood on the side of her cheek. "You know that I actually took him to court? He beat me so hard that I called the cops. You guys hauled him away."

"What happened?" Peterson asked.

"A couple weeks before the trial he called me at home. He couldn't see me, you understand. On conditions. But he threatened me if I testified he'd burn the house down. With me in it. So I pulled my statement. Withdrew everything. He was back here the next day. Put me in the hospital for three weeks."

"Why didn't you report the threat?"

"I did. You guys said I had no proof. My word against his. What was I supposed to do?"

Peterson had no answer for that, so he didn't even try. Lindsay Beasley fit well into the cycle of domestic abuse that he had seen time and time again. Some of the luckier women escaped. Most didn't.

"What happened here tonight, Ms. Beasley?" Peterson probed.

She sniffed again, rubbing the back of her hand across her nose. Her description was given in rapid fire, born from the shock of witnessing such an event. Single male came in. White. Sharp looking with a crew cut. Produced a handgun of some kind and shot Turner in the face. What she said next shocked Peterson.

"He said, 'Merry Christmas'?" Denly asked Beasley, just as amazed as Peterson.

"Yeah," she said. "Seemed real pleased about it too."

They asked Beasley a series of questions, not learning much more. Turner owned a car dealership, was generally hated by his employees. His parents were dead. Two sisters on the east coast. Born and raised in Seattle. Enemies? He was a prick, of course he had enemies. Did they hate him enough to kill him? Who knows?

Peterson looked around the kitchen, then hooked a head toward the SPD officer. He asked Beasley, "Do you have anywhere else you can go? Neighbours, family? They're going to be here for a while, and I can't imagine that you want to stay here."

She drew on her cigarette and resumed staring out the kitchen window. "I got nobody, Detective. Nowhere else to go."

Both men stood up and pushed the chairs back under the table. Peterson said, "We'll be in the other room with…your husband. Please let me know if you need anything." Without looking at him she waved her cigarette hand lazily toward the living room, as if to say, "he's all yours." When she did so, the curl of ashes finally dropped from the tip of her cigarette, falling on the leg of her housecoat. She made no move to brush it away.

Four

Officer Barnes moved aside as the two detectives went into the living room. The floor was beige carpet, the walls a muted yellow. A couch and a love seat, dark fabric, were up against the far wall, and a recliner was placed strategically in front of a large, flat screen television. Beer cans littered the floor, their contents tipped and staining the carpet. Blankets were tossed, and a small table had been knocked over, the wood cracked from where it had struck the ground.

"Seems like there was a struggle," Peterson offered to Denly.

"There was," a voice answered from the left side of the room, "but not directly related to the murder." A figure, dressed head to toe in a white Tyvek suit typically called a "bunny suit" came around the corner and stood in the center of the living room. The white hood was pulled over the person's head, and under the clear goggles and white mask little could be discerned about the individual. With gloved hands the person reached up and removed the hood, tugging off the mask and goggles, stuffing them into one of the side pockets of the cumbersome suit.

Denly sidled up next to Peterson and took care of the instructions. "Jack, this is Graham Matthews, one of the new forensic people. Graham, meet Jack Peterson."

Mathews reached out to shake Peterson's hand, the Tyvek suit crinkling like newspaper. Peterson looked down at the hand, which was cucumber green with the latex glove Matthews was wearing. Streaks of blood trailed across the glove's fingers and on the back of the hand, dark red against the green.

Peterson kept his own hands firmly in his pockets, and it took Matthews a moment to catch on. "Ah, sorry about that," he said, taking his hand back and wiping the blood off on his white suit. Fortunately, he made no move to shake his hand again. "Glad to finally meet," Matthews said. "I've heard a lot about you."

"All good, I hope." Matthews was in his late twenties or early thirties and his face wore a serious expression. Peterson nodded toward Matthews's Tyvex suit. "Should we suit up?"

Matthews considered and finally shook his head. "Not necessary. I got all the DNA samples I probably need, just try not to step in any of the mung that's out there."

"Are we alone?" Peterson asked, looking over Matthews shoulder. "I thought I heard other voices."

Matthews looked confused for a moment before nodding, pulling a digital recorder out of a side pocket. "It's easier than taking notes," he said and pressed the *play* button. His digitized voice came tinny through the small speaker. "Victim Caucasian male, mid-thirties. Entrance wound upper forehead." He turned off the recorder and tucked it back into his pocket. Giving Peterson a smile, he said, "Can't tell you how many pens I've had to throw away."

Peterson offered a small smile in return and nodded toward the damage in the living room. "So, this was all related to Turner hitting his wife?"

Matthews. "Seems so. They were in the thick of things when the shooter knocked on the door. Turner went to answer, and lights out."

"Good timing," Peterson said.

"For her, maybe," Matthews commented. They went from the living room to a small foyer that acted as a quasi mud room that led to the front door. The floor was white linoleum. At least, Peterson thought, it had been white at some point in time. Most of it now was covered with blood, which surrounded the body of a man like a carmine lake.

Turner was on his back, a large red hole in the center of his forehead. The dead man's face was collapsed inward, the orbital bones and the nasal cavity pulverised by the force of the impact. The air was heavy, dense with the smell of blood and feces, a sickly-sweet smell that reminded Peterson of honey. Feeling lightheaded, a knot forming in his throat, Peterson reached out and a put a hand on the wall. He heard Denly ask Matthews what he thought of the scene, and the forensics member cleared his throat before speaking.

"Well, the wife said that the killer opened the door and shot the victim at fairly close range, which is consistent with the wound and the stippling pattern you see here." Matthews bent at the knee and pointed to the entry in the center of Turner's forehead. The skin had split in this area, tiny cracks spreading outward a few millimetres from the hole. It was blackened and powdered, like burnt paper, which was common with close-entry gunshots. "Once we saw the size of the exit wound and the hole in the wall, we more or less ruled the wife out," Matthews continued.

"Why's that?" Denly asked.

"The responding officers got here within moments of the call," Matthews responded. "And they reported that the wife wouldn't have had enough time to change. Her shirt was clean, except for a few passive droplets from where Turner had smoked her." He pointed again to the wound, which seemed to pulsate the more Peterson stared at it. "With an entry like that, the gun we're probably looking for is a .45. At that close range you'd expect to see a fair amount of blowback." To Peterson's eyes, the entry wound looked like it had been made with a cannon. The shooter would have been practically bathed in tiny droplets of the victim's blood. Matthews continued talking, listing off facts and deductions, but Peterson barely heard him. Matthews's voice sounded like it was coming from a long corridor, muffled and fuzzy, and Peterson's head was beginning to swim. He couldn't take his eyes off the bullet wound on Turner's ruined face, and he became dimly aware that Denly was staring at him with a concerned expression.

"Are you okay, boss?" he asked.

"Hmm?" he responded. "I'm fine. Fine. Why?"

"You just look a little pale, is all."

Peterson closed his eyes for a moment and coughed into his free hand. He was worried that if he let go of the wall with the other he would fall over. Or worse, fall into the corpse lying there in a bloody mess on the floor. "Just something I ate," he said. "I…uh…just need some fresh air," he said, and pushed past Denly to get outside, leaving a stymied Matthews still hunched over the dead body. He didn't trust threading back through the house, so he went out the front door, the edge of which barely cleared the dead man's foot. The air was cool and damp but did little to clear his senses, and he half-walked, half-stumbled down the concrete steps, making it to the paved walkway while the uniformed officer called after him, making sure he was all right. A moment later Denly was there and put an arm under Peterson's armpit to lead him back to the CSI bus. They made it to the covered awning, Peterson wheezing like he had just run a marathon, and Denly leaned him up against the side of the bus, levelling a serious expression on him as he wiped rain from his own brow.

"What they hell did you eat?" he asked.

Five

They left the crime scene later in the morning, most of the time spent canvassing the neighbourhood. It was one of those areas where people kept their heads down and ignored what was going on around them. The immediate neighbours had heard the gunshot but didn't see anything. A neighbour to the south may have seen a dark-colored sedan driving away but couldn't comment on a make or model. Video surveillance? Laughable. Most people had enough troubles making ends meet; a security camera was a luxury they couldn't afford.

The grey December dawn was cool and crisp by the time they left the scene, and they drove in separate cars toward WestOps through an early afternoon drizzle. Up until this year, all major crime sections had been run out of headquarters downtown, but a recent reorganization had moved most specialized units to a separate building on the west side, a non-descript glass paneled six-story property that looked more like an apartment complex than a police building. With the threat of terrorism looming, perhaps that was the idea. WestOps would make an unlikely target as most didn't even know it existed.

Denly pulled around the rear of the building, and Peterson followed, steering his car down a steep concrete embankment that led to the underground parking. This was the first time he had been to WestOps, and he parked beside Denly in a stall that had been marked for him. The air was stale and musty, exhaust fumes mixed with standing water, and out of reflex he locked the doors to his vehicle, forgetting that the parking garage was secured. Old habits.

Denly was waiting outside his own vehicle, and the two men fell in step beside each other as they walked over to the elevators.

"Easier to find parking here than in downtown," Peterson commented.

"Cheaper too. I had Judith set up your desk for you, hope that's okay."

Peterson said it was as they approached a double set of blue metal doors that Denly opened with his key card. He held it up for Peterson before attaching it to his belt on a clip. "Got you one of these too. It'll let you in and out of the building. Just make sure you have it displayed at all times or else Gregor will have your ass."

Peterson walked through the open door, shooting Denly a look. "Gregor? As in Sergeant Gregor?"

Denly closed the door with a click, and they proceeded to the elevators. "It's Captain Gregor now." He pointed to a posted notice attached with scotch tape on the elevator door. "Check it."

Peterson did, leaning forward to read the note, which was an official memorandum from Seattle Police Department headquarters. It was a notice to all employees to follow proper dress and deportment, which included instructions to display their name badges at all times. This pronouncement followed a laundry list of other rules that needed to be adhered to, and it promised swift retribution for any noncompliance. At the end, it was signed "Captain Elias Gregor, OIC WestOps Division."

Peterson cringed inwardly. He knew of Gregor from his Homicide days, when the younger man had been a detective with Professional Standards, the unit primarily charged with handling code of conduct investigations of their own members. Peterson said, "How did that snake become captain?"

Denly pressed the button for the elevator, which hummed in response. "Kiss enough ass, something good is bound to happen."

Six

Their new office was typical in the fashion of police design, bland and conformist. A reception area at the front was normally occupied by Judith Cairnes, who had made the transition from HQ to WestOps. However, she was not there this morning, and Peterson assumed it was her day off. Each detective had a single cubicle with an L-shaped desk, a double set of computer monitors, and a large filing cabinet for storing active case files. A stand-alone computer was in the center of the office where the members could run suspect information in a system called CABS. A large window on the far side of the office faced over the Duwamish River, which looked choppy and cold in the late morning haze.

      Denly was true to his word, and Peterson found his desk already neatly organized, though there were no personal accoutrements of any kind. A banker's box stood at the foot of the desk labeled "Peterson," which he knew contained most of his personal articles from HQ, plaques and certificates, photographs of Laura. Without opening it, he pushed it under the desk with the side of his foot.

      A square, gunmetal grey box sat on one corner of the desk, secured with a large Stanley lock. Peterson fished his keys from his pocket, flipping to the one he wanted, and tested it on the lock, finding that it fit in easily. He opened the lid and found his old service pistol, a black Glock 40 cal, nestled in grey packing foam. A second compartment on the inside held a clip with fifteen rounds.

      He hefted the weapon out, feeling the weight in his hand. It was secured with a trigger guard, a two-piece kit that prevented the trigger from being depressed. The combination was a four-digit code on the action side, and he entered the code now, Laura's date of birth.

Swallowing down a lump in his throat, he placed the trigger guard back in the box and removed the mag, slamming it home in the butt of the pistol and cycling the action back. The round easily slipped into the pipe, and the weapon was ready to go.

Peterson had been unaware that Denly had been watching his moves. "Been a long time?" he asked.

Peterson slipped the weapon into the shoulder rig he had put on in the morning, which had been empty during the early morning investigation. "Too long," Peterson said finally, snapping the gun in place.

They settled into a rhythm at the office, but by the end of the day Peterson and Denly learned little more about who might have had motive to kill Bryce Turner. The financial checks concluded that Lindsay Beasley had not made any large withdrawals from their bank account. Paying off a hitman to kill her husband was costly work, and it would have shown up in the records. Denly called the dealership and managed to find a receptionist with a loose tongue. Through her, he found that Turner had employed at least fifty people, the general consensus being that they hated their boss with a passion. Any number of them would have reason to want to kill their boss; whether they would do it was another question. Denly, at one end of a long grey table, shuffled notes and paperwork aside, and rubbed at his eyes. Both men were operating on little sleep, and they sipped from white ceramic mugs filled with a dark murky liquid that had once been coffee but now tasted suspiciously of battery acid.

"We got a long list of suspects here," Denly volunteered, pushing back from his desk and holding the mug between his two hands.

Peterson nodded as he drank from his own cup. "True. We'll have to run checks on all of them. See if any have criminal records, any history of violence. Maybe we can contact Polygraph section to put a questionnaire together." Often when dealing with a large pool of suspects a probative questionnaire would be drafted, one with questions and answers that were designed to differentiate between the potentially innocent and the obviously guilty. It wasn't perfect or foolproof, but it could help to narrow the focus of the investigation. "Did you learn anything about Turner?"

"That's another matter entirely," Denly said, turning to his computer. "Our boy has a long history. Some juvy stuff when he was young: theft, break and enter, that kind of thing. No formal charges, he always seemed to get off with conditional discharge, alternative measures. There were numerous complaints of domestics with his common-law but only one criminal charge. About two months ago there was a trial, but the charges were withdrawn when Beasley recanted her statement."

"Tracks with what she told us," Peterson commented. "Did anything come out of the autopsy?"

Denly looked down and shuffled through the paperwork until he found the document he was looking for. "They haven't got to it yet, but the Doc gave me some basics. Close contact wound, we knew that. Matthews found a single casing on the scene, .45 calibre." He scrolled down with his finger. "One round dug out of the wall, but it was too damaged." He brought his eyes back to Peterson. "So ballistics is out."

Peterson shook his head. "I'm surprised that the casing had been left behind."

"I thought so too," Denly said. "But maybe buddy wanted to get out of there as quickly as possible. Matthews said he would check for prints on the casing but wasn't hopeful."

Peterson shook his head and pushed back from the conference table. He shrugged on his dark coat and buttoned it up. "We'll stick with Beasley unless something else comes forward," he told Denly. More often than not, the spouse ended up being the killer. He checked his watch and found that it was well past six p.m. "Why don't you take off, Charles? Sarah would probably like you home for dinner."

Denly got to his feet and shifted uncomfortably. "Why don't you come along?" he asked. "I'm sure Sarah would love to see you again."

Peterson felt his stomach tighten and made a business of trying to adjust the buttons on his coat. Charles and Sarah were a nice couple, as were their two children, and in the past Peterson probably would have said yes. Instead, he gave Denly the best smile he could summon and thanked him. "Thanks for the offer, but I'm pretty tired. I'll just head home, I think".

Denly slipped on his own coat and made an effort of doing up the buttons. "I'm a little worried about you, Jack. Just what happened at the house there, you looked pretty rattled. And…" He paused, searching for the words as he brought up his eyes up to Peterson. "Well, the thing is, you don't look so good. You're skin and bones, man. Sarah isn't the greatest cook, but she can put some meat on you."

Peterson laughed, though it sounded hollow to his own ears. He knew that he had lost a lot of weight in the hospital, which the doctors told him was normal with coma cases. The body self cannibalized in order to heal properly. He clapped his colleague on the shoulder as he led him toward the exit. "Rain check, my friend. Rain check." And he shut off the lights and locked the door, preparing to head home but planning on making a stop first.

Peterson pulled his vehicle to the curb and slipped it in park. Pedestrian and vehicle traffic was still heavy, even with the foul weather that continued to pepper the ground with rain. The street corner presented the usual hustle and bustle of people going about their affairs. Not many would notice him parked there, or at least he hoped that would be the case.

If the meteorologists were to be believed, the chill would continue to deepen as a cold front blew in from the Pacific, carrying with it the threat of freezing temperatures and possibly even snow. The women who were huddled underneath the awning of a tan and grey building across the street seemed entirely unaffected by the weather, despite the skimpy and revealing clothing that they wore. Even at this distance Peterson could see that their mismatched and tight leather and fur jackets had seen better days. They had probably been picked from the discount rack of a second-hand store, and most of the women kept their jackets open, allowing the passing motorists a quick glance as to what particular flavor they were offering that night.

His eyes scanned the group until he saw the one he was looking for. She stood apart only by virtue of being taller than the rest of her colleagues. Doing a quick mirror check, Peterson put the car in drive and inched forward until he pulled up beside the group of women on the corner. One of the girls, dressed entirely in black leather, elbowed the taller woman when she noticed the car pull up. The woman bent down and smiled slightly when she saw Peterson behind the wheel. Giving a parting word to her friend, she sidled up to the passenger side as Peterson rolled down the window. A dizzying wash of perfume splashed against Peterson as the woman, whom he knew only as Juliette, stuck her head in through the open window and gave him a seductive smile.

"Long time no see, handsome," she said in lightly accented French. Peterson couldn't tell if her accent was real or simply part of the façade that she used to help drum up business. Her face was long and narrow with thin lips painted dark red, which clashed with her maroon leather jacket. Her hair was strawberry blonde, which she usually wore down but tonight had tied to the top in a severe bun. Her frame with thin, accentuated by the tight black tube dress she wore. She said, "I'd ask if you were a cop, but I already know that you are" she allowed with a smile. He could see the red smudges of lipstick on her small white teeth.

"You busy tonight?" he asked.

Juliette brought a hand up to her lips and considered thoughtfully. "Depends on who is asking," she responded.

Peterson sighed and looked in the rear-view mirror, though it was impossible to say if he was being monitored or not. Finding the coast clear, or gambling that it was, he leaned over in the seat and opened the passenger door from the inside. "Get in," he said.

Seven

At 5:30 the next morning the sky was ashen as fat raindrops fell intermittently from the sky. They splashed against Kincaid's ball cap as he jogged down the tree lined path, the gravel underneath his running shoes crunching as he brought each foot down, the only sound to be heard other than a slight whisper of wind through the trees and his own shallow breathing. He jogged easily, his posture relaxed and measured, feeling the chill air as he sucked it into his lungs, the sweat already forming at the back of his neck. The black pants he wore pressed tightly against his quads, and he felt his muscles tense after each step, the loose-fitting rain jacket whipping around his arms and side as it flapped with the movement.

It felt good to be moving again. Kincaid frequently found himself stuck in one position or another, either behind the wheel of a car or wedged in the seat of an airplane. He breathed easily through his run, fully aware that he could push himself harder if he needed to. He was intimately aware of the limitations and stamina of his own body but he wanted to take this one slow. Slow for him, anyway.

Knotty pines flashed by on either side as he paced along, their dark brown fingers and mushroomed nodules collecting the rain and flicking them back to the ground, where they settled in dark, murky puddles that rippled in the breeze. As Kincaid rounded a tight turn, he came to a clearing where there stretched a horizon that featured a foggy grey valley with the mist settling in the lower levels like a thick blanket. He pulled up short, clutching at the back of his left leg, a look of pain etched on his face. He swore and slowed his pace, finally settling into a slow limp as he cleared the line of trees. A man sitting on a park bench on his right looked up sharply when he saw Kincaid, surprise flashing to concern as he noticed Kincaid's pained expression and pronounced limp. The man appeared to be in his early or late forties and was wearing blue jeans with brown hiking boots, a silver and black rain jacket that repelled much of the water streaking from the sky. Under a wide-brimmed hat, lively eyes tracked Kincaid as he stopped directly in front of the man, grasping on to the rear muscle of his leg.

"You all right?" the man asked.

Breathing heavily, Kincaid bent at the waist and began to rub at his hamstring, wincing in pain as he did so. "Yeah," he responded, looking under his ball cap toward the man. "Damn leg cramp." He took a few more deep breaths and tried to regulate his heart rate. "Sorry if I startled you."

The man shook his head indicating that the apology wasn't necessary. "You should probably stretch more," he smiled. "Or less, I'm not sure which is the popular theory these days." The man was sitting on the left side of the park bench, hands in his lap, evidently unconcerned with the either the rain or the cold.

Kincaid said, "You stretch for fast runs, don't stretch for slow jogs." When the man raised an eyebrow at him, he explained, "I'm a bit of a fitness buff." He straightened and placed his hands on his hips, looking out towards the horizon. "Though I'm not used to this cold, it would seem."

"Not from around here?" the man asked.

"No, southern California actually," Kincaid said as he turned back to the man. He motioned to the empty side of the bench. "Do you mind?"

The man said that he didn't, and Kincaid put his heel on the edge of the bench and bent forward at the waist to stretch his hamstring. With both hands, Kincaid grasped the sides of his running shoe to get the maximum stretch.

"What brings you up here?" the man asked Kincaid.

Kincaid winced in pain. "Business mostly. Just killing time right now before I have to see my next client." Kincaid looked around himself again and then back at the man, a small smile forming at the corner of his mouth "Do you often come out here and sit in the rain?"

The man looked out over the valley like he was drinking in the scenery. He breathed the frigid December air in deeply and exhaled. "Yes, I'm afraid I'm not built for running." He looked Kincaid up and down again. "Feels too much like punishment to me."

Kincaid switched legs, bringing up his right leg on the bench for a hamstring stretch. Like before, he brought both hands down to his ankle to lean into the stretch. "Some people deserve to be punished," Kincaid said, "Mr. Collins."

The man's eyes narrowed as he tried to process what Kincaid had just said. "I never told you my name," he said slowly, moving to inch away from Kincaid.

"I guess you didn't," Kincaid said and reached with his right hand, blocked from Collins's view by his shin, and grabbed at the boot knife that was sheathed between his shoe and his running sock. Blade flashing silver, Collins's abrupt scream pierced the silent valley, causing three nearby crows to take flight in alarm, their wing flaps beating a hasty retreat to safer parts of the valley below.

Eight

When Peterson awoke, Juliette had already gone, the only signs of her presence being a small dent where her head had rested on the pillow and her perfume, which hung in the air like camp smoke. This was the way it had been every other time Juliette had stayed the night, as Peterson, free from the nightmares that had been steadily increasing, would often sleep like the dead, her presence a somehow nulling affect that kept his dreams at bay. He had no idea how she got home, if she took a cab or walked, or indeed where her home was or what it was like. He was merely thankful that he was spared any awkward conversation that their strange relationship would undoubtedly require if he saw her in the morning.

      Kicking off the bedcovers, Peterson showered and changed, strapping his duty pistol into a black pancake holster that he secured on his belt. He checked the weather forecast on his phone, which still called for heavy rains and nearly freezing temperatures, and hastily packed a peanut butter sandwich before leaving the house. As he stepped out of the front door he wondered briefly if the neighbors had ever seen Juliette come and go and what they might think if they had. Green Lakes was an old area of Seattle, with 20th century colonial houses, most still bearing the original framework and design of their primary construction. The lake, for which the neighborhood was named for, was a shining jewel in the distance, nearly iced over from the unusually cold weather.

      His residence, which he and Laura had received from his parents following their death, had been heavily renovated but still retained the same theme as the surrounding properties, an intentional design idea that had mainly been Laura's. The newest addition to the house had been his own doing, and the "For Sale" sign posted in the center of the lawn creaked and waved in the slight wind that blew in off the lake. A month or two after getting out of the hospital Peterson had called a real estate agent, and the house had been listed on the market. The agent, a rail-thin man named Mason, had nodded with satisfaction during the initial walk-through, confidently telling Peterson that he was sure the house would be picked up in no time.

"Do you know about the history of this place?" Peterson had inquired, and when Mason shook his head he gave him a quick run down of the details, at which point the agent no longer looked so hopeful. Since then, there had been several showings but no actual offers. Seemed like people had a hang-up about buying a property where a woman had been shot and murdered only a few months before.

Before the shooting, Peterson had been close with his neighbors, often inviting them over for barbeques or the occasional block party. Since returning from the hospital he received mainly sideways glances and looks of quiet pity, muted hushes of conversations as he passed people in the street. Others looked toward him with disdain, as if his very presence was a blight on an otherwise perfect neighborhood. He noted their satisfaction when they saw the "For Sale" sign posted on the front lawn and imagined they were looking forward to the day when the moving truck arrived to take his belongings away, and with it perhaps the memories of what had occurred there.

The sky was a dusty grey as he backed his car out of the driveway and headed to Elliot Bay. He turned on the radio to listen to music but gave up after a few minutes, finding only Christmas and holiday songs playing in an endless loop. He switched the channel to the news radio and caught the tail end of the hourly report, the newscaster indicating that the body of a male had been found on the Watershed Loop trail. Peterson shook his head slowly as he listened, a familiar itch crawling down his spine as the slim details were transmitted through the radio.

"A heavy police presence is at the scene," the reporter stated, "and while few details are being released at this time, a police spokesperson is indicating that the death is being treated as suspicious."

Peterson's hands tightened on the wheel as he sped towards WestOps. Two murders in two days. He had picked a hell of a time to come back to work.

Peterson arrived at the office and took the elevators to the second floor, where he found Charles Denly and Judith Cairnes in the lunchroom watching the wall-mounted flat screen television that was tuned to the morning news. Denly nodded to Peterson as he walked up, a serious expression on his face. Cairnes, their primary receptionist, squealed piercingly when she saw him and pushed past Denly to embrace Peterson in a fierce hug. She was a short, pudgy woman, and Peterson felt her thick warm body nearly swallow his own thin frame as she wrapped her arms around his waist.

She looked up from her hug and peered through thick-rimmed glasses at Peterson. "I'm so happy you're back," she said in a serious tone. "How are you? Are you okay?" she asked rapid fire, eyes now round with concern.

Uncomfortable with the sudden display of emotion, Peterson drew her arms from his back and pushed her gently away. "I'm fine," he said, trying not to stammer. "Thanks, but I'm completely fine."

Her eyes brightened when he told her that it was good to see her again. Cairnes took Peterson's hands in her own, and a broad smile lit her face. "Would you like a coffee, sir?" When Peterson said yes, she practically bolted from the room, saying that she would be back within moments. Peterson watched her leave, sighing deeply.

Denly, a small smile forming at the corner of his mouth, chuckled around a silver thermos of coffee that he brought to his lips. "Someone missed you," he said over the top of the rim.

Peterson sighed again and nodded toward the TV. On the screen he could see a news reporter standing in front of a copse of trees, mike in hand, saying something to the cameraman. The sound was muted, but Peterson inferred from the scrolling typecast on the bottom that it was focused on the body that had been found on the trail earlier in the morning. "Anything?" Peterson asked.

"Not yet, no," Denly drawled. "Sly is there now. I just spoke to her on the phone, and she said she'd be a couple of hours. Not much there to see."

Peterson squinted, and he thought he spotted Partridge in the foreground of the camera feed. Dressed in black cargo pants with a dark blue SPD wind blazer, her long black hair was being whipped up in the wind, strands sticking to the side of her face, which she absently brushed away. She was standing next to a yellow tarp that had been draped over the ground, the general shape of the emergency blanket suggesting that there was a body underneath. A few other officers, general duty and forensic specialists, were milling about performing random tasks. He watched as she glanced over her shoulder in the direction of the camera, discomfort clearly written upon her face. Whether it had to do with the proximity of the reporters, the scene, or the foul weather, Peterson couldn't say.

Peterson tapped Denly on the back and hooked his neck towards the office. "C'mon" he said. "We got our own work to do."

Four excruciating long hours passed, and Peterson learned frustratingly little about why a stranger would shoot Bryce Turner in cold blood inside the man's house. That Turner was disliked was beyond question, but while the potential suspects had motive, they lacked the means and opportunity to pull something like this off. Only thirty-five years old, Turner had racked up a litany of police entries: cause disturbance, drunk in public, lewd behavior, assault. Only one incident had lead to a formal charge, and that had been tossed out in the last minute when Laurie Beasley had changed her story. Compounding Peterson's aggravation was the fact that he felt rusty, his previously well honed skills and intuition no longer as sharp as he once remembered, as if the shooting had not only taken his wife, but everything that had once made him a good police officer.

Denly, sitting across from him in a grey-padded cubicle, seemed to be fairing little better judging by the sounds of frustration that drifted from his pit at regular intervals. At a loss, Peterson opened a web browser and typed Turner's name in a search engine. A few random social media links populated the top of the list, followed by several entries that seemed to deal with the automotive dealership. As Peterson perused the articles, a door banging at the front of the office drew his attention, and he looked up as a wet, dishevelled, and extremely pissed-off Sylvia Partridge stormed through the door.

"If I never see another ident member in my life, it will be too soon," she fumed. She stopped short when she saw Peterson sitting at the desk, and a hand went to her throat. "Jack," she said, seemingly stunned by his presence. "I'm sorry, it's so strange to see you there." A small smile formed on her face that took away some of her fury.

Tall and thin, Partridge had jet black hair that framed severe and angular cheekbones. In her late fifties, the last time Peterson had seen Sylvia Partridge her hair had been mostly silver grey, so he assumed that she had dyed it since that time. The dye job, coal black, highlighted her age instead of reducing it, and made the crows feet around her eyes and the wrinkles at the corner of her mouth seem more pronounced by comparison. She was pretty in a way that a diamond is pretty, with sharp edges and aquiline features, only belied by her kind eyes that looked at Peterson with deep concern.

"Kinda strange to be back," Peterson agreed. He looked beyond Partridge and could see a muddy trail that she had left from the door to his desk, her boots caked in a black silt. He smiled slightly and said, "Did you have fun out there?"

Her body tightened into a coil. "No, I did not." Each word spoken like rifle fire. "I should have been back hours ago, but the forensic weenies were going through every blade of grass. Meanwhile, the worst storm of the century is blowing in."

"What was the call about?"

She shivered and flipped open a notebook that was streaked with rainwater. "Arthur Collins, forty-two. Single stab wound to the neck." She looked up at Peterson. "You should have seen it. The guy nearly took his head off."

"Suspects, witnesses?"

Partridge shook her head. "None. According to the victim's wife, Collins goes for a walk every morning, like clockwork. No one was around at the time, but a dog walker discovered the body. The coroner figured he had been dead for an hour or so. I got the uniform guys doing door-to-door inquiries now near the trail heads, but nothing so far."

Peterson nodded, taking it in. If things continued like this, they would have to farm out for more resources. Their department was small and stretched thin as it was, but there were other units that could assist and take off some of the load. He looked Partridge up and down, whose wet clothing was sticking to her body. "You should probably change," he commented with a smile. Partridge nodded, muttering something under her breath that he probably didn't need to hear, and stalked out of the office to the change room. Peterson chuckled to himself and continued the internet search. As he scrolled to the bottom of the search page his eye was drawn to a strange tagline. The line "State versus Turner, B (1995)" was a familiar format indicating a previous criminal case that had been brought before the courts. There was nothing in the man's criminal history regarding a criminal charge from 1995, and Peterson clicked on the link. The URL brought him to an intergovernmental website, the icon on the top of the website telling him that it was connected to the Seattle Criminal Courts.

Peterson leaned across from his desk and called Denly over. Denly, looking bleary eyed, spun his chair over to where Peterson was sitting.

"What is it?" he asked.

Peterson shook his head, confused. "Not sure. I searched for Turner on the internet and it brought me to this site, but there's nothing there." On the screen, in large bold letters, were the same words that Peterson had read before: State versus Turner, B (1995), followed by a list of court and docket numbers. Below this, Peterson read aloud: "Error 404. URL not found. Please contact the local administration office for more information." He scrolled down to the end of the page and stopped, feeling his stomach drop. He felt Denly swing his head toward him, a look of shock registering on his face. He heard a door open and saw a fresh-faced Partridge stride toward them, her hair back in a stiff bun. Both men looked at her, and she stared back at them self-consciously. "What?" she asked, coming to stand next to the two men.

Peterson pointed to his computer screen and asked, "What was the name of your victim again?" She told them and then bent down to squint at the computer screen, her eyes growing wide in alarm.

At the bottom of the webpage, written in small italic letters, were the words: *See also: State versus Collins, A (1995).*

Nine

It was late in the afternoon when Peterson pulled up to the Kings County Superior Court, the brick tan building glimmering in the intense sun that had escaped briefly through thick grey clouds. He had left Denly and Partridge back at WestOps, giving them instructions to pour over the police history of Collins and Turner, seeing if they could find any connections between the two men. It seemed clear to Peterson that the murders were linked, as the chances of two known associates being killed a day apart were beyond the possibilities of any kind of coincidence.

This far into downtown, Peterson immediately felt the press of the heavy traffic and the monolithic skyscrapers that probed the suddenly bright blue sky. The old west coast adage remained true, if you wanted the weather to change, you just had to wait fifteen minutes.

He walked up to the building, holding the door open for a pair of smartly dressed lawyers that were engaged in a lively conversation, and then entered through the double glass doors. Peterson waded through security, eventually flashing a badge at a bored guard who waved him through a metal detector that chimed red when he stepped through. Peterson opened his jacket to reveal the bulge of the pistol attached to his waist, and the guard wrote his name on a sign-in sheet and parcelled him forward. The courthouse was the typical controlled mayhem of a governmental legal building—the clients, witnesses, and judicial officials moving through the hallways, ferrying to the assigned courtrooms they had been subpoenaed to.

The interior of the building had held its age well and still retained much of the original furnishings, brick-lined walls that were a reddish brown. It had the general sense and smell of a historical building, and Peterson could well imagine what it had looked like in the 1920's, pre- and post-war times.

Peterson made his way to a set of elevators where the offices and departments were listed on a clear glass display case. He found what he hoped was the right department, Transcriptions and Records, and pressed the button for the elevator which he rode the elevator alone to the fifth floor. Stepping out, he followed an arrow to the left that announced the area he needed. He passed through a set of glass doors and approached a receptionist typing on a computer, glasses perched on the top of her brown hair.

She looked up when she saw him. "Yes, sir, how may I help you?" The woman, whose name tag read Jessica, was probably in her mid-thirties and pretty in a plain sort of way. Her thin, brown hair was tied in a ponytail that draped over her shoulder. Inquisitive green eyes stared at him, the cheekbones lined with freckles.

Peterson took out his badge and displayed it for Jessica before putting it back in his jacket pocket. "Yes, I was hoping you could help me out with a sealed file." Peterson explained what had happened, that he had found the case number but couldn't read any of the details.

"That is strange," she said after a moment's pause. "Once a file moves through the court process, it usually becomes public record." She moved the glasses from her head to the bridge of her nose. The frames were thick, chunky, following some sort of style that Peterson usually ignored. Jessica's fingers raced over the keyboard, faster than Peterson could keep track of, digits flying on the keys like a piano savant.

"How fast can you type?" Peterson asked, unable to conceal his amazement.

She stopped typing abruptly and looked at her fingers like they weren't her. She let out an embarrassed laugh. "Pretty fast. I was a real computer nerd growing up, spent a lot of time in chatrooms. And I do court reporting duties half the time, so I've gotten even better."

Peterson nodded. The court reporters were a vital part of the court process, though often forgotten and over-looked. Usually positioned in front of the judge or jury, the court reporter would document the entire court case, mostly doing so short hand and on a stenotype machine. The information, typically a phonetic code, would then be fed into a computer, which would translate the information into a final transcript. Looking at Jessica's fingers, which practically blazed over the keyboard, he wasn't surprised that she moonlighted as a stenographer. She looked up from her computer back to Peterson. "What did you say the docket number was again?"

He read it off a sticky note and her fingers continued to fly. She stopped suddenly, confused.

"What is it?" he asked.

The receptionist shook her head, taking off her glasses to chew on the ear piece. "That's weird," she said finally, and swung the computer screen to him. "It says the file is locked down." He looked at the screen, which appeared to be some kind of MSDOS program, the black screen flooded with green characters.

"Is that abnormal?" he asked, feeling out of his depth.

"I've never seen it before," she said. "But then I'm not up here very often." She swivelled her chair around and opened a lower drawer, taking out a set of keys on a brass key ring. Then she smiled at Peterson and stood up. "C'mon," she continued, "we'll pull the file." Jessica walked past the desk and disappeared for a moment, only to appear a second later through a locked door beside the desk. She was shorter than Peterson had originally noticed, barely coming up to his shoulders, and it made her appear younger than she probably was. She wore a black maxi skirt, and a button-up blouse that reached a thin and delicate neck.

Jessica waved for him to follow her and Peterson fell in step as they left the transcription office and headed for the elevators he had taken up a few minutes earlier. She pressed the down button, and he could hear the elevator engage as it rose to their level. She looked sideways at him and asked how long he had been a police officer.

He thought for a moment, counting back the years. "Getting to be twenty years soon." *Has it really been that long?* he thought to himself, and with a start he realized that it had. Suddenly he felt like time had gotten away from him, that the older he got the more quickly time advanced, as if it was a ball tossed down a steep embankment that simply built up speed as it got closer and closer to the bottom. And what did he have to show for it? Laura was gone, as was his only likely possibility of having children. She had been nearly three months pregnant when her life was brutally taken. He hadn't even had the heart to find out what the gender of the child had been. What it would have been, he supposed. He felt himself swallow and found Jessica staring at him intently. "What?" he asked quietly.

"Oh," she said, concerned. "You looked lost there for a moment."

Peterson absently rubbed the back of his neck with his hand. "A lot on my mind lately," he said lamely. The elevator dinged, saving him from having to explain further. As they stepped inside, he repeated his earlier statement. "Yeah, twenty years now. Quite the job."

Jessica pressed a button for the level marked "Sub-B," and the elevator shuddered as it began to descend. "I couldn't do what you guys do, all the stuff you must see," she said.

Peterson felt himself nodding. "It's not all gum drops, for sure." He regarded her and added, "But you see a lot of it too, working as a stenographer, I imagine." He noted that she considered his words before nodding herself. "All those trials, witnesses, and victims."

Jessica crossed her arms and held them to her chest. "Yeah, some of the cases can get to you." The young woman shuddered involuntarily, and a tremor ran through her entire body. Her eyes took on a haunted look as she stared intently at the elevator wall, rooted in the spot by whatever memory was flashing through her mind. "It's horrible what people do to each other," she said. "And what they get away with sometimes." She gazed at him sadly. "Makes you lose faith in the system."

They left the elevators and entered a long, damp corridor with buzzing fluorescent lights. The walls were yellow concrete, textured and bubbled, and even without knowing which floor they had landed Peterson could tell that they were deep underground. Jessica's stubby heels clicked loudly on the polished laminate flooring, and he followed her down a set of hallways before they came to a steel door marked "Case Files."

Jessica ran a plastic access card over a black box that was secured to the wall, and it glowed a faint green. She entered in a four-digit code in a keypad beside the box, the electric locks disengaged, and the door opening with an audible whoosh.

Once they had both stepped inside, she put her weight into the door and locked it again. She brushed her hands off and explained, "The code is to disengage the alarms. We have to lock it back up to keep the air controlled, as some of the files here are old and difficult to preserve." She must have read his confusion, as she smiled and continued, "The air will actually eat away some of the older documents if it's not circulated properly."

The area was dark, and Peterson found himself trying to adjust his eyes to the sudden gloom that surrounded him. From his right side he heard Jessica muttering as she ran her hands down the side of the wall, searching for a light switch. She grunted in satisfaction as he heard a click, and the cavernous room was suddenly bathed in an intense halogen glow. The storage area was huge, and its open space momentarily took Peterson by surprise, causing a wave of vertigo to wash over him for a moment before he could pull it back in. The room was easily the length of a football field and two stories deep, filled floor to ceiling with thick steel shelving units. The units themselves contained hundreds and hundreds of boxes, the sides labeled with white stickers or simply written on with black permanent marker. It was a massive repository of data, and the scope of it nearly took his breath away.

"Pretty impressive, huh?" Jessica said from his side.

He nodded. "You ever see *Raiders of the Lost Ark*?" He asked, referring to the scene where the Ark of the Covenant had been stored in a room like this. Judging by Jessica's expression either she hadn't or simply didn't understand his reference. "Never mind," he finally said.

Shrugging, she pulled a piece of paper from her pocket where she had written down the docket and case numbers from the Collins and Turner trials. Her eyes swept over the shelving units that were labeled with similar numbers, denoting locations like books in a library. She pointed to the right and said, "This way." As he followed her she explained how the case file repository worked. "We receive all the case files for the local and district counties in the region. Minor files get purged within five years. Serious matters have a retention period of about twenty-five years. And some of the more important files might be kept indefinitely. Your case isn't too old, 1995, so it should be just in the back here. There we should find pretty much everything, disclosure, judges reports, crown and defense arguments."

"Do they keep the evidence here too?" Peterson asked. Often evidence related to the trial would be entered directly into the court proceedings. The police retained the evidence until the trial and then the submitted evidence would transfer to the court.

"No," Jessica said, "that's a separate department that only a few people have access to. I couldn't get you in there even if I wanted to." At a long row of shelving Jessica finally stopped, reviewed her note once again, and peered down the length of corridor. "Ah, here it is," she said, and pointed to a box that was about knee high. Peterson bent to look at the box, finding that it was labeled with a black marker.

State versus Turner, Collins, & S.C. (1995)

He looked up at Jessica. "That's different from my internet search." He pointed to the lettering. "What does S.C. mean?"

She frowned, bent down beside him. "Usually the initials refer to a young offender. They're not allowed to publish the full name."

Peterson nodded and reached to lift the box out of the confined space. It was the size of a banker's box, and he prepared himself for a heavy weight as he pulled it forward, but it was surprisingly light. He set the box on the cool concrete and closed his eyes.

Jessica stared at him with concern. "What is it?" she asked. Not offering a response, he gripped the edges of the lid to pull the top off. He already knew what he would see, but still he felt crushing despair in his chest as they peered into the box. It was empty.

Ten

By the time Jessica and Peterson walked out of the Kings County Courthouse a few hours later, the sun was gone. It had been replaced by a darkness which carried with it freezing cold that caused the small puddles of rain water on the pavement to form ice at the edges. These crunched underneath their feet as they walked down the cement steps outside. The two had searched diligently for the missing case file, moving aside boxes and searching areas that contained similar docket numbers, hoping that there had been a simple mix-up. Eventually they admitted defeat and rode the elevator back to the main level, finding the courthouse nearly deserted save for security guards who prowled the hallways. Once outside, they stopped at the base of the stairway. Jessica pointed to the left where she had parked. Peterson hooked his thumb to the right. "My car's that way," he said.

Jessica breathed into her hands and rubbed them together for warmth. Shivering in the cold, she said, "I'm sorry that we couldn't locate the file. It was probably misplaced."

Peterson looked off into the distance, where a few vehicles were moving slowly through the city streets, skidding on the ice already forming on the pavement. If the weather continued like this, it was going to be hell to drive in the morning. "I don't think so," he said finally.

She sent him a questioning glance, and he explained. "Did you notice how much dust we were kicking up, moving those files around?" She nodded her agreement. Each time they had moved an older case file, a blast of dust broke free and whirled around their heads, the particles reflecting the halogen lamps that blazed above. "There wasn't anything on the Turner file, it was clean." From the look on her face he could tell that she didn't understand. "It means it was emptied recently, probably in the last few weeks I'd say."

She digested this for a moment. "What does that mean?"

Peterson shook his head. "I have no idea." He breathed out his frustration and looked over her shoulder. "Do you need a walk to your car?"

She smiled, showing him a set of perfectly white teeth. Despite her mousy demeanor, she was quite attractive, he thought. "No, but thank you, detective. I should be able to handle it from here."

"Jack," he said. "You can call me Jack." They shook hands, and he watched her walk away.

She looked back at him once before she rounding the corner of the courthouse and then disappeared from view.

Jamming his hands into his pockets, he walked to his own car, finding that the windows had frosted over completely, encasing the vehicle in a thin sheet of ice. He had to use a credit card to scrape the ice away that had formed on the windshield and two side windows, his hands freezing from the effort. He climbed inside and started the engine, cranking the heat to full power as he waited for the windows to defog.

He took out his cell phone and connected it to the car's Bluetooth, which sounded tinny in the car's interior but at least allowed him to rub some warmth into his painfully cold fingers while the phone rang Partridge's number.

She answered on the second ring, barking a curt "Yeah?" that blasted throughout the car's speaker. He winced and turned the volume down, asking her if she had made any progress.

"None, and I mean literally none. Denly and I have been riding the phone all day, but we can't find any connection between the two. Turner's wife is basically a hermit. Can't say for certain who he hung out with or who his friends might have been. Ditto for Collins, though he was a decent enough guy, according to neighbors and friends."

"Did you get my message about S.C.?" he asked as his window had finally cleared enough for him to see out the front. A tiny archway of clear glass allowed him to put the car in gear and pull out into the street, and he kept his head low to stare out the small porthole in the front.

"Nothing there, either. Turner didn't have anything for social media, but Collins did. None of his contacts had those initials." She paused on the phone. "Could be a false name. The initials don't always represent the real names in those youth charges."

Peterson considered her words, frustrated that they hit another dead end. "Are you still at the office?" he asked.

"Yes."

He told her to head home. "Denly too. We'll hit it fresh in the morning."

She wished him a good night and he told her the same, the line clicking off. As he drove down the slick city streets tiny snowflakes began to pepper his windshield, settling onto the ground outside like ashes. Usually, this close to the Pacific, any snow melted immediately on contact with the ground, swallowed up by the rain-soaked grass or pavement, but this stuff looked like it was here to stay, at least for a little while. Should make for an interesting commute in the morning.

Peterson came to a red light and brought the car to a skidding stop. He was familiar with the area, too familiar as of late. If he went straight ahead it would take him out of downtown and toward home. Left would take him deeper downtown, toward Juliette. Already he could feel the shame crawling over his skin, and his chest constricted at the thought. He wondered what Laura would say if she knew of what he did with Juliette. Would she understand or be as sick and revolted as he was of himself? Perhaps for this reason only when the light turned green Peterson did not hesitate but continued home. And maybe to the nightmares waiting there.

Eleven

The dawn brought a white so intense that Peterson had to shield his eyes when he opened the blinds in the living room. The sun reflected off the thick blanket of snow that had settled over his lawn and bounced back through the window, glinting with silvery brilliance that left after images burning in his vision. The world seemed utterly calm and still, a serenity so divine that it made Peterson's own ravaged mind seem all the more damaged through the stark comparison.

As he had expected, his dreams had been filled with thoughts of Laura. Each time he had been jolted awake and had struggled fitfully to fall asleep, only to have the scene repeated over and over in his mind, as if on a constant loop, the record of his consciousness skipping in place for an interminable length of time.

He rubbed at his nose, feeling the pressure of a headache building behind his eyes, the lack of sleep increasing the pounding in his skull. Painfully, like a man with a terrible hangover, he wandered to the bathroom, showering and then dressing for the day. He gunned up and stepped outside, the air biting at his lungs as he half-jogged, half-skated toward his car. The windshield, roof, and trunk held about eight inches of snow, and when he opened the driver's door a mountain of snow poured inside, dousing the seat and gear shift in a thick sheet of the wretched stuff that he knew would soak through the upholstery and leave him with a wet backside. Swearing under his breath, he looked up to the white sky, not a streak of blue to be seen, and sighed heavily.

It took him nearly an hour and a half to get to the office, a trip that requires only twenty minutes on a bad day. The snow plows were out in full force, doing their best to clear the heavy shroud of snow that had settled on the city, but it seemed like they were fighting a losing battle. The snow had begun falling lazily from the clouds again, and its presence seemed to rob most motorists of any shred of sensibilities or driving skill. The bulk of the people on the road, whether old or young, seemed to drive either too fast or too slow, bent over the wheel with white knuckles and a look of abject terror on their faces, as if they were navigating their Toyotas or Nissans through a white apocalypse. Peterson, who had spent all his childhood and a good deal of his teenage years in North Dakota, handled the poor driving conditions well, and mainly kept an eye on the other drivers, who skidded and slid through intersections like it was a *Stars on Ice* performance but with wheels. He didn't envy the general duty members, who would be flooding to one accident call after another, taking statements and filling out boring and repetitive accident collision forms.

When he arrived at WestOps, the parking lot was almost empty, and he assumed that the other officers had been similarly delayed by the state of the city streets and the general melee and chaos of the traffic. He pulled into his stall, noting that neither Denly's nor Partridge's vehicles were present, and took the short ride to his floor, shaking the snow off his jacket which fell from his shoulders like dandruff as he passed through the doors.

He frowned as an odd sound filtered through the office toward the entrance. The office was dark, and he could hear the lunch room TV blaring. Frowning, he strode in that direction as the sound of the TV became clearer, the individual overlapping voices becoming more distinct.

"I'm tellin' you," a voice said, *"I'm not that baby's daddy."*

"Well, let's see what the genetic test revealed," an announcer exclaimed, to the roar and clapping of the crowd.

As Peterson turned into the room he looked up at the wall-mounted screen, which flashed an image of a talk-show host reading the genetic results from a card. A black male and black female were sitting on separate chairs on a large stage, flanked by thick chested security guards, and they glared at one another in hatred.

In the lunch room, a figure sat with his back to Peterson, his feet up on the table, muddy boots dripping water on the tabletop. He yelled at the TV. "C'mon already, tell me who the baby's daddy is!" The host announced that the male was not, in fact, the baby's daddy, and the crowd erupted in hoots and cheers. Peterson cleared his throat, and the guy in the lunch room looked back over his shoulder, a smile forming on his lips. "Hiya, boyo," Archie Prince said. "Long time no see."

Twelve

Peterson strode to the table and yanked the remote out of Prince's hand. He stabbed the *off* button with his thumb and slammed the device back down, causing Prince's eyebrows to raise in alarm. Prince removed his muddy boots from the table and placed them on the floor, wiping the stain from the table with the sleeve of his jacket. He looked Peterson up and down appraisingly, seemed to consider for a moment, then spoke. "You look terrible, son."

Annoyingly, Peterson saw, the same could not be said for Prince, whose general appearance had greatly improved. In fact, he looked better than Peterson had ever seen him before. The man's face was no longer so weathered and grey, and his stomach, which could at best have been described as fat bordering on extremely fat, seemed to be only half the size it had been before. The neck wasn't so thick, his cheekbones more defined, and he had shaved his head, abandoning the comb-over that had only served to highlight his baldness. His clothes were still terrible and hung off the older detective loosely, as if he had lost a significant amount of weight and hadn't bothered to purchase better fitting apparel.

"What are you doing here, Prince?" Peterson asked, irritated. He didn't have anything against the man specifically, but the old detective had a way of grating on one's nerves.

Prince looked offended, holding his hands out defensively, though a small smile played on his lips. "Well, you don't call, you don't write…" When Peterson didn't respond, Prince continued, "Two things," holding up his right index and middle finger. "First, I wanted to ask you if you've called Harriet."

A frown creased on Peterson's face and he sighed, blowing the air out of his mouth. "No, actually. I haven't."

Prince shook his head, almost sadly, and looked away. Harriet MacAllister had been called to investigate the shooting and death of his wife, eventually finding the person responsible, the killer closer than anyone could have possibly imagined. In the end, she had saved his life. After waking up from the coma he had been told all that had transpired. Peterson had struggled with the idea of contacting Harriet and thanking her for all that she had done. But in the end he simply…hadn't. If pressed, Peterson wasn't sure if he could have even explained why he hadn't called her, and it made no sense, even to him. Somehow, she seemed too close to the event. Harriet had left him a few messages over the months, but Peterson found that he didn't have the heart to return her calls.

He sat down heavily across from Prince, placing both hands on the table and staring at the wall behind the man's shoulder. "Not sure why I didn't," Peterson said. "I should have, but I haven't."

Prince leaned forward in his chair and fixed Peterson with a sharp gaze. "Yeah, you should have. She sacrificed a lot coming here and helping you out. She deserves it."

Peterson nodded. "How is she, anyway?" he asked quietly.

Prince cocked his head to the side, considering the question. "Surviving, I think. Going through some shit with her ex right now that she's trying to sort out. Same old story." Prince leaned forward in his chair and levelled a gaze at Peterson. "Look, man, people been talking around here. Saying you walking around like a zombie or something. What's going on with you?"

Peterson shifted uncomfortably in his chair and met Prince's stare. "Nothing's going on, just trying to get my feet wet again." He cleared his throat and checked his watch. "You said there were two things?"

Prince stared at Peterson for a long stretch of time, as if wanting to say more but then opted to move on to other business. "I heard that Partridge was asking around about an old file, Turner and

Collins?" When Peterson nodded, Prince said, "I got curious because it sounded familiar to me, though I couldn't find anything in the old case files."

"Yeah," Peterson said. "1995 was around the time the SPD switched the record management systems." Back then, all files were collected and collated in hard copy, with little to no electronic record. Since that time, the bulk of the files were kept in electronic format, reports and forms completed on a computerized system. When they searched the old hard copy files, just like at the courthouse, they had found no record.

"That's right," Prince agreed. "You were just a recruit back then, but I had about five years in at that time. I don't remember much about the file." A smile played over his lips. "But I remember who the investigator was."

Thirteen

"No. No way, not happening." Sylvia Partridge waved her hands wildly, as if trying to swat a particularly annoying and large insect. She and Peterson were in the break room, a glass-paneled conference room off the main office. Through the semi-frosted glass, he could see Prince talking to Denly, punching the southern detective playfully on the shoulder, illustrating some kind of point. Denly, who looked the least bit impressed, nodded patiently and sent a long-suffering glance in Peterson's direction. Partridge and Denly had just arrived at work, both surviving the commute through the snow-choked streets. Peterson had unleashed Prince on Denly, telling the two that he needed to see Partridge alone. "I mean, seriously, Jack, I don't care if Prince has information or not. We can go and talk to the guy ourselves."

This was true, and a point that Peterson had already considered. After giving his colleague the information, Prince had sat back, crossing his arms over his thick chest. The details he had provided were slight, probably because he didn't know much beyond what he had heard. During his time on the street, Prince had heard whispers and rumors of a case involving those two names, Turner and Collins, and that it had turned sideways for reasons unknown. The primary investigator, Howard Nielsen, was not so subtly convinced to take early retirement shortly after the investigation was turfed, and he quietly disappeared from the collective gaze of the police force. During that time, Peterson had just started, and as a recruit he had heard little of Nielsen, and through the hallways his name was spoken in hushed terms, with a hint of shame and embarrassment. It had taken Prince to awaken the slim memory in Peterson's mind. One thing Peterson remembered was that Nielsen had been a cantankerous bastard even then, and according to Prince, his mood had improved little with age.

Prince had told him with a wink, "But I bet I can get him to open up a little."

Beyond that, Peterson felt like he owed it to Prince to bring him along on this little field trip, as they never would have obtained the information had it not been for him. He told this to Partridge. "It won't be so bad," Peterson said. "A little trip to talk to Nielsen and then we'll be back in time for dinner."

Partridge crossed her arms tightly over her small chest and set her jaw tightly. "I've worked with Prince before," she told him. "He's not human." She sent a baleful glance toward the man in question before snapping her eyes back to Peterson. "Last scene I went with him, he slapped me on the ass and said, 'Good job, champ.'"

Peterson felt a chuckle rising in his throat but forced it down. Then he clapped Partridge on the shoulder. "C'mon. The sooner we start the sooner we're done." They left the break room and approached Prince and Denly just as the former finished the punchline of a particularly crude joke.

Denly was kind enough to lend a pitied chuckle, though he eyed Peterson as if to say, "About damned time." Peterson nodded to Prince as he approached. "Okay, we're all set. Charles, I want you to follow up with Forensics. See if they got anything at either scene and what they figured out at the autopsies. Sylvia, Archie, and I will head out to Nielsen and see if he can tell us anything." He regarded Prince and added, "I assume you know where he is?"

The older detective responded with a simple nod of his head, flashing Partridge a toothy grin. Peterson raised an eyebrow at her as a low grumble rolled in her throat. "You ready?" he asked her.

Her exaggerated sigh was answer enough.

The sign indicated that Burberry Meadows Retirement Home was where "Comfort Found a Home", and from the outside it certainly looked better than a lot of the long term seniors' facilities that Peterson had seen in the past. With the crush of newly fallen snow, Peterson could barely read the sign posted at the front gate as he weaved the unmarked police vehicle through a narrow, cobblestoned lane. The snow continued to fall throughout their drive, the windshield wipers working at double speed to maintain visibility. Partridge sat in the passenger seat, giving one word responses to the slough of questions that Prince threw toward her from the backseat. Peterson had never heard the man talk so much, and, if he didn't know better, could have sworn that Prince was a little sweet on his colleague. Not that he was going to mention this to Partridge, who looked like any moment she would reach across and take the steering wheel, careening the vehicle into oncoming traffic.

    Peterson pulled the vehicle into a visitor's stall and they got out, each adjusting their jackets to battle the cold that greeted them. Three stories tall with a wide, gabled brick and mortar roof, the main residence facility of Burberry Meadows looked more like a country school than long-term care. Peterson wondered how Nielsen, likely living off a paltry policeman's pension, could afford to stay at such a place. Either he had invested and planned well or his children were flush in greenbacks. Either way, Nielsen, unlike the balance of seniors from coast to coast, was living the relatively high life.

    They pushed through the front doors and came to a silver-haired receptionist who was manning a sign-in area. The woman, with a red wool-knit sweater that featured a smiling snowman riding a sled down a snowy embankment, gave the trio a warm smile as they stopped in front of a narrow desk flanked by stubby, twinkling, Christmas trees. To their left, coming from a wide hallway, Peterson could hear Christmas music peppered with the sound of overlapping voices. A whiteboard on the far wall announced that it was the Burberry Meadows Annual Christmas Party, and an arrow pointed down in the direction where the music wafted from, the lettering blocky and pleasant, with small Christmas ornaments illustrated throughout.

    Peterson removed his badge and showed it to the woman, who blinked in surprise. She looked past Peterson to Partridge and Prince, who had held back and were thumbing through a set of pamphlets that were displayed in a corner cove by the door. The receptionist wore a handwritten nametag over her left breast that proclaimed her name was Eldridge.

"Sounds like you have a bit of a party going on over there," Peterson said, hooking his head toward the music. As he said this he tried to keep his eyes fixed on the woman, but found them drifting to the set of felt reindeer horns that she had fixed to the top of her head, the tiny bells threaded to the top chiming lightly as she nodded.

"You bet," she said in a high and pleasant voice. "We even hired a band this year." Her beaming smile spoke volumes to how proud she was of this fact, but it disappeared quickly when Peterson told her who they were looking for. She looked down and shuffled some papers absently, swallowing twice before answering. "You'll find him in his room, I imagine," she said after a pause, winking at him knowingly. "He's not much for partying, you see."

Eldridge provided Peterson with directions to Nielsen's room, handing him three visitor badges. He clipped one to his jacket collar and gave the other passes to Prince and Partridge as he met them in the hallway.

Prince took his pass and tucked it into his pocket while Partridge connected hers to her belt. "Pretty swanky place," Prince grumbled. Peterson had to agree, as the interior felt more suited for a five-star resort than an assisted living center, and as they proceeded down the hallway, the crescendo of the music climbing with each step, he found himself studying the furnishings in surprise. The floors were polished to a high gloss, reflecting the rough stone walls. Gilded mirrors were set above mahogany and marble desks that served only to decorate, an opulence Peterson found unsettling.

Remembering that the other two detectives had leafed through the home's display of pamphlets Peterson asked, "Did you see what the rent is for this place?"

A hard line creased over Partridge's face, and she set her mouth into a frown. Peterson knew that her own mother was living in a facility, and he imagined that it looked nothing like Burberry Meadows. "You don't want to know," she replied.

Peterson found himself frowning as well. While not unsubstantial, a policeman's pension, especially during the mid-nineties, would be unable to support living at such a place. He found himself wishing that he would have done more substantial background checks on Nielsen and not relied upon Prince's spotty recollection.

The three detectives passed through a burnished archway, coming into a large open room where the music was almost painfully loud. The room was two stories tall, shaped like a cube, the walls and ceiling made entirely of glass. A sign at the front indicated that this was the Redmond Solarium, and even with the sun hiding behind thick white clouds, he found the air stifling and warm, as sweat began to form under the collar of his suit. Two massive air conditioning units on a far wall probably worked overtime in the heat of the summer to keep the place liveable, though for now with the cold weather they sat motionless and silent. The staff had decorated them with tinsel and ornaments. Peterson looked up to the ceiling, the glass-panelled roof covered with a thick blanket of snow. The interior was criss-crossed with large steel I-beams, in place, he imagined, to support the weight of the unique glass design. Through the snow he could see at least three pairs of boots as workers struggled to clear the snow from the glass panels.

A large stand had been erected in the center of the room, and a four-member band, three young women and a man, were belting out familiar Christmas tunes. Many chairs had been set around the stage and were occupied by what he assumed was most of the residents of Burberry Meadows. They ranged from the moderately old to the near-death's door, and white-coated staff, festooned with their own felt reindeer horns, wandered through the attendees bearing trays of what looked like snacks and blister packs of pills. Only a handful of the residents, the relatively younger and spryer, danced slowly, shuffling side to side on stiffened legs.

The detectives waded through the throng until they reached the opposite side, walking down a long L-shaped corridor. The music faded as they ranged closer to Nielsen's room while a new sound reached Peterson's ears, decidedly less festive than the party songs they had left in the solarium.

"Get the hell outta here!" a scraggily voice yelled, and through an open door they saw a white ceramic mug fly through the door frame, where it smashed against the opposite wall.

A young woman, dressed in green hospital scrubs, bolted from the room, tears streaming down her face like the coffee that was slowly seeping down the wall.

She pushed past them and Peterson heard her mutter under her breath, "The bastard." He felt Prince smiling beside him and looking almost pleased.

"Same old Nielsen," he said.

Fourteen

The room had the pervasive air of urine and unwashed clothing, the general sense of sickness that reminded Peterson painfully of his own time spent in hospital during his convalescence. Howard Nielsen was sitting in a wheel chair by a large bay window that overlooked the grounds, the snow pelting the glass like pebbles. He sat stooped, his right side presented to them, a thin tube of plastic running from the old man's nose to a set of oxygen canisters that were secured in the rear of the wheelchair. Even from the doorway Peterson could hear the struggled, raspy breathing, a wet, sucking sound that labored to pull the oxygen in before releasing it in a wheeze. Peterson cleared his throat, and the head swivelled on a too-thin neck to regard the visitors.

Nielsen was wearing flannel pajamas, the hem on the leg too short, revealing a thin ankle threaded with blue veins that disappeared into black slippers. Nielsen shuffled his feet out of the stirrups and placed them on the floor. The old man slowly swung the wheelchair to face his newly arrived company.

"Yeah?" His reedy voice scratched through his throat.

Peterson made to speak, but Prince beat him to it, gently pushing his colleague out of the way as he stepped forward. "My man, Howard, how's it going?" His voice was genial, light.

Nielsen squinted at Prince, the watery eyes attempting to focus on the man. Peterson noticed that the irises had the faintest tinge of yellow, a patina that circled the black of the iris like a solar eclipse. "Am I supposed to know who…" Nielsen paused, recognition slowly dawning on his weathered face. "Hmm…Archie Prince," he said finally, without a hint of humor or happiness. He looked him up and down for a stretch of time before concluding, "You've gotten fat, boy."

From his shoulder, he heard Partridge mumble, "You should have seen him before."

If Nielsen's insult bothered Prince, the detective didn't show it, merely shook his head as if he had anticipated the comment.

The leather on the wheelchair seat creaked loudly as Nielsen leaned to look past Prince to where Partridge and Peterson were occupying the doorway. "I suppose you guys are cops too?" he muttered. "Well, come in, come in, I don't have all damn day." As Nielsen labored to roll his wheelchair to the foot of the bed, shuffling his feet on the polished floor, Prince sidled up to help, but the old man pushed him off with a wave of his hand, muttering something unintelligible. Prince sat on the bed, which groaned painfully under his weight, while Partridge took a chair and Peterson leaned against the wall.

Prince swung his head around the room, whistling in appreciation. "Pretty nice place you got here, Howard."

Nielson's room contained the similar tasteful design and decoration that Peterson had noticed in the hallways; the only difference was that the flooring, unlike the polished tile found outside, was a light shag. Peterson assumed that even a thin carpet like this would at least prevent a broken hip should a resident take a tumble. The walls were a gleaming hospital white, and flowing curtains bordered a bay window. A single bed was on one corner with an expensive-looking armoire on the other, set up near a plush couch that looked seldom used. Near the bed a door was left closed, and Peterson assumed it was the bathroom, close enough that the distance travelled for a night-time need would be slight. There was a utilitarianism to the room, an absence of personality. There were no pictures or personal adornments of any kind, no gifts from any family, indeed no indication of family whatsoever. He wondered who was out there for Howard Nielsen, if there were any sons or daughters, nieces or nephews, who gave the slightest thought to the aging and decrepit man seated before them. Someone who might even say in passing, "We should really visit Grandpa," but who never got quite around to doing it. Mowing the lawn and grocery shopping took precedent, after all. Though, considering Nielsen's scowl and general disdain for their company, Peterson couldn't say he blamed them.

"It suits me fine," Nielsen said in response to the comment about his room. Dark eyes snapped to the doorway that the nurse had fled from. "But the damned staff is stealing from me."

Prince asked, "How do you know that?"

Nielsen muttered an untellable response, seeing from the look on their collective faces that they probably wouldn't believe his story anyway, the insane rumblings of a senile man, and he waved the question off.

From the wall, Peterson asked, "How come you're not at the party?"

Nielsen looked at him like he was crazy for even suggesting the thought. He hooked a head towards the solarium. "Those old fools, dancing like a bunch of damned teenagers. I got all I need right here." These words grumbled out of a chest that sounded wet and phlegmy, and a racking cough rolled through the old man. Partridge started to push off the chair to help him but stopped when Nielsen shot her a glance.

When the coughing had stopped there was a small peppering of blood between the man's index and thumb. He wiped it on his housecoat quickly though it was clear everyone in the room had seen it. Nielsen cleared his throat and looked at each of them in turn. "So, what do you want?" he demanded.

Partridge spoke. "We came to talk to you about an old case file that you investigated."

Nielsen twisted around and gave Partridge a crooked grin, revealing a set of filmy teeth that were black in sections. The incongruity of Nielsen in a place like this unsettled Peterson, and he wondered how the old man had held on so long without getting kicked out. "I've investigated a lot of cases, sweetie," he told Partridge, thankfully drawing his thin chapped lips to hide the ruin of his dental work. "You'll have to be more specific."

"Bad guys were named Turner and Collins," Peterson said.

Nielsen's eyes snapped to Peterson's, recognition flooding his pupils. The old man's shoulders started to tremble slightly, as if chilled. Throat working furiously, he drew heavily on the air tube connected to his nose. Another racking cough assaulted his body, and it was a few minutes before the old man could regain any sort of composure.

"I always wondered when this would come up again," Nielsen said, defeated. He looked directly at Peterson with eyes that had probably seen too much during his policing career. "The dead don't stay buried forever, y'know."

Fifteen

Nielsen didn't want to stay in his room, and he ordered Prince to get behind his wheelchair and push. Nielsen led them back through the solarium, grumbling at the "silly old fools" who looked like they were enjoying the festivities. He told the receptionist to "go to hell" when she asked him how he was doing. She reacted like this was nothing out of the ordinary, rolling her eyes at Peterson in exaggerated fashion. They took a set of elevators to the second floor and entered an indoor pool area, the smell of chlorine thick and biting, causing Peterson's throat to itch.

There were about ten other people in the pool, all seniors, exercising at the direction of a young pretty blonde. She had a black headset with a microphone placed firmly on her fine straight hair, and her voice was broadcasted through a PA system in the ceiling. *"You're doing great, everyone. Five more reps!"* Her voice was accompanied by a steady musical beat that echoed throughout the large space. From Nielsen's hungry gaze toward the blonde, Peterson had no doubt why he had wanted to come here. This was probably the highlight of his week, he thought with no small amount of disgust. As they passed her, she gave them a quick sideways glance before refocusing on the octogenarians in the water.

Prince rolled Nielsen to the far edge of the pool, near a plastic white table and chairs. While Prince adjusted the wheel brake, Peterson and Partridge took two chairs and set them up in front of Nielsen. Prince perched on the edge on the white table, half watching Nielsen while keeping an eye on the blonde instructor.

Nielsen looked around nervously, as if checking for eavesdroppers, and his eyes glazed over hauntingly. His already-withered frame seemed to shrink even farther in the chair as he began. "What's the sudden interest in the Turner case?" he asked Peterson.

Peterson gave him the basic rundown of the two murders, and Nielsen listened without speaking. "We figure it's all related," he concluded. "We were hoping you could fill in some of the blanks."

Nielsen was silent for a stretch, staring off into the distance, and for a time Peterson wondered if he would respond at all. When he finally did, his voice was drawn and tired. "I was nearing the end of my career," he began. "Finishing things out in Serious Crimes, just kind of coasting toward the end. I got the call from the hospital," Nielsen continued. "Girl had been brought in, teenager, been raped halfway to hell and left for dead." Nielsen rubbed his hands up and down his pant legs as if trying to dry off his palms and his eyes were unfocused and distant. "They really messed her up."

"What were her injuries?" Prince broke in.

"Some superficial stuff, cuts and bruises. One large gash on her neck that barely missed her carotid. She had been leaving school when the three boys got her, pulled her into an alley and had their way with her. Tied her up, taped her mouth shut."

"And two of the suspects were Arthur Collins and Bryce Turner, I imagine," Peterson concluded, and Nielsen nodded stiffly. "Who was the third?"

Nielsen shrugged. "Some kid named Chris Solk, younger than the other two and didn't really get involved. He said he just hung back, watched the show."

Peterson flashed back to the original case file designation and the initials used to represent the youth's name, S.C. It didn't surprise him that they simply switched the initials around, probably made it less confusing. But a memory nibbled at the back of his mind at the mention of the third boy's name. He knew that he had heard the name before, or at the very least seen it somewhere, but he couldn't nail the impression down.

Nielsen's voice brought him back to the present. "Turner and Collins came from money, found them at their mansions not too far from the scene, flanked by so many black-hearted lawyers that it made my head spin." He laughed without humor. "Still didn't stop me from hauling those two boys in."

An extended pause stretched before Nielsen continued. "There was an old circuit judge back then, Stevens was his name, I think. Rumor was he had itchy fingers, but it never could be proven. I had everything ready to go for court against those three lads when he called me in. My spineless captain and the defense lawyer were there and everything, and they…" He searched for the right word, his eyes studying the high ceiling. "*Suggested*," he said in an exaggerated tone, "that I make it go away. Ordered that I hand over all the evidence, all the reports and case files. Even offered me a hefty compensation for the effort."

"So, what did you do?" Partridge asked.

Nielsen's eyebrows raised, and a flush crawled up his cheeks. "At first? Told them to stuff it, but they threatened to take my pension away too." His mouth twitched and his eyes grew downcast. "Ashamed to say that I took the money and handed all the evidence over to Stevens." For a moment, it looked to Peterson as if Nielsen might break down, small pools of water collected in the corners of the man's eyes, shimmering ponds of regret and pain. "They told me that they had offered the girl and her family some money too, and they accepted it. Were willing to drop the charges."

"And did they?" Peterson asked.

Nielsen shook his head. "Not sure." He crossed his hands in his lap and looked up at Peterson. "I received pressure to retire shortly afterward and never did ask." He paused. "Didn't want to either, if I'm being honest. Didn't want to know."

"So, what happened then?" Peterson probed. From the back, he could hear the music cut out and the sound of water sloshing as the residents climbed out of the pool, excited chatter about the party that was continuing in the solarium. Odd that Nielsen would choose such a happy place as his retirement home, as grief and self-loathing seemed to radiate off the man like waves of tepid heat.

Nielsen's mouth turned down in a sneer. "Not much. I retired and lived on my own for a bit. My wife had passed a long time ago, kids all moved away to different parts of the country. Not much time for dad anymore." He looked around the room as if seeing it for the first time. "I had enough money left over to put myself up comfortably for a time, this place seemed as good as any."

"What was the girl's name?" Prince asked, his eyes travelling over the aquatic instructor as her lithe frame climbed out of the pool, water dripping off her smooth skin.

A deep sigh escaped from Neilson's lips. "Isabella Green."

"And do you know where we can find her?" Peterson asked.

A look of surprise flashed over Nielson's lined faced, as if stunned that the detectives were unaware of the simple fact. "Hazelwood Cemetery," he said.

Sixteen

"Yeah, it's all right here, Jack," Sylvia said as Peterson bent over her shoulder to stare at the computer screen. The computer displayed a still image of a silver Honda being pulled from the river, with the heavy typeset of the headline reading: "Late night accident results in one death, police investigating." His eyes travelled to the byline's date and saw that it was in the late spring of 2005, approximately ten years after the attack on Green.

After finishing with Nielsen they had left the old man at the pool. He had told them that he had no interest in returning to his room. Peterson had looked back before walking through the door, and Nielsen had angled his wheelchair to look through the large glass windows that surrounded the semi-detached room. The light was already fading, and the old man's face had been a dim reflection in the glass, backlit by the bright lights of the pool. He stared at nothing, lost in his own haunted thoughts. With a small shake of his head, Peterson had left the room and caught up with Prince and Partridge at the vehicle. After they had dropped Prince off at HQ the other two had returned to WestOps.

Partridge continued as she read the news story. "Seems like she took the corner too fast, slid off the highway and busted through the guard rail. They never did find the body, I guess."

Peterson crossed his arms, considering. "Not surprising, really. The water moves pretty fast on that river, and she could have easily been swept away."

Partridge nodded an agreement and continued to study the computer. "It's so sad," she said. "Make it through a terrible attack like that only to die so needlessly." Despite Sylvia's rough exterior he knew that she was soft at heart, given the right motivation. A dead young girl, cut down so tragically, would do it. Peterson didn't entirely agree with her statement, but he kept his mouth shut. A part of him, maybe a large part of him, saw her death as a mercy. Maybe it was better to die then have to live with the memory of something so horrible.

Pushing that thought aside, he asked, "What about Chris Solk?" The three detectives had discussed their third man on the ride over and agreed that the name sounded familiar, even if none of them could pin down on how or where they had heard it before. Pulling up a search engine, Partridge began to enter the name, only to have the engine auto populate the results before she had even entered *the l* of Solk's last name. Peterson was surprised to see *Chris Solk CEO, Solk Industries,* and *Solk destroying the ocean,* among the top search parameters.

Apparently, the results clicked something with Partridge who snapped her fingers and said, "Of course!" Whatever registered in her mind settled into place in Peterson's as well, the images of the many newscasts, radio ads, and paper ads flashing through his mind. Solk was the Chief Executive Officer of one of the largest oil and gas exploration companies on the west coast. He had drawn the collective ire of many environmental groups when he had begun development of several offshore oil rigs deep in the Pacific Ocean, great steel monoliths that would plumb the underwater rock and sediment for liquid money.

Peterson pulled a chair over and sat next to his colleague. "He's not the most popular guy right now," he said. "His last pipeline burst near Vancouver Island, spilt nearly 800 gallons of oil that took months to clean up." It was inevitable with any oil company that accidents would occur, and usually the clean up was swift and effective, but the damage long lasting, the complete scope of the destruction sometimes only apparent years later. That Solk would push ahead to deep sea drilling so soon after a major spill showed a recklessness that Peterson found deeply disturbance. The arrogance of it all was unsettling.

Skimming through the webpages, Partridge stopped on an article from the Washington Herald. She read from the page. "'Chris Solk, CEO of Solk Industries, to appear before Senate Committee to answer questions regarding plans to expand well sites to deep sea drilling. Greenpeace and other environmental groups calling for immediate veto into operations...'" Her voice trailed off as she looked sideways at Peterson. "That committee will tear Solk apart, look at everything from his past." He knew what she was thinking. It would not only be Solk's company and safety history under investigation, but the man himself.

Peterson said, "Being complicit in the rape of a young girl would do little to improve his reputation for such a large operation. What better way than to get rid of the skeletons in his closet than by burning the whole damn house down?"

Partridge nodded appraisingly. "Do you think he would knock his friends off to protect an oil deal?"

"For potentially billions of dollars? Yes, absolutely." He swung her eyes back to the computer screen. "And with Green already gone, his two buds were the only ones who could bring him down. Hell, maybe they even tried to extort money from him, I don't know."

Peterson stood from the chair and moved to his own desk, plugging in his password to access the DMV records. He entered in Solk's name and date of birth, and the computer listed his contact information. Fishing his phone out of his pocket, he called the number and it rang three times before a husky female voice answered. "Solk Industries, this is Katrina. How may I help you?" In the background, Peterson heard the low rumble of a man's voice and the unmistakable sound of bedsheets being ruffled. He checked the clock and saw that it was nearly ten in the evening.

Peterson cleared his throat, and out of the corner of his eye he saw Partridge walk up to the cubicle wall and lean against the frame, arms crossed. "Yes, this is Jack Peterson of the Seattle Police Department, I'm sorry that I'm calling so late but..." his voice trailed off as he could hear the woman put her hand over the receiver and whisper something unintelligible. When she came back on the line, he continued. "If this is a bad time I can—"

"No, it's fine," she interrupted. Her voice was casual and professional, without a hint of aggravation. "I assume you will want to see Mr. Solk?" she asked. Surprised, Peterson agreed, and Katrina suggested ten a.m. the next morning.

"Well, I wouldn't mind seeing him tonight," Peterson said. "We have reason to suspect that his life may be in danger—"

Once again the receptionist cut him off. "I assure you Mr. Peterson, Mr. Solk is taking every necessary precaution to ensure his safety." He heard what sounded like pages turning and imagined Katrine flipping through an appointment book. "Do you know where the Goldman building is?" she asked. Peterson said he did and was about to ask a question when Katrina rolled over him. "Great, ten a.m. it is," and she hung up the phone.

Peterson stared at the phone for a stretch of time while Partridge shot him a questioning glance. He snapped the phone shut and put it back in his pocket. "I guess we have a meeting tomorrow morning," he told her as he leaned back in his chair.

"Oh joy," Partridge responded from the doorway. "We get to see how the rich people live." Sighing, Peterson swung his chair around to peer through the window. Outside the world was dark, with only the occasional pelt of snow that struck the window to indicate that anything was beyond the cool glass.

He turned back to Partridge. "You should head home soon, but maybe call an unmarked to set up post at Solk's house. Keep an eye on him, track his movements."

"You got it," she replied, and she stepped back from the doorway and returned to her desk. Her voice echoed through the hallway as she yelled, "Should I tell the guys he's a suspect or a potential victim?"

"Both!" he yelled back as he continued to stare out at the black expanse.

Seventeen

At a quarter after ten in the morning, Peterson and Denly were seated on a plush leather couch on the twenty-third floor of the Goldman building. The waiting area to which they had been directed practically oozed money, with shining gilded furnishings and frosted glass walls, each pane displaying an expensive-looking mosaic that spelled out Solk Industries in acrylic letters. Gold-filigreed paintings with motivational slogans hung from the walls above dark, marble accent desks, each sporting carefully displayed flower arrangements. Every other available space was taken up with a green frond or tree. Their placement suggested that any visitor would look upon such displays and conclude that Chris Solk's first priority was toward the environment and not to the mountain of cash that his oil and gas revenue would rake in. When he was first directed to sit on the couch, Peterson had reached over to a four-foot-high palm in the corner and rubbed a leaf between a thumb and forefinger. He was not entirely surprised when he found that the plant was fake, plastic, a simple window dressing made to appear like something more than it was.

Partridge had called in sick earlier, and Denly had been all too eager to accompany Peterson to the meeting. Denly had spent the previous day with Forensics, pouring over evidence and autopsy results. By his report, it had been a fruitless and boring affair. The Collins scene offered almost no evidence, save for some footwear impressions that a CSI tech had pulled from the mud. The generic running shoe would do little to break the case wide open. No fingerprints had been pulled from the expended cartridge casing located at the Turner scene, but Matthews had swabbed it for DNA, telling Denly that the chance of a profile being developed off the item was between slim and none, with emphasis on the none. Given the compression and heat present in a gun's chamber when a round was fired, Matthews had explained, little would usually be left of biological material, DNA or otherwise. The only apparent hope was looking in the past. There seemed little question that Turner and Collins were targeted for the Green attack, and it seemed all too likely that Solk was either next on the list or had orchestrated the entire thing.

They had arrived early, hooking up with the police detail who told them that Solk had emerged from his downtown apartment with a leggy blonde and two thick men who could only be security guards. After catching up with the police detail and checking in with the main floor reception Peterson and Denly were met on the twenty-third floor by a porcelain-skinned Asian woman with features so sharp they appeared to have been cut from glass. She directed them to a couch where they were to wait for Solk to invite them in. She sat at a high desk at the front of the reception area, periodically looking over to them through chunky white frames. To Peterson she looked as manufactured as the plants, just a different kind of facade engineered to provide a certain image.

He heard Denly huff angrily on the opposite side of the couch, and he checked his own watch for the time. Almost ten-thirty. He wondered if Solk really was busy or if he was deliberately being obstinate. The background checks on Solk were unremarkable, gathered from police index checks, university transcripts, and Google. The fact that Solk had his own Wikipedia page was not all that surprising. Thirty-four years old, Solk had graduated at a local high school, finishing at the top of his class. He managed to make it out of his rebellious years without much difficulty and enrolled in bioengineering at the U of S. After, he got an entry level position at a petroleum firm. His intelligence and ambition allowed him to climb the corporate ladder quickly, and within ten years he had his own company and a large enough bankroll that it rivalled most GDPs of developing countries. It wasn't until he started work on offshore sights that the focus really sharpened on him. The deal, which was tentative at best, hinged on the upcoming senate hearing, his fate in the collective hands of state politicians, judges, and lobby groups. There were more than a few websites who had already concluded that Solk had more than half of the senate committee members in his pocket, the bribes all but ensuring that the decision would go in his favor. And perhaps it would. It wouldn't be the first time that the wheels were greased in an oil company's favor. Peterson wondered how many of the environmentalists and detractors came to the meetings in their own gas-powered vehicles, arguing against the industry but ignoring their own comforts that the sector ultimately provided.

Peterson's attention was drawn away when he heard a female voice say, "Gentlemen?" He looked up to see an gorgeous blonde walk toward them down the hallway. From the earlier description from the police detail, Peterson knew that this was the woman who had been seen leaving with Solk earlier in the morning. He and Denly got to their feet as the woman stopped short before them. Dressed in black leather heels and a blue pencil skirt, she towered over Denly and came to eye level with Peterson. The term "leggy blonde" that had been given to him hardly did her justice, as smooth white calves climbed from the leather heels to the dangerously high hem of her short skirt. With the belt of the skirt just under the woman's breasts, it lent an almost disproportionate length to her entire body, making it seem like she was more leg than torso. Tucked into the skirt was a white blouse, the buttons straining to contain her large chest, which seemed deliberately displayed. Peterson fought the unconscious urge to look at her cleavage and concentrated on her eyes, which were a deep shade of emerald green. She introduced herself as Katrina and apologized for the delay, and Peterson thought back to the phone call from the night before, the sound of her voice husky from sleep, a male's voice in the background. That she had been seen with Solk at his apartment this morning left little doubt in his mind that their relationship went beyond the strictly professional.

"Follow me, please," she said and strode purposefully down the long hallway. Both detectives surged to follow her, and Peterson saw that Denly was having a difficult time not staring at Katrina's rear end in the form-fitting skirt. Except for the front receptionist and Katrina, the office building appeared to be empty, and Peterson wondered where the rest of the employees were. Katrina led them to an impressive solid oak door, a gold-plated sign screwed to the front that said "Chris Solk – CEO", and she opened it and waved them inside.

"If you have a seat, Chris will be with you in a moment," she said before closing the door softly behind them. From Peterson's left, Denly whistled in admiration. The room was roughly U-shaped with large floor-to-ceiling windows that collected around the entire exterior, which looked out over downtown Seattle in a panoramic view. On one side was a lush, white leather sofa flanked by two dark wood stands; crystal bowls on top held clear glass orbs that reflected the slashes of sunlight that sneaked through the late morning clouds. The other side held a black grand piano and a sweeping wood desk that had probably cost more than Peterson's car.

"Guy's not hurting for cash, is he?" Denly offered.

From the right side a doorway led to another room where there came the round of running water, a tap being shut off. "If you got it, flaunt it," a voice yelled from the attached bathroom. Chris Solk, looking a few years older than the photograph from his Wikipedia page, emerged from the doorway, rubbing his hands dry on a small white towel. He threw this absently behind him into the bathroom and closed the door. With a warm smile, he approached them, stuck out his hand. "So, you like the living space?" he asked, eyes alight.

Peterson took the proffered hand and shook it once. He allowed his gaze to sweep across the room. "I guess it makes no bones about the amount of money you have at your fingertips," he said, making no attempt to hide his disgust at the ridiculous display of opulence. His mind drifted to people like Juliette and the other poor denizens of the city who were just trying to scratch out a living, keep their head down until the storm passed, though it never seemed to. Solk could buy and sell those types of people and not even break into a sweat.

"It's important to project the right image," he explained, and they followed him toward the bamboo desk in the corner. He sat behind it and propped his Italian leather shoes on the corner, laced his fingers on his flat stomach. "I have investors who come to this office building expecting a certain thing. They want to be assured that their funds are going to be paid back to them, in spades."

Denly asked, "How do your investors feel about your upcoming hearing?"

Solk nodded, meeting Denly's eyes. "They're understandably concerned."

"And you?" Peterson asked.

"And me, what?"

"Are you... 'understandably concerned'?"

Solk chuckled and took his feet from the desk, leaning forward to prop his elbows on the tabletop. "Look, Detective Peterson, I get it that the media has painted me as some kind of devil. Out to destroy the ecosystem and all that. What they don't report on is all the safety protocols I've enacted in my company. Protocols that go far beyond what any other organization in the petroleum industry is currently doing. Or the millions I have invested in renewable forms of energy, the technology that I have advanced and spearheaded to ensure that no marine accident occurs." A sadness passed over his eyes that looked to Peterson as genuine. "I care about the world, detective. I really do. It's my world too."

Peterson wondered if Solk's display of concern was real or all just an act, practiced before the senate hearing, the big show.

Peterson heard a soft click and looked back to see Katrina slide through the door. She carried a steaming mug of what was probably coffee and set it down on a coaster on the tabletop. Solk nodded to her gratefully, and she stood beside him, hand on his shoulder. "You didn't seem all that surprised when I called you last night," he said to the secretary, and from the physical closeness of the two there seemed to be no pretence of the other roles she filled in Solk's life.

Solk answered for her. "We watch the news, detective. Turner getting murdered is one thing, but Collins is too much of a coincidence. I had to assume that I was going to be involved in some way, or at least there was the possibility of it."

Denly nodded toward Katrina. "Are you sure you don't want to talk about this alone?" he asked.

Katrina gave him an icy smile. "We know everything about each other," she responded.

Peterson doubted that claim but let it slide. Perhaps she really believed that or maybe she didn't. In the end, he pressed forward.

"We believe that the death of Turner and Collins were related and that it has something to do with Isabella Green," Peterson said. He told Solk about the missing case file at the courthouse. "Did you have anything to do with that?" he asked.

Solk coughed, disbelief written on his face. "Me?" he said. "How the hell would I do that?"

"Money opens a lot of doors," Denly said. "Doors that are closed for most people." He leaned forward and fixed Solk with a sharp gaze. "Do you mind if I go ahead a little bit, Jack?"

Peterson waved a hand at him, *by all means*. "You're going to have a spotlight on yourself real soon, Mr. Solk. Everyone is gonna wanna know what kind of skeletons you got floating around in your closets." Denly's southern twang drifted like liquid smoke, but Peterson could see the outrage brewing under Solk's calm and confident demeanor. "Who's to say that you didn't hire someone to take your skeletons out? With Turner and Collins gone, it's easy to bribe someone to steal and destroy the case file for you. Then all you need to do is deny, deny, deny." He smiled with little warmth. "I think you're good at that."

Unexpectedly, Solk burst out laughing. The other three people in the room looked at him like the man had lost his mind, and it was a stretch of time before he gained control of himself. When the laughter subsided he rubbed at his eye with the back of his hand, apologizing to Denly. "You sound like those hippy dippy environmentalists, spouting that I'm some kind of black-hearted Satanist trying to raze the land." He stared very seriously at Denly and Peterson now, switching his eyes between the two men. "No, I didn't hire anyone to kill Turner and Collins. To say that we had a falling out over the…ah, incident, is an understatement." He sighed deeply. "You have to believe me, I didn't know what they were going to do to that poor girl, and if I did I would have told someone."

Peterson asked, "What happened with Isabella Green?"

Solk swallowed a few times, as if the memory was something unpleasant that had settled in the back of his throat. "Bryce and Arty were the popular kids, lots of money, good at sports, good looking, the whole thing. Girls flocked toward them, guys too, though for different reasons of course. They…" he searched for the right words, mouth drawn in and pursed. "…they had their own gravity, you know what I mean?" Peterson gave him no indication one way or the other and he continued. "Bryce was always confident with the girls, where I was a bit of a nerd at the time. I only found out later that the girl, Isabella, had snubbed Bryce, and, well…" He paused again. "He had a temper."

"If you guys were so different, then why were you friends?" Denly asked.

Solk gave a short laugh. "Money, mostly. All three of us were rich kids, and their parents probably told them they had to hang out with me. Who knows, maybe they even liked me. We had some good times before, well, before all of that happened."

Despite the halting details, Peterson felt his revulsion deepening as Solk went through the story. Collins may have been aware, Solk said, of what was going to happen with the girl, whereas Solk claimed that he had no idea. One night, Turner and Collins had invited him out to play basketball at the school. But instead of going into the school they waited outside of it, hidden away in a darkened alley. When Solk asked them what was going on, he was merely told to be quiet. Being the younger and smaller kid, he followed the order. When he saw Green emerge from the school shortly before nine and noticed the tense expressions settle over his friends, he knew that something bad was about to happen. He held out his hands in defense now toward Peterson and said, "But I had no idea they were going to do what they did. Bryce pulled her into the alley and threw her to the ground. Arthur took out a roll of duct tape and taped her mouth shut, used another piece to bind her wrists." Solk's eyes stared through Peterson with the memories. "I remember she had a red hat on. Isn't that weird? It fell in a pothole, covered with water. I remember thinking that she would have to clean it after."

A pause stretched out before Denly asked, "What happened then?"

Solk nodded, as if sensing the inevitability of this confession. Katrina stood to his side as still as a stone, looking down at him. "They told me to keep an eye out, so I went to the mouth of the alley and just stood there, watching for anybody, keeping my back to them. I don't know how long it went on for but eventually they came back out. And then we left."

Peterson raged against his own sickness and asked as calmly as he could, "What about the girl?"

Solk shook his head one, twice. "I didn't look back," he said quietly.

Eighteen

"Why should we believe any of this?" Peterson asked, drawing Solk back into the present.

The man leaned forward in his desk, placing both hands on the table top. "Because I didn't do it. Sure, I didn't like Bryce and Arthur, didn't even see much of them after that, and it had been their folks who had paid off the judge and everyone else associated to the file. They were all in on it—Judge Stevens, our lawyer. I was just a kid, what the hell did I know about the world?"

"Well, someone seems to be interested in taking you people out," Denly offered.

"Have you talked to Stevens?" Solk asked. "If anyone could steal the file, it would be him."

"He's been dead for years, natural causes," Peterson said. He frowned and shifted in his seat. "You said 'our' lawyer. What did you mean by that?"

"We were charged at the same time, so we had one defender to represent us." Solk pulled a drawer open in his desk and took out a pen and paper, writing the name of his lawyer down. He handed it to Peterson. "This is the guy. I don't know if he's still practicing, but at least it's someone that you can talk to."

Peterson pocketed the note. Katrina's hand was still on Solk's shoulder, and he reached up and squeezed it in his own. It occurred to Peterson that she must have heard this story before and wondered if his earlier assumptions that their relationship was purely physical had been a bit unfair. That she was still with him despite the admission either spoke to her own character or to the deep feelings they obviously had for one another.

"What are the chances that I am also a target?" Solk asked.

Peterson considered a moment before answering. "I don't know if the killings are related yet or not. There's still the chance that it was entirely random, or at least that Turner and Collins were killed for different reasons entirely. I do think we need to exercise at least some caution—" but Peterson didn't get to finish his sentence as there was a muffled pop, the sound of glass shattering, and then the side of Solk's head disintegrated. A splash of blood sprayed Peterson's face, and Katrina cried out in pain as the round passed out of Solk's left temple and entered her right side, throwing her to the ground like a sack of rice. Peterson sat motionless, stunned, unable to move, until he felt Denly's hands on his shoulders, the man yelling "Down!" as he was pushed to the ground where they struggled to the side of the desk opposite of the window.

Denly was on his left as they huddled behind the protection of the bamboo desk, and he could hear the other detective's ragged, panicked breathing. His own breath came in great heaves as he struggled with his own panic and fought to control his terror and surprise. He could feel Solk's blood dribbling down his forehead, and, sickened, he rubbed it off with the back of his hand as his thoughts bounced in his mind like rocks in a tin can. *Breathe, calm down, breathe,* he told himself and he finally remembered Katrina, whose strangled sobs floated somewhere from his right side.

She was partially over Solk, who was lying on his side from the force of the gunshot that had destroyed his head. The chair that he had been sitting on had been knocked over. With one hand she clutched at his shirt, crying, *"Chris, Chris!"* while the other she held to the oblique side of her stomach, a great tide of blood washing through her fingers and running down the length of her skirt.

In the fog of his mind Peterson realized that she was still in the line of fire, and he expected any moment for another shot to cut her down. Without thinking he grabbed her arm and bodily pulled her toward him, even as she fought to hold on to Chris Solk, where no amount of grief or tears could bring the dead man back.

He yelled at her with as much force as he could muster, "Get the hell over here!" and she finally released the corpse, collapsing into his arms as he dragged her the rest of the way. Periodically Denly would peer over the desk to the where the shot had come from, all the while yelling into his cellphone for backup and an ambulance. Peterson wasn't sure when he had taken the phone out, all of it was happening too quickly.

Peterson eased Katrina gently to the carpet; she stopped fighting him the second she had been detached from Solk, as if her physical contact with him had given her strength, and now that she was detached so had gone her energy. He placed both hands on the side of her stomach and applied pressure, the sticky warmth of her blood seeping through his shaking fingers. Her breath came in shuddering gasps, and her head rolled to the side where she stared at the body of Solk, her lips quivering and her eyes twitching at the sight of him. She had gone deathly pale, skin chalk white. There was the sound of a door opening from behind Peterson, and then a female voice shrieking in terror. The Asian receptionist was standing the doorway, hand to her mouth, taking in the scene with a horrified expression. Denly was telling her to get back, to get away, and Peterson was about to tell the other detective that the shooter was probably gone when there was a crack, louder now that the window was partially shattered, and a table lamp on top of the desk exploded in a shower of glass and plastic. Peterson swore, throwing his body over Katrina's, and he saw out of the corner of his eye that the receptionist had darted out of view. Denly was now on the phone, telling the dispatch or backup that the shooter was still active, and to get teams out to the building now.

Peterson could feel Katrina's body shudder underneath his own, and he pushed himself up off her. The blood was no longer flowing so freely out of her wound. It had slowed to a trickle. For a second Peterson was relieved, thinking maybe the pressure he was applying had stemmed the worst of it, but he took one look at her face and he felt his stomach drop. Her mouth was working slowly, eyes still staring at Solk's limp form, and her breathing was coming in slow pulls that ended with a quiet moan each time. She made one final sound, a soft cry through lips so pale they were almost hauntingly beautiful, and then she was still.

Peterson took his hands away and stared at the red sticky blood that was painted on his fingers. He was trembling violently, and the small droplets flew from his hands like crimson tears.

Nineteen

By the time the adjacent building was cleared, where the responding officers found an unconscious and tied-up guard on the rooftop, the blood on Peterson's hands had cooled and mostly dried, and he could only see the red staining faintly on his skin, like an after image that had burned into his retina. The guard had a broken jaw and other superficial injuries they were attempting to get a description of the shooter, but communication was difficult. The officers had managed to learn that the guard had been doing routine patrols when he had come across a maintenance worker on the roof. He was going to let the man go before he noticed a long-barrelled rifle poking out from a duffel bag that had been at the man's feet. When the guard tried to call for backup, the man had lunged at him, striking him in the face with an elbow and knocking him unconscious. On the rooftop, after hauling the guard away to an ambulance, the responding officer's found evidence that a bipod had been used to support a high powered rifle. The rifle itself was gone, packed up and taken away by the killer. They were working on security footage, but it seemed that it had been disabled.

     Peterson learned all of this from Partridge, who had shaken off most of her sickness to come to the Goldman building, where Denly and Peterson waited in the main reception area. Denly paced around the room like a man incensed while Peterson sat on the edge of one of the leather chairs, hands clasped before him as if in prayer. Every few moments he would pull his hands apart and the skin would stick slightly from Katrina's blood. He should really wash them, the bathroom was right there, but he didn't trust his legs to support his weight when he stood up. He didn't want to collapse in front of Denly and Partridge. So he sat very still as Partridge calmly detailed what she had found out thus far while at the same time trying to ignore Denly as he rumbled like a penned-up lion.

"That son of a bitch tried to kill me," Denly said, his face red with barely supressed rage. His hands were clenched into fists and held to his side, pressing into his thighs.

Peterson felt himself speak, voice hoarse. "No, he didn't."

"What are you talking about man, that bullet nearly took my head off!" Denly stormed.

Peterson was too tired to explain, so he said nothing to try and quell the man's overloaded anger. The shot that had killed Solk and Katrina, whose last name had been Ellis, Peterson had learned, had been the killer's first bullet, his cold shot, which typically had the worst aim. Usually, the shooter hadn't adjusted to the specific conditions yet, wind, yardage, or his own nervousness. If there was any shot that was going to go wide, it was the first one out of the pipe. But it had struck Solk exactly as intended. The second shot that had struck the table lamp near Denly's head had merely been for show, for fun, the killer showing off before packing up his gear and fleeing the scene. Had he known Denly and he was there, that they were police? He didn't see how, though there was no doubt that a scope of some variety had been used to make the kill. He would have seen all three of them in the office with Solk, along with Katrina. Given the precision of the kill shot, he could have easily shot all four of them should he have had half a mind to do so, and the thought should have filled Peterson with a choking rage, but the memory of Katrina's pale form played over in his mind like a repeating clip.

Partridge settled into the chair next to the Peterson, clearly trying to ignore Denly who was growing increasingly more agitated. Her eyes were red and puffy by whatever sickness had fallen upon her, but he read the concern there. She reached out a hand and placed it on Peterson's knee.

"Are you okay, Jack?" she asked, very seriously.

Peterson barely trusted himself to speak, but he nodded. "Yeah, I'm just thinking." Partridge seemed to accept the lie as she removed her hand from his knee and nodded slowly to herself. The truth was that Peterson's thoughts were a garbled jumble, and when he closed his eyes, if only for the smallest second, he pictured Katrina staring at her dead lover, and he couldn't help but draw comparisons to his own experiences. The terrible thoughts and memories that he fought so hard to keep pushed down deep in his subconscious were banging on the gates of his mind, and he knew that if he allowed them even the smallest crack that they would bust through and consume him.

Forensics had already been through both scenes, from the rooftop to Solk's office, and had found little evidence. They found no expended cartridge casings, suggesting the killer had taken them with him prior to leaving. The coroner had arrived and authorized that the bodies be removed and at the autopsy in the morning they would excise the bullet lodged in Katrina's side, using the ballistic information to run it through the NCIS database. Peterson was not hopeful that anything would be learned from this course of action. With the addition of the forensic evidence from this scene they had practically nothing to connect the killer or give any shred of information of what his identity might be. That they were dealing a professional was no longer in doubt, but Peterson wondered why the man had let the security guard live. Perhaps it was for the same reason that he and Denly were both still alive, their deaths would have served no ultimate purpose.

Partridge leaned back in her seat and sniffed loudly, and when she spoke it sounded like her mouth was full of cotton. "As soon as the guard is able to speak we'll get a description out of the suspect to the airports and bus stations. Maybe someone will be able to spot him when he leaves town."

"Why do you think he's leaving town?" Peterson asked.

Partridge gave him a look. "Why wouldn't he?" she asked, sweeping her hand back toward Solk's office.

The flash bulbs of the forensic members were lighting the hallway like the strobe lights at a rave party. "Turner's dead, so is Collins, and now Solk. Those were the three involved in the Green assault. What reason would he have to stay?"

Peterson didn't have an answer for that, but a niggling settled into his stomach. He had no logical reason or explanation, but a large part of him thought that the killer wasn't done.

After two gurneys had wheeled away the bodies of Solk and Katrina, mercilessly sealed in black, plastic body bags, they left Partridge to oversee the final release of the scene while he and Denly walked out to Peterson's car. They had to weave through a sea of police officers and reporters, the latter who, when they saw the bloody state of Peterson's clothes and Denly's ragged expression, threw microphones and cellphones with recording apps in their face, and barked rapid fire questions at them. A mixture of rain and sleet fell from the darkening sky, and Peterson did his best to ignore the reporters as he pushed past them. He cast a sidelong glance at Denly as a particularly aggressive reporter blocked his past, the young kid jamming his iPhone under Denly's nose. From the look on Denly's face, he thought he might punch the kid in the face, but instead used the outside of his forearm to shove the guy back where he slammed into another reporter behind him.

"Hey, watch it," the kid protested, adjusting a blue windbreaker and sneering at Denly, who stalked away.

Peterson settled into the driver's seat and asked Denly if he was okay. The younger man simply nodded, but a flush crept up his neck, and his hands were clenched so tightly that the knuckles had turned a ghostly white. Peterson put the car in gear and managed not to run anyone over, reporters and onlookers alike, until he was clear of the maze and speeding toward the north side. Peterson would have preferred to drive alone and grieved that he would be unable to see Juliette tonight, but Denly's residence was on the way to his own, and the man was wound so tight that Peterson didn't trust him to drive. Not that he trusted himself overly, and he kept his hands tightly on the wheel to prevent them from shaking. He was so focused on himself and Denly that he didn't notice the dark-colored sedan as it pulled out from a side street and began following them from a respectable distance three car lengths back.

Kincaid had waited patiently in the dark-blue, four-door Ford Escort, going through the evening's events in his mind. By the time the detective's beige Chevy Impala passed by the mouth of the alley, he had finished his introspection and, despite a few mistakes and regrets, had concluded that he had done the best he could with the information and time that he had. True, he should have killed the guard, who could now provide the police with his physical description. The death of the blonde that had been standing beside his intended victim had given him greater pause. He knew he had hit her approximately two seconds after he had pulled the trigger; the way her body had flopped backward like a rag doll had been evidence enough. The round of ammunition that he had fed into the M40 had little backstop, and once it punched through Solk's skull and brain it had obviously continued along its inexorable course. What he hadn't realized at the time was the severity of her injuries. After they loaded the second body into the meat wagon he had realized that the woman had died. To say that Kincaid felt regret would have been an over characterization. He admonished himself for the unprofessionalism and promised to rein it in and focus on the task of hand. Broken eggs and omelets, after all.

The decision to follow the detective, he felt, was a prudent one. Something about the sight of the man had triggered a memory, and he was sure that he had seen him before. He stayed behind the man's car by a few car lengths, enough that he wouldn't be noticed, but not so far that he would get trapped behind a red light should the detective speed through on a yellow. By the time they made it out of downtown the traffic thinned, and he increased the distance between their two cars. Kincaid's windshield wipers worked double duty, swishing side to side as their cars penetrated the inky blackness, and soon they seemed to be the only two cars on the highway. Kincaid drummed his thumbs on the steering wheel and hummed a tune to himself, the death of the blonde woman now completely forgotten.

Twenty

Peterson was concerned Denly was losing his mind. After leaving the office building, he wound through the city streets toward Denly's residence, while the younger man went through fits and spurts of increasingly agitated behavior. He would be at once outraged at nearly being killed then would yell in exultation about still being alive.

Peterson knew that Denly was in shock, still trying to process the terrible event that had just occurred. Usually the police were not witness to such extreme acts of violence and brutality, at least not when it was occurring. There was a big difference to arriving at a scene and finding a dead body versus watching two people die right before your very eyes.

Outside of downtown and heading toward the residential areas, they were alone on the highway save for a pair of headlights that bobbed in the far distance behind their car. Peterson was grateful for the light traffic, as he had found the intensity of the oncoming headlights dizzying and he was forced to shield his eyes each time a car passed them. A steady rain spattered the windshield, and small ribbons of rainwater trailed down the glass from outside the driver's window, and in the darkness they looked a lot like small rivers of blood.

"I mean I was right there!" Denly yelled and punched the dashboard for the second or third time. With alarm Peterson saw that the plastic framing was dented and the knuckles on Denly's right hand were bruised and reddened. One more punch like that and Denly's skin would crack open and the blood would start to pour. Denly, face flushed in the dying light, turned to Peterson. "Can you bloody believe it?"

Peterson told Denly to calm down and take it easy, and he cast sideways glances toward him while trying to keep focused on the road. Whereas Denly's emotions punched out, Peterson could feel himself drawing in, shrinking from his very center. He pictured himself getting smaller and smaller, his bones pulling in, snapping like dry tinder, collapsing in on himself as if being sucked down in a black hole that had somehow formed in the pit of his stomach, until the only thing that was left of himself was no larger than the head of a pin.

"I've never seen anything like it," Denly was now saying. He had both hands gripped on the dashboard, fingernails pressed into the hard plastic. "I mean, his head just went pop," Denly finished, shaking his own head with the memory.

Peterson had no need for Denly to mention this, as the recollection of the day's events were replaying over and over in his mind. The snap of Solk's head as the force of the bullet entered his temple, the red spray of blood and brains from the opposite side as the bullet rifled through and entered Katrina's abdomen. And this, inevitably, brought up carefully buried memories that were usually reserved for nightmares, the sight of Laura's dead eyes staring up at him.

Peterson tried to speak but found that his tongue was thick in his mouth, and it felt fuzzy and sluggish. He smacked his lips a few times, trying to work up some saliva, but it was gummy and the best he could manage was a kind of a croak that Denly in his tempest failed to notice. Peterson had his left hand on the wheel, the other resting against his palm, and he felt the sweat form under his palm and at his hairline, the temperature in the vehicle climbing as the thoughts of death and blood rebounded in his mind. The windshield and the roadway faded away as he saw flashes of the faces of the dead blaze through his mind.

It was so damned hot in the car. He went to raise his right hand to turn the thermostat down but found that his arm didn't respond to his commands, his palm remaining on his thigh like a dead fish. Tendrils of darkness edged along the outside of his vision, and with a sickening horror he felt his left hand slip off the wheel and his head began to loll towards the headrest, the back of his head butting up against the upholstery silently. With his vision failing he tried to say something to Denly, who had yet to notice that Peterson was no longer holding on to the wheel, but he couldn't form the words.

Peterson's foot pressed harder on the accelerator as his consciousness started to slip farther and farther away from him, and from what seemed to be a very far distance away he heard Denly yelling his name and roughly taking the wheel. The vehicle began to bounce over the rumble strips on the pavement. And as the darkness enveloped him, a great buzzing sound grew behind his ears. The ditch loomed and knew somewhere in the back of his mind that it was too late.

Half a mile back, Kincaid had watched curiously as the sedan began weaving slightly side to side, as if the driver were drunk. Moments before the vehicle hit the ditch it picked up speed and angled sharply to the right and shot toward the embankment. A great plume of water erupted from the front end as it nosed into the far side of the ditch, and even from this distance he heard the crunch of the front end as it jammed into the hard-packed earth.

Kincaid's eyebrows raised in alarm, but he said nothing as the rear end lifted off the ground and the vehicle slammed onto its roof, waves of ditch water shooting off the sides like a tidal wave. He closed the distance quickly now and stopped his vehicle on the side of the pavement parallel to the detective's car, the wheels spinning as power was still being delivered from the engine. It threw a whining sound in the air that pierced his ear drums as he stepped out from the car, the rain striking his head and shoulders, soaking him almost immediately. He looked over the hood of his car at the cop's vehicle, which was now partially submerged in the ditch water, the level of which had already reached past the steering wheel and rippled out from the broken driver's window.

Kincaid quickly checked his surroundings, finding no other cars in either distance. From where he was standing he could see the driver's left arm, hanging limply in the small lake that had collected in the car's interior. Kincaid was alone with the two police officers, who were slowing drowning in their own car.

Twenty-One

Peterson was having another nightmare. This time Laura's skin seemed to be made of glass, and each time she spoke a piece broke off, revealing the pink muscle underneath. Though it wasn't words that came out of her mouth, but a metallic beeping sound. The beeping that he heard slowly dragged him out of the memory and coalesced into a steady ringing. Peterson opened his eyes painfully, blinking away the stinging sensation as some kind of liquid, blood he thought, dripped from his eyelid. The ringing was coming from the car, some kind of alert or alarm. Beyond the thrumming of the rain, he heard gurgling water and a groaning, whirring sound.

He was initially confused by the sensation of being upside down, suspended in his driver's seat, the seatbelt cutting painfully into his hips. Like Laura's skin, the windshield was shattered, fracture lines running through the glass in violent and jagged angles. The airbag was deflated and hung from the module like a wet sheet. A waxy sheen of blood was present on the fabric that he figured was his own, though he had no recollection of striking the airbag.

He groaned and looked over to his right to find Denly hanging in a similar fashion in the passenger seat, his arms hanging above, or below, his head. Peterson couldn't see past Denly's elbows, the rest of his arms submerged in dark murky water, and the man appeared unconscious, a wide gash on his forehead that slowly leaked blood that looked black in the dim light.

Peterson had no sense of time and wondered how long they had been like this. He knew what had happened, and panic and despair settled into his mind as he started to focus on the situation. He had to get out, he had to get Denly out. He could feel the vehicle shifting in the ditch, sinking into the soft grass and mud, and the water line slowly crawled up the windshield toward them. Already he could see that the level had climbed past Denly's elbows and was now lapping against his biceps, inching ever higher as the weight of the vehicle drove it deeper.

His own arms were submerged in the water, above his head, and he lifted them painfully, pins and needles radiating across his skin after being in the cold water for so long. His body seemed to ache everywhere, the pain flaring up in so many places he couldn't focus on where it was coming from. He brought numb fingers to his face and breathed into his hands, tightening and relaxing his fists to exercise movement in them. He found it difficult to keep his eyes open, and his lids felt heavy, consciousness slipping through his tenuous grasp as a wave of nausea shuddered through him.

"Uh…" A sound escaped from his lips as he brought his hands up to the buckle. He squinted up as his right thumb found the latch and he pressed, the red rectangle hardly moving an inch as he struggled to detach the belt. It seemed to be stuck, and he pressed it again with all his strength, which seemed to be fading with every passing second. Already he could feel the water tickling the top of his head, a gentle lapping that marked its slow ascent. Gritting his teeth, he fought his own dizziness and pushed on the latch with all his strength, but it refused to disengage, and he let gravity take his hands and arms back into the icy water, a small sob of frustration threading through his chattering lips.

He looked over to Denly, who remained unconscious, the ditch water now halfway up his forehead. He found that he almost envied the man, who in his state would not have to suffer what was about to happen. Shame and regret crawled over Peterson, a sickening denseness in his stomach.

The cold persisted and settled into Peterson's bones, the claws of unconsciousness digging into him again, and he was about to give himself over to it when he heard a sound outside the driver's window. It was entirely shattered, the water halfway up the A pillar, and a small rippling tide accompanied by the sound of a male swearing petered through the space. A pair of heavy work boots, entirely sunk in the water, reached two pairs of legs, which appeared through the window.

"Help..." Peterson groaned. The person just stood there, the legs immobile, and panic itched over Peterson, and he would have screamed if he had the energy.

Finally, there was a grunting sound and the peal of metal as the door was forced open. In the darkness, and upside down, he could hardly make out the profile of the individual that stood before the window, hands on hips, looking down on Peterson. A shake of the head was barely visible as a deep voice said, "Now, what to do with you?" The voice, a man's, sounded to Peterson like it was almost amused, as if the person was looking down on something either entirely funny or strangely tragic. But the darkness that had been worming its way across Peterson's eyes now took hold again, and before he could answer the man, or think of anything to say at all, a blackness seized him again, and he heard no more.

It was the pelting rainwater that brought Peterson back to the world of the living, and he found that he was on his back, staring up at a black sky that sent an unrelenting shower into his open eyelids. His lower half was in the ditch, and he looked to his left to find that the back of his head was on the pavement, his body partially in the ditch and partially on the shoulder of the roadway. He heard a pained groaning beside him and saw that Denly was in a similar position, and he was slowly moving his head as if coming out of a deep sleep. Peterson didn't trust himself to sit up, but even in this position he could see the dwindling red taillights of a vehicle as it cut through the inky blackness of the impenetrable night.

Twenty-Two

Denly had suffered a broken right leg, a fractured left arm, multiple contusions and cuts, and probably had a concussion. Peterson watched the departing ambulance from the soaked roadway. Two uniformed patrol officers standing to his right were talking quietly, shoulders hunched against the cold. They watched the tow truck attempt to right his vehicle, which was settled into the ditch like a beetle on its back, tires uselessly pointing in the air. From their darted and wary glances in his direction, he could tell they were still wondering what had caused the accident. No skid marks leading to the entry site indicated that he hadn't tapped his brakes or lost control, which ran contrary to the story that he had given them. What was he supposed to tell them, after all? That he had passed out for no other reason than to escape the crush of memories that threatened to destroy him? He couldn't do it, and so had thought up the lie that made the most sense to him. He hit a patch of rainwater on the roadway that had caused him to lose control. Denly, who hadn't full regained consciousness by the time the patrol officers began their questioning, could neither refute or support this claim, and the two doubting officers had to rely on Peterson's account alone, though he knew that they suspected he had either been high, drunk, or incompetent at the time of the accident. And since they had no evidence to support drug or alcohol use, they had no choice but to accept his account, for now.

   Peterson shut his eyes against the flashing glare of the patrol car's red and blues, finding that the lights seemed to drill directly into the center of his brain, and jammed his hands as far as he could into his pockets. His clothing was entirely soaked through, and when he had reached into his coat pocket to retrieve his driver's licence for the cop, he found that his wallet was gone. When Peterson had asked the tow truck driver to keep an eye out for the wallet the older man had looked at the ditch and laughed. At least his pistol was still secured in his shoulder rig, and although the weapon was wet, it should still operate. He didn't want to imagine the bureaucratic nightmare if he had to report a lost service weapon.

Peterson had refused to go to the hospital, and the paramedics reluctantly and reproachfully left him on the side of the roadway, waiting for the taxi he had called with one of the officer's cell phones. They had bandaged him up sufficiently, but he could still feel the pounding in his head where he had struck the airbag.

The tow truck whirred as the winch tightened and pulled at the far passenger side of his partially submerged car. The operator had parked his rig parallel to the roadway, and its warning lights flashed a mustard yellow as the middle-aged man pulled on the red knobbed levers on the side of the flatbed. The silver cable pulled taut as his car settled on to the driver's side then fell roughly back on to its wheels. The roof was completely caved in, the metal ribbed and rippled from the impact on the soft earth, and water gushed from the interior where it joined the silty river that flowed through the ditch. The precipitation pinged off the now-flat roof like tiny pellets that Peterson found unbearably loud.

From his right, one of the uniforms nodded in his direction and approached him. "They'll have to get a flat deck to take this out," he said, jerking his head toward the ruined car. He handed Peterson a card that had his name and badge number. "In the morning, I'll need you to drop off a statement." The cop, a young-looking kid in his late twenties, gave him a measured glance that was only answered when Peterson raised an eyebrow at him. "You really don't know who pulled you out?" he asked.

Peterson shook his head and told him no. What he remembered of the man, his apparent good Samaritan, came back in flashes and snippets, like old photographs. The guy standing outside the window in the rain, his strange words, the feel of strong arms under his armpits, and a drawn face staring down at him from the darkness. These images flittered through his mind like butterflies, shapeless and formless, and the more he tried to catch them the more they skittered away. The cops had told him that they had received an anonymous 9-1-1 call about the accident and Peterson assumed it was the same guy. At least there were some kind people left in the world.

The cab smelled like cigarettes and rotten apples, and Peterson tried not to dwell on whatever crunched under his feet on the rear passenger floorboard. Once they had pulled away from the accident scene, Peterson had asked the Middle Eastern driver to take him downtown, away from his home, which held no attraction for him now. Relief flooded over him when he saw Juliette standing under an awning past the corner market, her black fur coat pulled up on her thin shoulders to brace against the cold.

Her hair was slicked back and hooded eyes glared at the cab suspiciously as it pulled to the curb. He caught the look of the cab driver from the rear-view mirror, likewise suspicious and more than a little reproachful, as Peterson rolled down the rear passenger window. He had probably already figured Peterson for a cop, given the situation, and knew beyond a doubt the tradecraft that the woman on the corner participated in. Peterson was too tired to care what the driver thought and ignored him as he stuck his head out the open window and called to Juliette.

Her suspicious glare dropped immediately, and she smiled when she saw him. Peterson swung the door open and slid over the cracked leather seat as she ran from the protection of the awning to the cab's interior, shaking off the rain from her head as she settled herself down.

Her look of happiness evaporated into concern as she took in his face, which had a large bandage on his temple and multiple bruises and small cuts. "Oh my god," she said, touching his face gently with a gloved hand. In the dim light of the cab her eyes were like dark sapphires, and they flicked from his injuries back to his own eyes. "What happened to you?"

Juliette gave the cab driver her address, which was on the second floor walk up of a ratty looking apartment on the far edge of downtown. On the cab ride over Peterson described the accident, surprising himself in that he held none of the details back, and gave her the complete truth. He spoke in hushed tones, inches from her ear, lest the cabbie overhear and be forced to report back the conversation to an investigator at a later date. Her skin smelled strongly of Irish Spring soap, but there was an undercurrent of foulness present, the smell of recently smoked cigarettes. She listened patiently, without interrupting. When he was done, she rubbed her thumb under his chin and sadly shook her head, whether at him or simply at the situation he could not say.

Juliette paid the cab driver in cash, Peterson's own wallet probably halfway to the ocean by now. The loss of his money, credit cards, and ID was one thing. The loss of his badge, which had been kept in the back of his wallet under a clear plastic divider, was something else entirely. He would call in the morning to report the loss and prepare for the inevitable investigation. Usually Internal Affairs followed up on any misplaced or lost badges, and they typically were not very gentle.

Juliette held his hand as they climbed up the two-story stairs to her apartment. Her thick, black, fur coat hung past her knees, revealing the smooth white skin of her shin and calf, each of which ended in a pair of severe pumps. He had never been to her apartment before; all the other times they had met had been at his own residence, and he had never considered where she might have lived. As such, he had no expectations of what her apartment might look like, but the cleanliness of it was a little shocking. During his policing career, he had been to many dwellings of prostitutes, being forced to as a follow up to them being either witness, victim, or perpetrator to a crime. If one looked hard enough you could usually find evidence that indicated their involvement in the sex trade. Needles, condoms, and drugs were all common denominators, but walking into Juliette's apartment, he found none of these things. What he saw was neat and orderly, filled with bright colors and simple designs. A bookshelf in the living room held many different genres, an even ratio of fiction to non-fiction, some of these with French titles.

Artful depictions of still life were hung from the walls with careful attention, and there was a simple but elegant flow of design throughout. Despite this, Peterson could subtly hear the city traffic outside, the honk of horns and the sounds of passing sirens. Juliette had done her best to create a refuge here, but the pounding of the city disrupted the effect and threatened the grace and beauty that was hiding here.

Juliette took one look at his clothing and ordered him to stay put, disappearing around the corner and returning a few minutes later with a change of clothing and a black garbage bag. She had removed her fur coat and stood in a striped, black-and-white top that was tucked into a tight black skirt. With her hands on her hips, she said, "You can throw your old clothes in the bag and change into those."

He eyed the set of clothing suspiciously. "Who did these belong to?" The last thing he wanted to do was slip into some John's clothing.

Juliette laughed, throwing a small delicate hand over her mouth to hide her amusement. "It's okay, Jack. I don't bring any of my clients home. Those clothes belonged to my brother." With that, she told him that she was going to have a shower and ordered him to change. She left him standing by the door, holding the garbage bag in one hand and the clean clothes in the other.

Without moving from the foyer, he undressed completely, placing his shoulder rig and pistol on the floor and throwing his dirty clothing in the garbage bag as ordered. He paused, nude, to inspect the rectangular bruise that extended from his left shoulder to his right hip, the wide ribbon of yellow and pink flesh indicative of the pressure of the seatbelt upon impact. Wincing, he dressed in the clothing that was provided, which was snug but did the job. He used his overcoat to wipe up the water from Juliette's floor, and then threw that in the bag as well. He tied up the bag, slipped back on the shoulder rig with the pistol, and went into the apartment. From his right a short hallway led to a bathroom and bedroom, and he could hear Juliette humming over the sound of the shower.

Peterson stood awkwardly in her apartment until she came out a few minutes later, drying her hair with a white towel. She was dressed in dark blue pajamas with a black tank top, and she regarded him with a curious and unreadable expression. Free of the makeup and the street clothing, the resemblance to Laura was striking, and he had to remind himself that the person that was standing before him was not his wife.

She crooked a finger at him, beckoning him forward. "C'mon. Let's go to bed."

Peterson lay on his left side in Juliette's bed, his legs pulled up to his chest like an infant, his arms wrapped around his knees. The room was dark, with a tiny sliver of light coming from the hallway. He felt the bed shift as Juliette climbed under the covers next to him, and she breathed softly. The scent of her skin, freshly showered, brushed at his senses and unwillingly caused a flutter in his stomach.

Her fingers tentatively brushed against his right shoulder, and he flinched at the feel of her touch. She hushed at him, running her hand across his skin. "It's okay, Jack," she said, her breath hot on his neck, warm. "I won't do anything that you don't want to do." He nodded into the pillow, a lump rising in his throat. "How long has it been now?" she asked. And when he didn't answer, she said, "Since she died?"

It took him a moment to answer, unable to find his voice, and when he did it came like a croak. "Nine months, four days, twelve hours." He had never spoken of Laura, indeed had never given any indication that he had, at any time, been married. All pictures and traces of Laura had been purged from his house as he had been unable to deal with the sight of her face in the many photographs that they had throughout the house. All these items had been carefully placed into boxes that he had stored into his basement. That Juliette was aware of Laura's death was not all that surprising. One simply had to enter his name into any search engine and the story would be clear, as he had been told the death of his wife and his own shooting had been mainstream news for the better part of two weeks.

"All this time," Juliette said, "you've never tried to…do what any of my other clients want to do with me." He felt Juliette lean up on the bed, and he could feel her staring at him in the darkness, propped up on her elbow and looking at the side of his face. He kept his eyes firmly shut, unable to face the woman, unable to face himself.

The first time he had approached Juliette, she had denied him outright. Doubtless she had been suspicious when he had told her that he was a police officer and that he would like to pay her for something specific. Eventually, after repeated visits, she had agreed and he had taken her back to his residence, his own heart shuddering with shame and confusion. He had told her that he needed someone to help him sleep. Peterson found that, if he simply gave himself over to the idea, he could imagine that it was Laura in the bed beside him, and that her murder had simply been a bad dream. That first night with Juliette he had slept better than he had in months, and no dreams of death had plagued him.

Juliette had left before he had woken up that first morning and had done the same on almost all subsequent encounters.

Juliette was speaking now, her voice inviting. "You could now, you know," she said, close to his ear. And he knew that he could and he found that, physically, he even wanted to. Juliette was a beautiful woman, who in so many ways reminded him of one love that he had lost so cruelly.

He felt a tear escape from his eye, where it travelled across the bridge of his nose and drip to the pillow below. This was followed by another tear which broke whatever floodgates had been erected in his mind. He began to sob. Juliette said no more and held him as if he were a child.

At two in the morning there was no traffic in the Green Lakes district of the city. Most of the residents, quiet professionals by all accounts, were likely in their beds, sleeping, and with all luck would not notice the old sedan as it drove through the neighborhood. As it was, Kincaid felt exposed, as being the only vehicle on the street was due to attract attention. He recognized that this next course of action was a risk, but his curiosity was peaked, and he convinced himself that this reconnaissance was necessary for the eventual success of his mission. With one eye on the road and his other eye on the cop's driver's licence, he found the address easily enough.

The decision to lift the cop's wallet, once he had dragged the two police officers out of the wreck, had been made quickly. Beyond the fact that he now had a policeman's badge, which could prove to be useful, he wanted to know more about the taller cop. Something about him had struck Kincaid as familiar. With nothing much to do, he figured a little reconnaissance was a good a move as any.

When he pulled up to the house he observed that the driveway was empty. The two officers had probably been taken to the hospital. The younger of the two seemed worse off than Peterson, but maybe the elder cop had sustained a head injury. Now, parked on a side street across from the residence, Kincaid's memory snapped into place. This was not the first time he had set eyes on the Peterson residence, though before it had been splashed on the front page of a prominent newspaper. The headline "Cop Shot, Wife Dead" popped into his mind, and he chuckled at the strange circumstance of fortune. By all accounts Peterson had been assigned to the Turner and Collins homicide. Now Turner, Collins, Solk, and assorted company. This was the man tasked with stopping him? The situation was almost laughable.

Twenty-Three

Peterson awoke early in the morning, the sun yet still a promise beyond the horizon, and in the near darkness he could hardly make out Juliette's form, but by her steady breathing he knew that she was still asleep. Carefully, he disentangled himself from her arm which lay on his and rose quietly from her bed. When his eyes adjusted to the gloom her small face and smooth skin was revealed. She was on her stomach, her right arm draped over the pillow where a few seconds earlier he had been lying, and her face was turned to him. He had fallen asleep from sheer exhaustion with her arms wrapped around him and a more perfect sleep he had not had. With the dawn brought the reality of things in stark realism, and he crept from her room silently with his depression settling over him like a shroud. Four people dead. Denly in the hospital.

Peterson paused long enough outside the bedroom to quietly close the door and picked his way with difficulty through the dark toward the kitchen, trying to remember the layout of the apartment from the night before. In the living room, he banged his shin against a corner table and bit off a curse.

The kitchen was dim, with a faint light slicing through the curtains from a street lamp. It cast a sickly, yellowish light into the small room but allowed him to feel along the walls like a blind man for the light switch. He finally found the switch and gave a muffled cry of alarm when he realized he was not alone.

Sitting at the kitchen table, previously hidden in darkness, was a small boy, who likely was no older than ten. He looked at Peterson with an inquisitive but calm expression. "Hi," he said and took a drink from a glass of milk that he held in his small hands. Unable to think of anything else to say, Peterson repeated the boy's greeting. The child took another sip of the milk and placed it on the table, pushing back his chair so he could stand up and walk up to Peterson where he stopped a foot away and stared up at him. The child was exceedingly small, the top of his head hardly at Peterson's beltline, and he reached out a small hand for Peterson to shake.

"My name's Adam," he said, and Peterson took the boy's hand in his own, surprised that the boy's grip was firm and strong, though the hand felt unbelievably tiny in his own, no more than a mouse. Adam had no shoes or socks on, only a pair of Spiderman pajamas with frayed ends that hung above small feet. He wore a plain, blue, long-sleeved shirt that seemed far too big on him, and hung at the arms like wizard sleeves. A curly mop of brown hair framed a smooth face that held many of Juliette's features, and there was no doubt in Peterson's mind that he was looking at her son. Juliette had never mentioned her son, though this fact did not surprise Peterson. Most women in her profession, if it could be called that, would probably want to keep their family separate from what they did. Made sense why Juliette had never taken a client home.

Peterson cleared his throat. "Um…my name's Jack," he said to Adam, who released his grip and padded back over to the kitchen table where he sat back down in the chair. Peterson stared at the boy for the moment before sitting down in the chair opposite, where they regarded one another. Despite his small size, Peterson saw that the boy looked at him openly, without fear, and held his gaze with curiosity. "You're probably wondering who I am," Peterson said, and Adam shrugged noncommittally. "I'm a friend of your mom's and I uh…just came over for a visit." He felt his skin flush.

Adam cocked his head to the side. "My mom has lots of friends. They usually call her, but they've never visited before."

Peterson had no response, and he shifted uncomfortably.

Dodging the statement, Peterson asked, "Do you normally sit in the dark so late at night?"

"Early," Adam said, and when he read the look of confusion on Peterson's face, he repeated, "It's early, not late. I woke up early and was thirsty," he said. He looked Peterson up and down and asked, "Why are you wearing Uncle Jaime's clothing?"

"Oh, sorry," Peterson said, looking at his own clothing as if noticing it for the first time. "My clothing was ruined, and your mom gave me these."

"Why was your clothing ruined?"

"I crashed my car."

"Why? Were you drunk?"

"No, why would you say that?"

"My friend's dad crashed his car, and he was drunk."

"That's not really my thing," Peterson said. "I'm more into despair and self pity at the moment." Adam didn't respond to this, so Peterson filled the silence with a question. "Do you think your mom will mind if I use the phone?" and he pointed to a land line which was secured to the wall on a hook. "My cell phone got wet when I crashed the car."

Adam told him to go for it, so he got up and dialed for a cab, putting his hand over the mouth piece when the dispatcher asked him for an address. "Hey, what's the address here?" he asked the boy. Adam told him, and he relayed it back to the dispatcher, thanked her, and hung up. Adam had finished his milk and put the cup back in the sink, was standing before Peterson with a quizzical expression.

"Are you dating my mom?"

Peterson blinked, stumbled over an answer. "I don't.... y'know, I'm not sure actually. I might be."

Adam nodded slowly, shook Peterson's hand, and padded back to his bedroom. Before he passed through the door he waved at Peterson, just an outline in the dark shadows of the hallway. Peterson waved back, and then the boy disappeared from view.

Twenty-Four

Peterson went straight from Juliette's apartment to WestOps, where he had a change of clothing in the first-floor change room. The guard at the front gave him a curious glance when he stepped through the exterior doors wearing black leather shoes, tapered grey jogging pants, and a long, black t-shirt. He had managed to find a grey windbreaker in a closet, and his pistol banged against his ribs as he walked to the glass paneled security station.

"Help you, sir?" the guard asked. Peterson explained the situation, or at least a version of it, that his wallet had gone missing and with it his building ID. The guard typed Peterson's name into a computer system which brought up his photograph and building access information and then looked from Peterson, to the computer screen, and back to Peterson again, before finally concluding his rightful identity. He made Peterson sign in and handed him a flat white visitors badge that would get him into the building. Peterson clipped it to his shirt and thanked the guard, who mumbled a response.

"Jack," Captain Gregor said in greeting. The man was leaning against the corner of the wall, arms crossed, wearing a pair of dark uniform pants and a white SPD long-sleeve shirt, tucked in revealing his thin and fit waist. The pants and shirt were perfectly pressed, with creases so sharp they seemed machine manufactured. His blonde hair was combed back, and the slick of his hair gel reflected the overhead lights with a greasy sheen. His eyes regarded Peterson with what seemed to be suspicion and contempt, and Jack prepared himself for the coming storm. Still learning against the wall, immobile as if etched in stone, Elias Gregor continued. "I read the briefing this morning. You and Chucky are fortunate to be alive."

Peterson sat down on the bench and began tying his shoes. "What can I say, captain, the road was shit. Lost control and hit the ditch. Just a good thing that we were both wearing our seatbelts."

"Hmm," Gregor said. "Good thing, yeah." Peterson saw out of the corner of his eye as Gregor pushed himself off the wall and came to stand before him. Gregor had his hands in his pocket and stared at Peterson like he was an exhibit in a zoo, a monkey that had suddenly caught his attention. "I've been thinking, Peterson, that maybe you came back a little too soon."

Peterson felt heat rise to his cheeks, and his pulse quickened. He put the palms of his hands on his knees and leaned up to stare at Gregor. The man looked down at him, the challenge in his eyes unmistakable. "What the hell is that supposed to mean?" Peterson demanded.

A bemused smile formed on the captain's face. If not for Peterson's dislike for the man he could have probably said the man possessed classical handsome features. The chin was strong and square, the eyes bright and intense, but beneath it all there was a foulness. Elias Gregor would do anything to succeed, sacrifice anyone to continue climbing up the ladder. Peterson had seen it before, perfectly capable officers who in their grasp and scramble for power lied, cheated, and essentially sold out their own morals and character simply to get another rank, to get one step closer to whatever height they were climbing.

"See, here's the thing, Jack," Gregor said. "Some red flags were raised during your last psych eval, and while the doctor couldn't say for certain, he thought you were being evasive." Peterson kept his face impassive, but inside his stomach was roiling. After passing his physical examinations, he had sat down with the force shrink and had completed several personality and psychopathology tests, including the MMPI, or the Minnesota Multiphasic Personality Inventory. He had taken the test before, on two previous occasions, as part of a routine health assessment, but this had been the first time after the shooting. He thought he had deftly skirted around some of the more challenging questions as he was reluctant to give an indication of how deeply Laura's murder had affected him. Somewhere in that test, which had such marvelous questions like, "I love my mother and if my mother is dead I *loved* my mother, true or false?", he must have screwed up, and concerns had been raised. To his recollection, Peterson believed that he had dealt with most of these during the follow up evaluation with Dr. Richie, the force's head shrinker, but clearly he had been overconfident.

"You know those tests are bogus, Captain."

"Be that as it may, I have a duty to ensure my *employees* are safe within my building." Gregor was one step away from gloating and made no effort to hide it. The man was a pompous prick, always had been, always would be, but the rank and file structure demanded that Peterson be, at least on the surface, deferential.

"What are you planning to do?" Peterson asked.

"I've already done it," Gregor said, taking his hands out of his pockets and turning to walk out. He paused at the open door and looked back at Peterson. "The force doctor will be calling me later today to set up an appointment. I *expect* you to be there." He flashed Peterson an unkind smile. "Oh, and don't bother phoning Denly at the hospital to get your story straight. I already spoke to him this morning and know the whole story." He called out as he walked away. "Be safe out there, Jack."

Twenty-Five

In a gloom, Peterson rode the elevator up, where he leaned against the glass-paneled interior wall with his hands in his pockets, studying the grey carpet. When the doors opened, he was surprised to see Sylvia Partridge and Archie Prince engaged in what seemed to be a heated argument. She had leaned forward at the waist, her right hand on her hip, which pushed back her black jacket to reveal a blue blouse underneath. Her left hand was held up, jabbing a finger in Prince's face. Her expression was one of anger and disgust, and her thin lips were pulled back in a snarl.

Prince was dressed in a customary rumpled, dark-blue suit, and the sleeves of his jacket were rolled up to his elbows. He held out his hands so that his palms were facing Partridge, trying to calm the irate woman.

As Peterson stepped out from the elevator neither seemed to notice his approach, and Partridge continued her lacing into Prince. "I swear to God, you make me so angry sometimes I feel like I'm going to shoot you."

"I don't know what the big deal is," Prince said. "I thought I was giving you a compliment."

Sylvia's jaw clenched tighter, her cheekbones jutting from her skin like marbled stone. "You called me old," she said.

"No, I said you *looked* hot for an *older* lady." Prince responded, holding a finger. "Bit of a distinction."

Peterson cleared his throat audibly, probably cutting off whatever laconic retort Partridge was about to fire back. She gave

Prince a final snarl before nodding curtly to Peterson and stalking off. Prince watched her walk away with the ghost of a smile on his face and a wistful look in his eyes.

"What I wouldn't give for her to be the next ex-Mrs. Prince," he said.

"Don't say that too loudly," Peterson warned. "If she hears that she'll shoot you on sight."

Prince sighed and clapped Peterson on the shoulder. "Women, right? Can never say anything right." He spied Peterson's clothing and raised an eyebrow but said nothing. From his inner jacket pocket Prince removed a handwritten note where Peterson saw the name Michael Green and the address of a business in the city. The words "Helping Hand" were written on the top in Prince's scrawl. He pointed to the note with a thick index finger. "While you and Chucky were joyriding in the ditch, I looked into the dead girl's father."

"And this was all you were able to find?" Peterson asked.

Prince nodded and pressed the button to call the elevator. "Yeah, there wasn't much," he said. "After the accident, he and his wife divorced. No sign of her that I can find, but it seems like she remarried and moved up north somewhere. The husband, Michael, dropped off the map, but I was able to get some information on him at a local shelter. Seems like he runs a non-profit homeless shelter on the east end." A smile played on his lips as the elevator arrived, and he stepped on. "I was going to suggest that we all go and pay him a visit, but I don't think Ms. Partridge wants my charmed company right now." He waved his hand toward Peterson as the doors closed. "Enjoy," he said as the doors clicked shut.

Peterson pocketed the address and found Partridge at her desk, sitting hunched at the computer with a sour look on her face. Nor did her mood brighten when Peterson told her about the accident from the night before, and she finally took stock of his clothing and bruised features. "Did you not hear about it at all?" he asked.

"No," she responded, concerned. "After I got home last night I shut everything off." She waved a hand toward the elevator where

Prince had just left. "I was so flustered from that jackass that I barely knew my own name. Are you okay? How's Charles?" Peterson told her that he was fine but that Denly might be in the hospital for a couple of days. He skirted around the question of what had caused the accident and let Sylvia come to her own conclusion.

He tossed her the note from Prince, and as her eyes scanned the address he said, "Maybe we'll check out the hospital once we've talked to Green."

Her eyebrows raised as she read over the note. "I'm surprised that jerk wad took the time to find this guy, it's not even his case," she said, referring undoubtedly to Prince.

Peterson didn't have the heart to tell her that Prince had probably put in the effort simply for her, and so he let the matter drop. From the wistful expression on Archie's face it was clear that he had feelings for Sylvia, even if he had almost no chance of any affection being reciprocated.

He waited by the elevator as Sylvia Partridge gathered her things and they headed out into the cool dawn to find Isabella Green's father.

Twenty-Six

Helping Hands was a rundown looking homeless shelter buried between equally rundown and abused buildings along a narrow road that appeared seldom used. It was a place that you would never know existed unless it was your sole intent to find it, or you were one of the unfortunate denizens that had to rely upon its services to survive. Even during the winter, the temperature was usually above freezing, with only a few days out of the year presenting any real sort of challenge to those who found themselves, whether through situation or choice, living on the streets. The relatively mild climate afforded the ability to live almost year-round outside. Cities with harsher temperatures provided a unique challenge for people without a home, and in those areas death from extreme exposures was a real and present danger. As such, the west coast metropolis had an unusually large amount of homeless people, and funding toward shelters was sparse and abysmal. Judging from the outside, the *Helping Hands* homeless shelter looked in a state of encroaching condemnation, and Peterson imagined that the amount of government support given toward such an establishment was pretty much nil.

As Partridge pulled to the curb and put the vehicle in park, Peterson said, "It doesn't really make sense to me. The timing of it all." Through the window, Peterson stared at the square grey concrete building. The roof was flat and black, and two crows fought over some kind of food scrap on the roof line, their beaks clawing and gnashing at one another. A sign on the exterior wall announced the name of the shelter, and a crudely painted sign stated that it was a "Healing Ministry for Those in Need." Peterson continued, "Why now, after all this time? I mean, if we think Green paid off a hired killer to take out his daughter's rapists, why wait twenty years to do it?"

Partridge shrugged. "Maybe he just had enough, couldn't take it anymore. Tough, living with that kind of knowledge. Your daughter is gone while these dudes are enjoying their life."

This didn't track with Peterson, and he breathed out in frustration. The Greens had probably been paid out to rescind their complaint, likely given a hefty settlement like all the other players. It would explain where Green would have gotten the funds to open the shelter, and perhaps it was his way of giving back to the community. But would have it been enough money to hire a killer to take out three people? And why sit on it all this time only to act now?

No answers were coming to Peterson sitting in the car, so he and Partridge got out of the car and walked up to the building. There was a handful of people who were outside, some sitting on the sidewalk or braced up against the building, mostly with their heads down and their hands in their pockets. They were mostly men, but it was difficult to tell the specific gender underneath the thick and tattered clothing that they wore. They bore the haunted expression of someone who had spent too much time on the streets, struggling through hard lives that were probably filled with torment and sadness. Peterson wondered what decisions or circumstances had led them down this path. Did they get in with the wrong crowd, make poor decisions, or had luck simply not gone their way? How could one person lead a normal and apparently happy life, get a successful job, get married and have kids, while another spent his life on the streets, scratching out the barest existence? Peterson wondered if there was an element of choice involved, or if people were simply victims to a cruel and pointless fate that predestined how some lived and died.

The people outside barely acknowledged them as they entered the building. It was harshly lit inside, with intense bulbs streaming a sharp and buzzing light that was curiously loud to Peterson, a sound that seemed to intensify the farther he entered the property. He forced the sensation away along with the sudden nausea that came with it, tamping it down to focus on the woman who sat behind a counter directly past the front door.

She was an older woman who looked up at them through thick bifocals perched on the end of her nose. She had a pencil in her hand

and a half-finished crossword puzzle sitting open on its spine on the desk. She put the pencil down as they approached and pushed back the glasses on her nose so that they settled directly in front of her eyes.

Her voice was kindly but wary when Partridge produced her badge. Sylvia gave Peterson a quick glance up and down when he made no move to show his own ID, but she focused back on the woman. "Yes, what can I do for you?" the woman asked. Her voice was guarded as likely the only time the police visited the shelter was to place one of the residents under arrest. She was wearing a grey, knitted shawl that she adjusted around her shoulders, and she wore no jewelry or accoutrements of any kind, and Peterson wondered how many times her personal possessions had been lifted by the bums to sell for booze or drugs before she started coming to work with as little decoration as possible.

After sliding her badge back in her pocket, Partridge asked, "We were hoping to speak to your manager, Michael Green? We just have some questions for him."

The woman pulled her head back as if surprised. "Michael Green? We have no manager of that name." She scratched at her cheek absently and looked between them. "In fact, we don't even really have a manager. The shelter is run through a community organization, and we have a board of directors."

"The information we got was that he owned this place and gave this as his address." Peterson produced the note from Prince and gave it to the woman, who adjusted her glasses to inspect the writing. "Michael Green.... Green..." she said quietly, pondering, before nodding to herself. "Ah," she said finally. "I think I know what happened." She pushed her chair back and told them to follow her, and they fell in step behind the clerk, who led them past the desk toward the rear of the shelter. Here, as they descended farther, the smells of foods and poorly washed bodies intensified, and Peterson looked over to see Partridge trying to keep her expression level. The smells did not seem to bother the clerk, who walked purposefully toward the back. She had probably grown used to the odor.

There was muffled conversation and the sound of clinking silverware as they passed through a hallway into a large seating area.

Four plastic tables were set up in the center of the room, each flanked by wooden pews that looked to have been donated from a church. Every available space was occupied with vagrants whose abused clothing spoke to their level of homelessness. Some looked halfway decent. Others looked halfway dead.

In the far back a pair of white-aproned workers were safely secured behind a five-foot glass sneeze guard. Steam rose from behind the glass and drifted toward the ceiling in a lazy roll as they spooned up dark soup to a pair of homeless women who were wearing torn skirts and heavy woolen jackets.

Their guide stopped under the arch that separated the hallway from the soup kitchen, and she arched on her toes to spy over the heads of those sitting and standing in various locations. From his left Partridge asked, "Does the shelter run year-round?"

The woman settled back on her feet and put her hands on her hips. She fixed them with a dry look. "No, we barely get enough funding for the winter months as it is. We are all volunteers here, don't get paid for what we do, which can be hard. A lot of the people that come here have substance abuse problems or mental instabilities. Sometimes they are violent, and we have to call the cops when they get out of hand. Other times they yell or scream, throw stuff maybe. But a lot of these people wouldn't have anywhere to go and would have to sleep on the streets otherwise. Maybe get robbed for the meager things they own, maybe even worse."

"Why do it then?" Peterson asked. "Why volunteer here?"

She pushed the glasses farther up her nose so she could look at him directly in the eyes. "My son was homeless, got mixed up with the wrong crowd and just drifted away. Died out east, terrible thing." Her eyes traveled over the people sitting at the pew, which Peterson figured had been donated by some church. Like the volunteers, this shelter probably subsisted on charity and not much else. "I guess this is my way of making sure it doesn't happen to someone else's mother." She chuckled humourlessly, a hopeless sound. "Who knows, maybe I can even get someone off the street for good." She didn't seem to believe it herself.

Her eyes scanned the assembled group for a moment before focusing on the very back of the long table. She walked toward the end, flanked by Peterson and Partridge. The detective felt studied as he walked, and the bums looked up over their soup to watch the officers pass. The woman stopped before the end of the table, where a man sat alone. He had in front of him an empty bowl that looked like it had been licked entirely clean, and he held the spoon in a shaky fist that he had propped up on the table. His left hand disappeared beneath a tattered black-and-gold jacket, and from the movement of his arm it appeared as if he was madly scratching his abdomen.

"Excuse me, Mike," the woman said, her voice strained. At her voice, he began rocking back and forth; dark, filthy hair waving slightly with the movement. His head was down, and Peterson could hardly see the man's face, only the outline of a dirty and unkempt beard framing an equally dirty face. Peterson wondered where Prince had gotten his information from. Michael Green didn't own the shelter or run it. He was a guest.

Twenty-Seven

Michael Green rocked back and forth like he was on a ship in rough waters and began humming to himself, though with no discernible rhythm. There were small twigs and leaves in his long brown hair, probably from where he had slept in previous nights, or previous months. He was wearing a green army jacket that had holes patched up with duct tape, the edges of which had begun to pull back and curl, the shoulders a faded color with loose threads where the epaulets had been torn off. He wore a pair of gloves with the fingers cut out, showing nails chewed down to nothing, with the skin red and raw.

He avoided their eyes as Partridge and Peterson sat down on the bench across from him. The clerk had told them that she would give them space to talk. Peterson saw her having a quiet conversation with one of the soup dispensers in the back, the pair of whom were looking in their direction and nodding.

"Mr. Green," Peterson said. "We have a few questions regarding your daughter, Isabella." The old man's head twitched to the side upon hearing her name, and both his rocking and moaning increased in intensity.

Peterson and Partridge shared a look, and he knew that they were both thinking the same thing. The idea that Michael Green had hired a professional killer to take out his dead daughter's attackers now seemed truly far fetched. Buried underneath the rocking and moaning Peterson thought he could hear Green saying something, so he leaned forward, trying to ignore the fetid smell that rose off the man in waves. He listened for a moment then settled back into his chair, leaning over and whispering to Partridge. "Sounds like he's saying, 'The river ate her.'"

Partridge nodded, partially to herself, and whispered back, "From her accident, they never did find the body."

Peterson looked back at Green who continued his rhythmic motion and wondered when the man's mind had truly broken. Was it after his daughter's attack or after her death? Perhaps the crack had always been there and it simply needed the right wedge to bust it wide open.

They tried asking Green a few more questions, things they felt were relevant to the investigation. "When was the last time you talked to your wife? Do you have any other family members that might want revenge? Is there anything you can tell us at all?" Each question was met either with no response or the same broken words that the river ate his child. They shared one last look between them and stood up to leave Green with his ghosts, passing the clerk at the front who asked if they had learned anything useful.

"Not really," Peterson told her.

She nodded as if this wasn't a surprise at all. "He's fairly withdrawn. I don't know if I've heard him string a word together since I've worked here." She looked back toward the soup kitchen where Green was probably still muttering nonsense to himself. "It's sad, really," she said.

They asked the clerk a few more questions, wondering if Green had been absent for any significant amount of time, if anyone had visited him recently. She answered no to both queries, and after he and Partridge shared a look he thanked the clerk for her time and they returned to Sylvia's car.

As he opened the passenger door and sat down, her cell phone rang and she answered it with one hand as she was doing her seatbelt up. "Sylvia here," she said, paused. Listened. "Yep, he's right here actually," giving Peterson a glance. "Do you want to talk to him?"

Peterson couldn't hear the voice on the other end, but an ill feeling crept across his mind. "Yep..." Partridge was saying. "Okay. Yes. Okay, I'll tell him." She hung up the phone and put it back in her jacket pocket. She twisted her body and placed her right elbow on the seat back so she could stare at him straight in the face. "Seems like you have a meeting with the doctor. Anything you want to tell me?"

Twenty-Eight

Partridge told him that Gregor had been trying to get a hold of him for the past two hours but that his cell phone kept going straight to message.

"I lost it," he said. "Along with my badge."

She looked at him for a long stretch of time before responding. "I can't help you if you're not honest with me, Jack."

He could feel her eyes on him but he continued to study the street ahead.

"Look, Gregor basically ordered me to take you back to HQ to sit down with the shrink. What's going on with you?"

The seconds ticked by in the interior of the car, and Peterson felt the heat rise on his cheeks. An oppressive air seemed to settle, and he found it difficult to breathe. Peterson chewed on the side of his lip, wondering how much, if anything, he should tell her. *Well, what the hell.* "I've been having blackouts lately," he finally said.

"Lately? Since when?"

He shook his head ruefully. He explained how he had passed out while trying to go upstairs at his house. "After the Goldman shooting, I lost consciousness and crashed the car into the ditch."

He checked Partridge and saw that her jaw was set in anger. "What's wrong with you, man, you could have killed yourself, killed Charles. Why didn't you see someone, get some help?"

He locked eyes with her. "C'mon, you know how it is, you tell a doctor what happened and it'll find its way back to health services.

They'd take my badge away in a heartbeat." He crossed his arms over his chest. "I'm trying to work through it, just takes time."

"No, you're not," she said in response. "All your doing is burying that shit, and it's going to keep coming up again and again."

"I know you're upset with me. You have every right to. But I need to finish this case, do you understand?" His voice was pleading. "I'll get help then. You can tell Gregor, I don't know…you tried to take me but something came up. I ordered you not to, whatever. Please just do this for me."

She swore quietly under her breath and she sat for a long while, considering his words. He felt a mixture of hope and dread as he watched her weigh the consequences, the positives and negatives of what he was asking of her. In the end, it seemed, the negatives won out. Her wide eyes held concern for him. "I don't want to come to work one morning, or open the newspaper, to find out you've crashed your car again or ate your gun in the middle of the night." She started the car and drove away from downtown, toward HQ. "I'm taking you to the doctor."

They drove in silence to HQ, still out of the periphery of the city. Partridge stared straight ahead, though Peterson could feel her head swing toward him at regular intervals. He gazed gloomily out of the passenger window, watching featureless grey clouds streak past, feeling much like the disobedient child who was being taken to the principle's office. Before long, he began to get a sense of where they were, and he sat straight up in his seat, looking around to confirm their surroundings. Partridge glanced at him in question.

"Take the next right," he told her, pointing toward the service road that they were approaching.

She took her foot off the gas but didn't slow entirely. "Look, Jack. I'm sorry but I gotta take you—"

"Please indulge me," he said. "Just take the next right."

She sighed audibly and hit her blinker, slowing the car down enough to take the turn. They entered a winding highway that pitched left and right, running alongside the Stewart River, which rolled with white froth, glimpsed intermittently through knotty pines and brush. Partridge opened her mouth to speak, but Peterson got there before she did.

"Pull over here," he ordered. A sign indicated a roadside turnout on the edge of a bend in the road, and she pulled the car into this and put it in park. Peterson immediately undid his seatbelt and stepped out of the car, closing the door behind him and walking toward the edge of the road. He heard Partridge exit the vehicle and stand beside him.

"What the hell are we doing here, Jack?" she demanded.

The guard rail was waist high, the metal cool against Peterson's hand as he leaned over it. There was an eight-foot drop off to the water below, a steep incline of shale rocks that were razor sharp. The river was a hundred feet across, the water churning from the nearby runoff from the mountains. It looked icy cold, and the wind that wiped off its surface seemed to crawl right underneath Peterson's skin. A mile or so downstream the river dumped its contents into the ocean, whose depths would swallow whatever was carried across it.

"Don't you recognize this?" he asked. Partridge shook her head. Peterson turned and looked back down the roadway. It ran at a slight decline as it entered the curve, and he imagined someone coming down it picking up speed, heading toward the curve, heading toward the river. "This is where Isabella Green crashed her car. She came around the corner, blew through the guardrail, and plunged into the river."

Partridge swore, looking back over the water. "I didn't even notice. This is where she lost control of her car?"

Peterson joined her at the end of the guardrail. "Either lost control or deliberately drove into the river."

She looked sideways at him. "You figure she might have killed herself?"

"Could you blame her?" he responded. "Maybe the pain was too much, who knows?"

They were silent for a time before he felt her hand on his shoulder. "You don't have to end up like this, Jack. You can make the choice."

He continued to stare out over the river, the dark water cool and hungry. Odd that Green's grief would cause her to take her own life, whereas his own grief was the only thing he had left to hold on to. Who was he without it? There were no mementos here, no sign at all that a young desperate girl had died, no crosses, no memorials. The guard rail had been replaced, all signs of the accident wiped from the trace of memory. No one left to remember Isabella Green. Without looking at Partridge he went back to the car, spoke to her over his shoulder. "C'mon. I have a doctor's appointment."

Twenty-Nine

Dr. Cecelia Walters tapped a pencil on the notepad at a steady beat, the *click click click* grating on Peterson's already frayed nerves. Walters was a plain woman in her late forties with straight brown hair that was already greying at the sides. Her face was weatherworn and wrinkled, as if she had spent too much time in the sun or at the beach, and she wore loose-fitting capris that showed off calves lined with varicose veins. She wore little makeup, and her lips looked too pale for her skin, giving her a grey pallor that made her look older than she probably was. Her handshake was firm, however, and her eyes shone with a fierce intensity.

"Thanks for coming on such short notice," she said, releasing his hand and directing him to a green armchair in the corner of the office. Her voice was deep and husky with a faint hint of an accent that he couldn't place.

"Well, I didn't have much of a choice, to be honest," Peterson said, sitting down and taking in the surroundings. The room was not overly large, and its space was diminished by what Peterson felt were too many knickknacks and small decorative pieces that occupied every available shelf space. Many of these had an African bent to them, tiny gilded elephants and brass hippos; near Walters's framed medical degrees he saw a photograph of her and an older man atop a rusted and beat-up Jeep on what appeared to be an African plain. Both were dressed in dirty khakis and camo gear, digital cameras slung around their necks like black charms.

A desk was set in the corner of the room, with a small lamp throwing off a triangular glow over an open folder. He imagined it was his medical profile and Walters had been reviewing it prior to his arrival.

Peterson waited, with the *click click click* of the bouncing pencil the only sound in the room. Walters stared at him, not aggressively, but calmly with a look of detachment on her weathered face. It struck Peterson that this was like an interrogation, but for the first time in his life he was on the opposite side of the glass, sitting in the wrong chair. He knew what she was trying to do, make him wait it out, cause him to speak first. It was a technique he had used himself, from time to time, and while he was aware of the process, he found his discomfort growing with each passing second. The difficulty was that here, in this room, the control was immediately hers, and both knew it.

After what seemed an interminable amount of time, Peterson broke, and he quelled at the own irritation in his voice. "So, are we going to do this or not?"

Walters cocked her head to the side, a minute twitch that made her look like a dog who had just heard a high-pitched noise. "Are we going to do what?"

He held out his hands to indicate her office. "This, talk. I can't imagine you just want us to stare at each other all day." After the morning's events the afternoon had waned on, and the large brass clock in the one corner of the office gave the time as well after five p.m. Most of HQ would already have emptied, and Peterson imagined that the good doctor would rather be home than sitting with him in this tiny, cramped office.

"I'm fine not talking," she said. "I don't want to do anything that makes you feel uncomfortable."

"Who said I'm uncomfortable?"

She laughed, and her eyes blazed bright. "Look at yourself, detective. You look like you're ready to snap."

She was right, and he knew it. His arms were crossed and his shoulders were hunched forward, and he held his chest as if he were cold. One leg was crossed over the other, and his defensive body language was unmistakeable. Sighing, he released his chest and placed both feet on the floor, flexing each shoulder and arm to work out the tension that he could now feel.

"See," Walters said. "Isn't that better." She placed her notepad and pencil on the side desk and leaned forward, placing both elbows on her knees and clasping her hands together as if in supplication. "Tell me, what brings you here, Jack?"

"I was told to come here."

"Well, I know that, but something must have happened for that order to be given in the first place. You can speak freely; everything between us is confidential."

Peterson doubted these words but didn't say so. Walters probably couldn't speak of specifics to the upper brass but in the end she would have to give a formal report that would outline whether he was mentally fit to continue duty. But this all felt like a formality to him and that his fate had already been decided.

"There was an accident. I blacked out and crashed my car, nearly killed my colleague."

Walters sat back in her chair as if surprised by the sudden confession. "How long have these blackouts been happening?"

"A few months now."

She put her hand to her mouth and rubbed her chin. "And why not get some help? You must have known that it wasn't normal."

Peterson shifted uncomfortably in his seat. He could feel his arms begin to cross at his chest again, closing up, and forced himself to relax. "I don't know. Didn't want it to be acknowledged, I guess."

"Maybe," Walters said, but she didn't sound convinced. "I've noticed that cops are pretty reluctant to get help. Something about the whole *macho-macho* attitude. If you get help, then you're seen as weak. For you, I think it runs a bit deeper than that."

"What do you mean?" he asked.

"Well, have you ever stopped to think that maybe you're punishing yourself?"

Peterson shook his head like he had just been slapped. "For Laura's death? Why would I punish myself?"

Very casually, Walters said, "Well, it was your fault after all."

Peterson was so stunned he could barely take in a breath. "How could you say such a thing?"

"I've had time to review your file, detective," she said. She waved a hand absently behind her where the file was splayed open on her desk. "It's all there in black and white. You had the chance to act, but you didn't. You essentially opened the door to allow the killer to walk right in and kill your wife and try to kill you, did you not? If you had simply done what you were supposed to do, what you knew to be right, then Laura would still be alive. Instead of doing your duty, you allowed your friendship to Wilson Gage blind you, and in the end your wife paid the cost."

He felt his jaw hanging down as if on a broken hinge and he forced himself to close his mouth. "Has anyone ever told you that you are an absolutely terrible doctor?"

She looked up to the ceiling as if seriously considering his question. "No, not really," she said and levelled her gaze back to him. "But, then I'm not really here to be your friend or your buddy. I don't care if you're afraid of spiders or that you don't like public speaking. I'm here to assess if you're a danger to yourself, your colleagues, and the Seattle Police force in general."

Walters sat back in her chair, crossing one leg over the other and putting a hand to her chin. "PTSD is funny thing, detective. Did you know that it's not necessarily the event that the causes it, but more specifically the person?"

"What does that have to do with anything?" he asked, growing irritated.

She shrugged. "I thought it might help you to know that it could simply be part of who you are. If not for the death of your wife you might not suffer from it so greatly, but it could have happened to you, regardless." Walters spoke at him as if he was a student in one of her classes. "I had a colleague who was dealing with a patient who had been involved in a horrific car crash. The man had been rendered a paraplegic and was burned quite badly. You would think, given the situation, that his mind would have simply been shattered. But when he got out of the hospital he thanked the staff for a wonderful stay and was, by all accounts, very happy. Some people are just prone to PTSD. It might be a series of little things that build up over time, or in your case, one giant shit storm that finally broke your mind." She leaned in toward him, and her eyes bore a challenge. "The question is, what are you going to do about it?"

"What can I do about it?" he said. "You just told me that it's a problem with my brain, that it's me."

"That doesn't mean there aren't strategies. I could give you medication, antidepressants, anti-anxiety, but this is simply going to treat the symptoms and not the underlying problem. You need psychotherapy." Walters reached out and touched his knee, and he saw that her eyes were tender and caring. "There is always something to hope for, Jack. You have to believe that."

She removed her hand and settled back into her chair, and a period of silence stretched out in the room. He had never given much thought to post traumatic stress, though he knew somewhere in the back of his mind that he was deep in the throes of that disorder. The general attitude toward PTSD had improved in the police force, though there still was a prevalent attitude of just manning up and soldiering on. And he had a basic idea of what she was asking him to do, to relive the event in order to find a way to cope with it. But in a strange way it felt like a betrayal to Laura and her memory. His flashbacks felt like the only thing he had left of her, a physical connection that made him feel, in some small way, that she was still around and in his life. It felt too much like letting her go.

Finally, he spoke, looking Walters directly in the eyes. "Okay, so I sign up for therapy and I can keep my job?" he asked.

She nodded. "Yes, essentially. You don't have to sit down with me, but there are several registered psychologists that you can connect with. I have a list-"

"You'll be fine," he said, interrupting her. "I'll get a hold of my secretary and have her call your office. We'll figure out scheduling around my work, and—"

Now it was her turn to interrupt him, and she held up a hand to stop him in midsentence. "I'm sorry, Detective Peterson. I should have made myself more clear." She put her hand down and gave him a grave look. "There's no way I can recommend you for active duty right now, you're simply too much of a liability to work for the SPD." She picked up her notepad and pencil where she scratched something on the top. "I'll be recommending that you be placed on a medical suspension from this day on. Until such time as you are deemed mentally fit to continue your duties."

Thirty

The car ride back to WestOps was deathly silent. Partridge had been sitting in the waiting room reading from a *People's* magazine when Peterson stormed out, and he almost had the elevator doors closed before she stuck her hand in and forced them open. From the look on his face, she knew better than to engage him in conversation. She couldn't be blamed for what had just happened, but he didn't have to pretend to like it either.

They had said nothing in the car, and remained silent when she pulled into a parking spot at the office. It was only when they passed through the front doors that she said, "It's probably for the best."

"Maybe," he said in reply, riding the elevator to Gregor's floor and leaving Partridge standing alone, watching him go. She had told him that Gregor had wanted to see him the moment the meeting ended, and like a lamb led to the slaughter he followed the order. The secretaries were all gone, but Gregor's office door was open, revealing the man himself sitting behind his desk, scratching something on a legal pad. Gregor looked up when Peterson came in. "You can sit," he said.

Peterson reluctantly took a chair and looked around the office. Numerous plaques and certifications lined the walls, all dealing with some kind of commendation or another: a letter from the mayor, a cut-out from a newspaper. It was a shrine to the illustrious career of Captain Elias Gregor.

When Peterson looked back Gregor, the man was staring at him, his expression unreadable. Gregor was wearing a set of thin, silver-framed glasses and he folded them, placing them in the front pocket of his crisp white shirt. The man was perfectly manicured and unflappable, and fixed Peterson with a measured gaze. "Dr. Walters called me a few minutes ago and told me the results of the assessment. It's a raw deal, for sure, but we all have to abide by the rules." He waited a few moments for Peterson to respond, and when he didn't the captain continued, looking off and shuffling a stack of papers on his desk, unexpectedly uncomfortable. "I'll put the paperwork in and arrange it with Health Services to get you regular appointments with the physician. Give it a few weeks, and we'll see where your progress is at."

On a corner of Gregor's desk Peterson noticed a cardboard box, a few items poking out that he recognized. They were the personal articles from his office, packed away what must have been hours ago.

And now Peterson looked past Gregor's caring expression to see the dark satisfaction, the glint to his eyes that spoke the truth. Peterson's voice was like ice. "You must be real proud of yourself. Don't give me that shit about getting a call from Walters." He pointed to the box on Gregor's desk. "That was packed long ago. How long were you going to wait before you let me know I was locked out?"

Gregor dropped his mask, and his manner reflected his apathy. "Okay," he said, pushing back his chair, getting to his feet and walking over to stand in front of Peterson. "You were reckless, Peterson, and you almost got Denly killed in the process. Not only that, but you've cocked up this investigation long enough. Four bodies and you're no closer to catching this guy. How many corpses need to be laid at your feet before you realize you need to step aside?" He leaned forward and stared in Peterson's face. "Face it, *Jack,* you're just a shell of what you once were. I'll give it to you that you were a good cop before your wife got shot, but you're not the same anymore. I'm tired of people pussyfooting around you just because you got something taken away from you. It's life, deal with it."

Peterson gave no conscious thought to punching Gregor in the face. The next thing he knew Gregor had toppled over the desk, crashing to the floor, and Peterson's knuckles felt like they'd been broken. Cursing, Gregor shot up from behind the desk, red faced and enraged, angry blue veins pulsating in his forehead like thick ropes. Already his jaw had turned a fireplug red and he rounded the desk to grab a fistful of Peterson's shirt, but Peterson batted his hand away. Peterson was taller than Gregor by more than a foot, and maybe it was for this reason that Gregor paused.

He pressed in close to Peterson, his breath hot and angry. "You son of a bitch," he said, barely a whisper to his strained voice. "You just wait. I'll have a code of conduct investigation on your ass so fast your head is gonna spin." He held out his hand as if begging for change. "Gun, badge, now."

The men stared at each other, the tension so thick you could skate on it, and Peterson finally relented, pulling his service pistol out of his holster and slamming it down on the table.

"Now the badge," Gregor demanded. "Where is it?"

Peterson glared at the man, thinking of his badge in his wallet, halfway to the ocean by now.

Thirty-One

"I'm sorry, detective…" The secretary trailed off.

"Detective Peterson," Kincaid said, bringing out the stolen badge and flashing her the ID but keeping his thumb over the picture. They looked similar, both white with brown hair, but beyond that their dissimilarities could be noticed in an instant. As he expected, she saw the shiny gold shield and little else.

"Peterson, yes," she said. "It's just that Mr. Prihar isn't here right now."

"Well, that's okay," he said, slipping the ID back into an inner coat pocket. He had on leather shoes, dark slacks, and a black sports coat over a white, button-up shirt with a tie. He looked the part of a police officer, with his muscular build, but more than that he projected the confidence and self-assuredness that he recognized was a familiar trait with most cops.

The secretary occupying the front area of the law firm Sachs Parker and Prihar hardly gave his story a second thought and had taken it on face value that he needed to talk to the defence lawyer for an active investigation. He looked around the spacious waiting area appraisingly, where several civilians and lawyers were occupying high, leather-backed chairs, reading from the golf and law magazines that had been left on careful stacks on the glass and gold tables.

"Can you tell me when he'll be back?" he asked.

The secretary, sitting in front a large, flat-screened computer, clicked through a series of windows until she brought up a schedule.

"He's back in tomorrow at eight a.m. Do you want me to make you an appointment?"

He gave her a smile but said no. "I'll just stop by if I find the time."

Peterson was escorted off the premises by Gregor and two beefy SWAT members. Gregor went from angry to incensed when he learned that Peterson's badge was MIA, and he promised swift consequences as Peterson stalked from WestOps across the street toward a 7-Eleven. The sun had slunk beyond the horizon, the sky darkening quickly. By the time Peterson convinced the convenience store clerk to let him use his cell phone, the sun had disappeared completely, and soon he found himself shivering and alone, standing on the corner of the 7-Eleven, arms crossed over his chest and stamping his feet. He had called the only person that he could think of, and she showed up twenty minutes later, behind the wheel of a battered and rusted Nissan Pathfinder.

Juliette pulled up to the curb and rolled down her passenger window. He leaned down to make sure that it was her, and she had a rare and warm smile, genuine by all appearances, on her youthful face. "Well, this is a first," she said, apparently finding humor in the role reversal on him standing on the curb and her behind the wheel. "Get in, hot stuff," she said, and he climbed in the passenger seat. She rolled up the window and cranked the heat as Peterson held his hands up to the blessedly warm dry air, stretching his fingers against the biting cold that had settled into his skin.

She was dressed in tight blue jeans, and her hair was tied into a ponytail with a pink elastic, and in the absence of any makeup Peterson found her stunning. It was easy to forget the life that she had, but he found that his mind bent towards it, more so now that he had learned about Adam. "Why didn't you tell me you had a son?"

Juliette slipped the car into park and twisted in the seat to look at him. They were still at the 7-Eleven, and the harsh glare of the street lamps cut through the windshield and gave her a haunted expression.

"It's not something that I usually discuss with my…" she paused, "clients."

"Did you have him before or after you started working on the streets?" he asked. There was now a duality to the woman that he found difficult to process.

"More like during," she responded. She turned back in her seat and leaned over the steering wheel, placing both forearms over the vinyl and staring beyond the windshield. "I came down from up north and ran into some trouble. I met a man who told me I should try some drugs, and after I got hooked he started selling me on the street." A bitter smile formed on her pale lips, and in the dim light her skin looked like ivory. "He would use me sometimes too. Adam is his son."

"Is he still around?"

She barked a laugh, cool and empty. "No, he left a long time ago."

"So, why do it? Why continue working on the streets. You're not stupid, Juliette, you could do something else."

She considered a moment before answering. "I guess you get used to a life. And it's hard to think of doing something else. It becomes a part of you, even if you know that it is terrible." She looked at him, and her eyes were deep pools that threatened to pull him in. "You know this, I think."

There was a tragic truth to her words that Peterson found painful to think of. His grief and his pain had become so integral to his understanding of himself that he found it difficult to think of being anything else or what he had been before. After his coma, it had been like a rebirth, although his transformation had not been an improvement. There was what he had been before and what he now was, two lives that were wholly separate from one another, two different men who could not occupy the same space.

Juliette was still staring at him, her blue eyes luminous and dangerously beautiful. Without fully realizing what he was doing, Peterson reached out and touched her cheek with his hand. Her skin was cool and soft and she shut her eyes, breathing deeply and evenly, lips parting. He leaned in and kissed her, and for a moment he forgot himself.

Thirty-Two

They drove to his house without speaking, stealing glances at one another, hoping the other wouldn't notice. She parked in the driveway, and they walked beside each other to the front door. After he had unlocked it they stepped through, and without a word she grabbed his hand and led him to the bedroom. With practiced hands, she removed his clothing, sliding his shirt over his head and throwing it at the foot of the bed. She ran her fingers down his chest, her hands pausing on the puckered scar below his sternum, the flesh white and rippled from where an assassin's bullet had narrowly missed his heart and with it prolonging his unenviable life.

    He felt consumed entirely by the feel of her, the smell of her skin, as she bent forward, and soft lips trailed an outline down the side of his neck, down his chest. He shut his eyes against the sensation and he felt rooted where he stood, unable to move, his breath coming in sharp gasps. It was only when her hands touched his hips did he finally react.

    His voice sounded ragged and drawn. "Don't." And he placed a hand over hers and pulled it away.

    She straightened and looked up at him, hurt, rejected. "What's wrong? Don't you want me?" she asked.

    He drew in a deep breath and let it out slowly, willing his heart to slow down, to resume some kind of normal rhythm. "It's not that. I…don't know how to explain." Which was true enough. The physical desire that he felt for this woman, more so in the last couple of days, was undeniable. And he would be lying to himself if he at least didn't acknowledge that he was beginning to feel an emotional connection with her as well. In the past, she had been a kind of conduit, a way for Peterson to fool himself that Laura was still alive, even if the perversion and depravity of such a farce would nearly stop his heart if he had the mind to dwell on it.

He put a hand on her cheek, running his thumb down her cheekbone and over her soft lips. He could see her take in a breath, and she swallowed. How could it possible that she could have feelings for him too? "I'm a broken man, Juliette."

She laid her own hand over his and held tight. "We all are," she said.

And it occurred to him that perhaps that was part of their connection. She recognized in him part of herself and felt drawn to it. In an imperfect world it made a disjointed version of sense.

With nothing else to do, Kincaid had returned to the detective's house and Green Lakes and was parked in an alley within eyesight of his residence. The night was still and calm and a rare display of stars danced overhead. It was cold, frost settling in on the window of his car that he scrapped absently with a fingernail.

He kept the vehicle turned off and sat low in his seat, not wanting the neighbors to notice a running car parked in the alley. With the engine turned off, however, the interior of the vehicle had grown quite cool, and he sat with his fingers buried into his jacket pockets, his breath puffing out in a pale mist.

A red SUV was parked in the driveway of Peterson's house, and for a time he thought that the cop had borrowed a vehicle. He sat a bit straighter when the front door opened, and a woman stepped out. She stood underneath the porch lamp as the detective himself stepped through the open door and held her by the shoulders. She was a taller than average woman, nearly coming up to the cop's chin, and they stood there for a long time looking at one another, not saying anything.

They shared a long embrace, the woman's head buried into Peterson's shoulder, and then they released. Kissing her on the forehead, he stood in the doorway as the woman got into her SUV, put her seatbelt on, watched the cop for a moment, started her car, and drove off. Only when the vehicle was gone did Peterson step back inside the residence and close the door.

    Kincaid waited a few moments before he started his own vehicle. He went in the direction of the departing SUV, eyes scanning for the sight of her taillights, curiosity welling up within him.

Thirty-Three

The law firm of Sachs Parker and Prihar was in the business district of downtown, and its smooth and polished exterior fit well with the surrounding towers that practically dripped money. The note that Solk gave Peterson had nearly been destroyed in the accident, the ink had blurred almost entirely, but he could still make out the name "Dharm Prihar" on the front, the defence lawyer that Turner, Collins, and Solk had used on the original sex assault charge. A web search quickly brought up the prestigious law firm that Prihar was apparently a partner in and with it an address.

Peterson had showered and dressed in a navy-blue suit. He skipped the tie and kept the upper buttons open, hoping the clothing would be enough to get him in through the front doors. He prayed that no one would ask to see a badge. He was already facing at least two code of conduct investigations, one for losing his badge and the other for punching Gregor in the face. He wouldn't be entirely surprised if the latter infraction also resulted in an assault charge, but there was nothing he could do about it now. His only hope, or so it seemed to him, was to get a bead on the killer and thus perhaps find redemption. If it was reported to some higher up that he was continuing the investigation while on medical suspension, his goose would truly be cooked, but he had already resolved himself to this course of action and he was determined to see it through.

Juliette had left late last night, and he was undecided on how he felt about their parting. A large part of him, larger than he thought possible, had wanted her to stay. But in the end he felt his own grief and logic pushing his physical and emotional feelings aside. He was a police officer, for the moment anyway, unless Gregor pushed extremely hard to have that fact changed. And she did what she did, though he tried not to dwell on her choice of occupation. More than those things, Laura was still an ever-present thought in his mind, and probably would be for some time to come.

Juliette had seemed hurt but showed understanding when he asked her to leave, and he had kissed her on the forehead. Spending the rest of the night tossing and turning, the thoughts of the case, of Laura, of Juliette, consumed him. He had maybe fallen asleep around three or four and awoke bleary eyed but with a hastily formed plan in his head.

Peterson walked through the front doors of the twelve-story office tower and found a list of businesses on the one side of the bank of elevators. A security guard off to the right watched him with disinterest, and when Peterson smiled at him the man nodded and continued to read a magazine that he had set on the desk in front of him. Judging by the names displayed in blocky, white, stenciled letters the office tower mainly hosted professional departments. He saw that the Sachs Parker and Prihar firm was on the fourth floor, so he hit the button to go up and stepped inside the elevator when it stopped at the main floor.

He rode the elevator up and stepped out, following a sign that pointed him to the left toward the law offices. As he rounded the corner, he walked full on into a man coming toward him. The impact was hard, mainly because the other guy, a well-muscled guy in his mid-thirties, seemed to be in a hurry. His eyes, an intense shade of blue, widened slightly when he took in Peterson's face, and his hand drifted toward his waist for a moment.

"Sorry about that, buddy," the guy said pleasantly, whatever shock that had originally shown on his face vanishing in an instant.

"No, it's fine," Peterson returned. There was something about the man that made the detective feel uneasy, though he couldn't exactly say why. He looked familiar but couldn't place him, though if he was a lawyer or a client there was a good chance that Peterson had dealt with him over the years. He certainly looked like a professional, with a neatly pressed dark suit and severely polished leather shoes. The man's face was what set off that interpretation as he had a hard, square jaw, and carried his body as if geared for a fight.

"Is everything okay?" the man asked.

Peterson took a moment before answering, trying to organize his thoughts. "You just look familiar is all," he said finally.

"Ah," the man chuckled good naturedly. "Name's Pete Forbes. I sometimes do *ad hoc* duties downtown. Maybe that's where you saw me." The introduction came so freely and without so much of a hint of hesitation that Peterson found himself relaxing, even though alarm bells still drummed in the back of his mind.

"Yeah, that's probably it," Peterson agreed. He tried to ignore the warning in his heart. "Anyway, sorry about jamming into you like that."

"It's all good," Forbes said, slapped Peterson on the shoulder before going past him towards the elevators. "Have a good day," he called back. Peterson watched him go, still feeling unsettled but unsure why, as he continued toward the glass doors at the end of the hallway that read, "Sachs Parker and Prihar, Law Firm."

He pushed through the doors and approached a dark-haired receptionist who was sitting at a cream-colored, oval desk. She was talking through a headset that disappeared underneath smooth, black hair that reached past her shoulders down to her mid back.

"Yes, they will be able to make it for three," she said into the phone as she looked up to Peterson, raising her index finger to indicate she would be a moment. "No, we received the disclosure from Crown, but I think Mr. Parker will be arguing there was a charter breach." She finished her conversation, took the headset off, and placed it on the desk. "Can I help you?" she asked.

Out of reflex, Peterson reached into his inside coat pocket to remove his badge but then remembered that he didn't have it. *Might as well just go for it,* he thought. "I'm Detective Jack Peterson with the Seattle Police Department. I would have called ahead but…" he let the thought hang on, let the receptionist fill in the story however she wanted. "Anyway, I know it's short notice, but I really need to speak with Dharm Prihar. It's extremely important."

She gave him a curious look, as if confused by something that he had said, and then swung over to her computer screen. Her fingers beat out a few keys before she glanced back at him. "Mr. Prihar is already with a Detective Jack Peterson," she said. "Do you have some ID that I can see?"

What she told him made absolutely no sense, and he was about to ask her to repeat her question when from the back came a blood-curdling scream, and then everything fell into place.

Thirty-Four

Peterson flew past the receptionist, pushing past lawyers, clients, and office staff, trying desperately to get to the source of the screaming. He moved through a throng of people who were jammed in the doorway and saw an older woman dressed in a business casual suit being led away by two guys. A plaque on the door said, "D. Prihar, Attorney."

Her skin was pale, and she looked on the verge of throwing up or passing out, or perhaps both.

He pushed the onlookers aside and poked his head in the office doorway. There were two other guys in Prihar's office, both lawyers by the looks of them, and they were performing first aid on an East Indian man whose beige turban was lying crookedly on his head. They were in the corner of the office near a bookshelf and the victim, who Peterson assumed was Dharm Prihar, was lying on his back, one hand down by his side, the other held limply to his throat where a silver-handled letter opener protruding from his flesh.

The one lawyer had a shirt pressed to the wound and the other guy was yelling for someone to call an ambulance. From the splash of blood on the walls and the pool collecting under Prihar's neck, Peterson knew that there was no point. Dharm Prihar was not moving, and his eyes were staring sightlessly up to the ceiling.

"Shit," Peterson yelled, earning a surprised glance from the people nearest to him, as he ran back from the direction he had come, sprinting past the receptionist who was frantically speaking into her headset, calling for the police and an ambulance. She yelled at him as he pushed through the doors, saying, "Hey you! Wait!" but he was already down the hallway and crashing through the emergency exit to the stairs, ignoring the elevators completely. He half ran, half stumbled down the four flights of stairs, his heart pounding against his chest as the full realization of what had happened dawned on him. The killer had rescued him and Denly following the car crash and had stolen his wallet. He had then used his police ID to gain access to Prihar so he could kill him. Peterson had been face to face with the killer and had let him simply walk away.

On the main floor, he crashed through the doors and ran for the exit, rushing past the security guard who made a move to stop him but only came up with air as Peterson blazed past him. He hit the exit doors at a full sprint, using his shoulder to bang the door open and then stopped on the sidewalk, looking in all directions, but the killer was nowhere to be seen.

A voice yelled from behind him, and he turned to see the security guard jogging toward him, shouting into a radio mike, probably for backup and maybe even communicating with the police who were surely on their way. Without hesitation Peterson broke for it, running to the left and then down an alley, forming a hasty plan in his mind even as he fled the scene. He had maybe an hour before they would put it together that he was involved. Probably enough time to get home, pack a bag, grab some cash, and find somewhere to hold up until he figured out what to do next.

His name would be circulated, and either they, in particular Gregor, would assume he killed Prihar or had been at the scene for reasons yet to be identified. Either way he was royally and judiciously screwed.

Thirty-Five

Sylvia Partridge was having a shit day. It had started out as a shit morning, as she had woken up with a pounding headache from the three gin and tonics she had downed the night before. She had gotten out of bed, wavered there for a moment as the blood seemed to rush up and in through her damned temple, and then staggered to the shower. The four ibuprofens she had popped with her cinnamon bagel had pushed her pain from an intense wave down to a dull throb, just enough to let her know that it was still there, like a relative who had overstayed their welcome.

She was not normally a drinker, but she felt like crap after her actions with Jack, which seemed to her as if she had served him on a silver platter to Captain Elias Asshole Gregor. After Peterson had been escorted from the premises by those two meathead SWAT members, Gregor had sidled up to her, chummy like, and had placed a hand on her shoulder like they were old buddies.

"Got to weed out these bad apples," he had told her, and she had barely stopped herself from either decking the pretentious bastard or throwing up in her mouth. Her mood had brightened only slightly as he noticed the welt on Gregor's chin from where Peterson had clocked him.

That evening, on her second of three G and T's, her cat Toby had eyed her curiously, taking his favorite post on one of her old armchairs as she raged around the apartment, the liquid from her drink sloshing on her wrist as she paced in the living room like a caged animal. The problem was, she realized, that she knew she had done the right thing. More than that, Jack probably didn't blame her for what she did, which seemed only to make her own guilt double and then redouble after that.

Given that Denly was still recovering from his injuries, and Peterson was on a forced medical suspension she assumed that the office would be empty when she finally arrived shortly after nine. Her headache thrummed a little harder when she stepped off the elevator and saw Captain Elias Gregor standing by her desk, checking his watch periodically.

She grumbled in her throat, too quiet for him to hear, as she approached him. He looked as resplendent as ever, with not a hair out of place. Her appearance resembled, however, a bag of smashed apples and she knew it, which made her even more annoyed by his perfect complexion and shining, golden hair.

"Where the hell have you been?" he asked. "I've been screwing around here for nearly an hour."

She fought the urge to smack him and did her best to keep her voice level. "It was a long night." She adjusted the bag on her shoulder, sensing now that he wasn't there for idle chit chat. "What happened?"

He flipped a set of car keys, and she caught it with her right hand. "Grab your gear. Your boss screwed up royally, and I plan on grabbing him by his short and curlies."

Well shit, she thought. Seems like this day was going to get a hell of a lot worse.

Thirty-Six

The letter opener jutted out of Prihar's neck like a silver lawn dart, buried deep in his flesh up to the hilt. The smell of blood was sharp in the air, and the tangy metallic odor left a bad taste on Partridge's mouth; it intermingled with Gregor's pungent cologne, all the stronger as he was standing so close their shoulders were nearly touching.

"Son of a bitch," Gregor said, wringing his hands in great exasperation. This expression was betrayed by what seemed to Partridge as glee that alighted in the man's eyes. He had already formed his opinion on the car ride over, Partridge behind the wheel. She had been forced to open her window three inches, despite the cold, simply to provide some air to combat Gregor's Italian shower body dousing. "Early reports are that Peterson made an appointment to see Prihar and then stabbed him in the neck," Gregor told her as she sped through the city streets, her dashboard-mounted red-and-blue strobing into her already pained eyes.

Neither she nor Gregor proceeded very far into the crime scene and thus were spared the annoyance of having to suit up fully. Inside the office there were two forensic officers working the scene. Another white-suited figure was roaming around, hovering over Prihar's body like a vulture, reaching out a tentative hand to probe the wound around the neck. Partridge didn't recognize the person, who had the vague body shape of a woman, but she figured her for a coroner, who would at the very least assign a tentative cause of death.

One of the ident members, who Partridge thought was a guy named Matthews, was snapping off photographs of the scene while the other was doing a quick search of the room itself, pushing aside papers on the desk on the opposite side of the room.

"What do you think?" Gregor asked the detective, giving her a sideways glance.

Partridge sucked on her teeth for a moment, trying to form the picture of the events in her mind. Prihar lay near a bookshelf, with the arterial spray of blood arcing on the wall. It appeared to be uninterrupted, and it seemed like the man had been stabbed from behind. She told this to Gregor, who nodded sagely. "Doesn't appear to be any defensive wounds on his hands," she added. "And you'd think the blood spray would be disrupted if buddy came from the front. The vic probably got up to check something out on the bookshelf, buddy grabbed the letter opener and stabbed him from behind." No part of her thought that Jack was involved and her mind was racing for other explanations.

"Found something," the ident guy near the desk said, and they ambled over to see what was going on. With a green latex thumb, he pointed at an address book that was splayed open on the desk. Under today's date a neat hand had written, next to 9:00 a.m., the words, "Meet with Dt. Jack Peterson, SPD."

"Got you," Gregor said, slamming his fist into his palm.

"Now, just wait a minute," Partridge protested. "That could have been anyone, Jack lost his wallet after all."

"*Claims* he lost his wallet," Gregor chimed. He turned to the ident member. "What about surveillance?" he asked. They had both noticed the cameras leading into the office building, as well as the ones in the elevators and the fourth floor as they stepped off.

Behind his mask and goggles, the ident member shook his head. His voice sounded muffled behind the 3-M mask that he wore. "Nothing. The feeds were cut to the cameras on the elevators and the fourth floor, someone had broken into the security office and disabled the connections. The cameras were still up at the main exit, and there's someone checking it out now."

Gregor wheeled on his heels and strode purposefully out of the office, and Partridge felt obliged to follow, leaving the crime scene to the two ident members and the coroner where they would probably spend the next day or two checking for fingerprints and DNA. She caught up with Gregor as he was passing the receptionist desk, and a uniformed officer called to him as they rushed past.

"Captain, sir," the uniform said, a youngish guy wearing the standard blue-black gear of a street SPD member. He was standing next to an attractive, dark-haired woman in clothing that looked too tight for office wear, her boobs practically spilling out of her top, which to Partridge seemed an intentional act of dressing. Partridge and Gregor approached the pair, and out of the corner of her eye she saw the captain take a long look at the chick's exposed cleavage before turning to the uniform.

"What?" Gregor barked, and the uniformed guy, probably a rookie judging by his smooth youthful face, quailed in his shiny black boots.

"You, uh…wanted to know if we found anything," the uniform stuttered. He pointed to the blonde beside him. "She says that she talked to Detective Peterson."

Gregor straightened and waved the uniform officer off, who looked relieved to have the captain's attention diverted elsewhere. "Sorry I didn't catch your name, Ms…" Gregor drifted off.

"Stacy," she said, voice like velvet silk. Partridge saw Stacy scan Gregor up and down quickly, a speedy approving appraisal judging by the woman's vapid smile. Gregor smiled back in kind, but for Partridge his demeanor was feral, wolfish, making her feel as if she had wandered into a *Wild Kingdom* episode featuring two baboons. She was already irritated enough without having to endure a mating dance between Malibu Barbie and Captain Awesome.

"You got something to share, Stacy?" Partridge said, making no attempt to mask the annoyance in her voice. The younger woman turned to her as if noticing her for the first time and gave Partridge a chilled smile.

"Only that the detective, Peterson, asked if he could see Mr. Prihar."

"And when was this?" Gregor asked her.

Stacy put a finger to perfectly plump lips and considered. "Oh, right before Mrs. Akins started screaming. I ran back there and saw Mr. Prihar, so much blood, so horrible." Stacy shuddered with the memory, and Gregor reached out a hand and squeezed her shoulder.

"It's okay, dear, it's all over now," he said.

Partridge made a gagging sound, and Gregor looked at her sharply. Stacy took no notice of the exchange and was crying in a tinny sort of way that reminded Partridge of those little barking dogs, though no tears were falling from the woman's eyes. She rubbed one away anyway and looked gratefully to Gregor.

"Did anyone else speak with Mr. Prihar?" Partridge asked.

Stacy shook her head. "No one else came up to the front desk to ask for him, no."

"How much time passed between you speaking to Peterson and when Akins started screaming?" Partridge asked.

"Oh, I don't know," she said. "So much was going on."

"Well, was it two minutes before, five minutes before, or right when things started to go down?"

Stacy gave her a blank expression and shook her head. Partridge fought the overwhelming urge to dropkick the woman, and asked instead, "All right, how about this. Do you know what time it was when you spoke to Peterson?"

She was afraid she was going to be given another negative answer, but a dim bulb flashed off somewhere in the back of Stacy's mind. She grabbed Gregor's hand and looked him deep in the eyes. "I know! I was just talking to Peter Ackland about the Clarke deposition, and I looked at the time, this was right when Detective Peterson asked to see Mr. Prihar. And it was 9:10 a.m." From the smile on the woman's face, you would have thought she had just won the bonus round on *Family Feud*, but at least she had given something in Peterson's favor.

Partridge turned to Gregor. "There you have it, Sir. The victim made an appointment with Peterson at nine. Jack was here at nine-ten, so it must have been someone else with Prihar at the time of the murder."

Gregor was unfazed. "Or it was Peterson and he was simply late." Gregor thanked Stacy the receptionist and gave her a long stare as she sauntered away. Gregor managed to drag his eyes away after a period of time to regard Partridge once more. "C'mon," he said. "Let's look at the video feed."

It was not normal for the big brass to attend a crime scene like this. Then, of course, it was not normal for an SPD detective to be implicated, even peripherally, in a crime of this scope. A lawyer is murdered in the middle of the day in a highly affluent downtown district apparently under the eyes of over twenty witnesses with no one offering any real shred of evidence, beyond Stacy the dim-witted receptionist who maybe sorta thinks she spoke to Peterson at one time or another. The whole thing made Partridge want to scream.

What was interesting, she noticed, was how the rank-and-file members, from the uniform cops manning security, to the other detectives on scene, deferred to Gregor in an almost beat dog mentality. Gregor had never been a really good cop, she knew. Unpopular and abrasive, he had been disliked by most of his colleagues and had been all but washed out of patrol duties. No one wants to work with someone on the streets if they're not a hundred percent confident that the person would have their back if things happened to turn sideways. She had heard, though it had never been confirmed, that he and his last partner had pulled over a drunk driver on one of the abandoned side streets in the city. His partner had gotten out and spoken to the guy while Gregor had stayed behind to run checks on the mobile work station. The drunk had attacked his partner outside the vehicle, and the fight was on. Instead of rushing to his partner's aide, as any other cop would, Gregor had remained in his vehicle and actually locked his doors.

The partner had managed to get the drunk in cuffs, and Gregor still refused to open the door. This may have been because his partner had probably indicated, in colorful language, that some kind of harm would befall him the second he got his hands on Gregor. That had been the beginning of the end for Gregor's general duties days, and he had been shifted, rather unceremoniously, to an admin position, and then through various misdeeds, another rumor she had heard, he had slowly risen in the ranks, usually on the backs and careers of his colleagues and subordinates. It was a sad aspect of the policing world that duplicity, not honor, was often rewarded.

By the time they reached the security office on the main level, Partridge had grown tired of cops jumping out of Gregor's path like he was a rampaging bull. The officer standing guard over the security station practically fled from Gregor as if he had just been told his house was on fire, and Partridge soon found herself alone in a security office that was no larger than a jail cell. Gregor took a seat at the computer terminal and deftly navigated the keys, seemingly at ease with the program.

"I graduated with a computer sciences degree," he explained to the question she had no intention to ask. "Give me a few minutes and I'll pull everything up, no problem."

"Good for you," Partridge said under her breath as she went to the door. There didn't appear to be any damage to the locking mechanism, though there were tiny scratches on the outside key hole. *Picked, maybe?* she thought and then moved back to where Gregor had shifted excitedly in his seat.

"Got it," he said, as he brought up a multi-monitor view of the building's security system. The image on the screen featured eight security feeds, segmented into equal spaces on the monitor, though two of these were black. The rest showed what appeared to be live images of the comings and goings of the building employees, though most of the people were now cops interviewing various people.

"Why wasn't the security guy here at the time the feeds went down?" Partridge asked.

"I guess he got a call to go somewhere else, and he left his post," Gregor responded. "The call turned out to be bogus, so Peterson must have planned on getting the room empty."

She bristled at the casualness of Gregor's interpretation of Jack's guilt, but she let it go for the moment. Now was not the time to fight this particular battle. With little difficulty, Gregor navigated the security system and rewound the feed. Partridge watched with a sick feeling in her stomach as Peterson came through the main floor doors at 8:50 a.m. The resolution was clear enough that he was easily identifiable with his short brown hair and dark suit. Four minutes later, the security feed to the elevators and fourth floor hallway cut out. And five minutes after that she saw Peterson racing through the main floor exits, being chased by a security guard.

"Got you, you son of a bitch," Gregor said, his feral grin reflected in the computer monitor.

"Now, just hold on a minute," Partridge began to protest. "This is nuts. You're making out like Jack murdered Prihar. Where's the motive? Why would he do it?"

"Who the hell knows?" Gregor said, turning to face her. "Beyond the fact that he's crazier than a loon, and that's documented in his records. Doesn't it strike you as odd that all this stuff went down as soon as he got back to work?"

"What does that matter? He was with Solk during the time of the murder, there was no way he could have done that."

"So he has an accomplice. Look, maybe he heard about the Green assault, saw these guys living the high life, and it reminded of his own screwed-up life. He can't avenge his wife so he settles on some new targets. There's your motive." Gregor pointed to the screen where an image of Peterson was frozen as he fled through the exits. "And you got means and opportunity."

Partridge stared at the screen, felt Gregor's eyes on her, and a great weight settled into her stomach. *Jack, what have you done?* she thought.

Thirty-Seven

It took Peterson thirty minutes to get from the office building to his house, transported via a cabbie that paid him almost no attention. He hoped that the driver wouldn't remember him, but he doubted such a thing was possible. They would get to the taxi driver eventually, track Peterson's movements through the various CCTV scattered around downtown. It took him another ten minutes to pack his duffel bag with a change of clothes and cash. From this point on he wouldn't use any of his credit cards unless absolutely necessary. In the basement, he turned on an overhead lamp and pushed aside the washer and dryer, revealing a section of concrete that had been cut out into a box shape. A grey silver pistol case, covered with a thin sheet of dust and cobwebs, was buried in the back. He removed it, entered in a combination on a roll lock, and opened the case, revealing a black matte Smith and Wesson 9 mm pistol. The handgun was already loaded, fifteen rounds in the mag with another in the pipe. He hoped he didn't need anymore ammunition. Hell, he hoped he didn't need any ammunition at all, but from this point he was planning as he went along, and he couldn't exactly say what he might and might not need. Better to have the gun and not need it versus need the gun and not have it.

He tucked the handgun into his rear waistband, the metal cool against his skin, and pulled his shirt over it. He already felt the press of time and wanted to get out of there as soon as possible, but he knew that he couldn't get far without a set of wheels.

Peterson climbed the stairs, turning off the light as he went up, and closed the door. He knew that when his fellow SPD members came to the house, and eventually they would, they would find evidence that he had been here and had packed in a hurry. There was little he could do to hide that fact so made no attempt in trying to conceal it.

From his duffel bag he removed a blue ball cap and pulled it low on his forehead, giving his house one last look before he went outside. He wasn't entirely sure he would ever come back, and he had mixed feelings about that. He had so many good memories here, memories with Laura. But this place also contained so many nightmares, so much darkness that proceeded most of his waking thoughts.

He left through the side door of the house. The afternoon was crisp and clear, and though he knew most of the neighbors were at work, he still felt exposed as the afternoon sun hit him. He had lingered too long and felt the need to escape press against him. His next-door neighbors to the east, Bill and Linda Miller, were gone for the next two weeks, and had asked him to watch over the place while they were away. Their houses were connected by a cobblestone walkway that cut through a thick green hedge, and Peterson hurried as casually as he could between the two properties. They hadn't given him a key, but Bill had told him that there was one under the mat at the side door that led into the garage. He found it quickly enough and opened the garage door, closing it quickly behind him.

He was swallowed in a cool darkness, only diminished by two small windows on the garage door, which were frosted over and nearly opaque.

The garage was neatly organized, with white shelving installed in the walls, packed with blue Rubbermaid containers. An older model Ford F150 was parked in the garage, a fine covering of dust on the exterior. From one corner of the garage Peterson found a red-and-black work bench, and he searched the drawers until he found a medium-sized slotted screwdriver. He returned to the truck and tried the driver's door, finding with relief that it was unlocked.

He opened the rear cab and threw his duffel in, closed the door, and climbed into the driver's seat. He closed his door and sat back in the seat, caught his reflection in the rear-view mirror. There was sweat beading on the top of his forehead and he looked pale, sickly. His haunted eyes stared back at him as the realization of what he was doing finally took shape. He should phone Gregor, turn himself in, and explain what happened. From this moment on, everything that he did would only shift more blame and suspicion on to himself.

Peterson pushed the idea aside; the thought of turning himself in to that blowhard was bad enough. He needed to do this. With his right hand he moved the mirror up and to the side, adjusting the reflection away from himself, and got to work. Years ago, he had dealt with a prolific car thief whose favorite vehicles to steal were the Ford F models. "Damn easy, man," the thief, whose name Peterson could not recall, had given him that particular nugget while he had fingerprinted him in a concrete-lined cell at the Remand Center. "All you need is a screwdriver."

Peterson had never tested the theory, but it now seemed as good a time as any. He fit the blade of the screwdriver into the ignition. He used the palm of his hand to strike the base of the screwdriver until it wedged itself into the key slot and twisted. Nothing happened, and the screwdriver refused to move. He put more torque into the turn, grunting with the effort, and something in the internal housing gave way with a crunching sound.

Now the screwdriver moved freely, and he turned it in the ignition. He was surprised when the engine rumbled to life and the vehicle started. Peterson gave Bill Miller a silent apology and hit the garage door opener, which was suspended from the visor on a plastic clip. The door opened slowly, he pulled out and closed the door with the opener. As he drove away he thought of his mounting sins and decided that vehicle theft rated low on the list.

Thirty-Eight

Twenty minutes later, keeping his vehicle under the speed limit and observing all traffic laws, Peterson hit the I-90 and travelled over the bridge, Lake Washington a silver flat disc that stretched beyond him. The edges were frosted over from the recent cold, small reaches of ice that would probably melt in the coming days, and he could see a few brave souls on the edge of the black ice fishing with large cork rods.

He had been to Denly's house a handful of times, but the Mount Baker neighborhood was designed like a labyrinth, and he worked from memory to try and find the place. On a police officer's salary, Denly would have been hard pressed to afford a house in that district, but his wife, Sarah was a plastic surgeon, and her bankroll had been enough to afford their house, though just barely. With its scenic views of the mountains and access to waterfronts most of the people who occupied the neighborhood carried with them six-figure salaries.

It was a quarter after five when Peterson drove past their house, finding with relief that their car was in the driveway and there were lights on in the house. He parked a block away, shooting for a place with no streetlamps. While he was confident the vehicle wouldn't be reported stolen, the Millers being unaware he had borrowed their car, the damaged ignition would have been enough for even a causal passerby to take notice. Last thing he wanted was to have Denly connected with his most recent bout of thievery.

He got out of the truck and grabbed his duffel bag, leaving the doors unlocked, hoping no one would steal his stolen truck. He went on foot, crunching on half-formed ice, down the sidewalk which was lined with streetlights and bare birch trees. Denly's house was on the south side of the street, two cars in the driveway, and through the white, drawn curtains he could see the outline of their Christmas tree, red and blue twinkling lights throwing shadows on the blinds. The house was a two-story affair, with dark-cream siding, the newel posts bordered with dark stone masonry. A puff of chimney smoke snaked lazily toward the sky.

From inside he could hear the faint sound of Christmas music and the peal of children's laughter. He walked up the steps and hesitated near the door, now questioning whether he should draw Denly in like this, or even trust the man. He didn't blame Sylvia Partridge for essentially turning him in; she had been completely justified in her actions, and Denly had more than enough reason to do the same. He and Denly were both lucky to survive the accident that had occurred because of Peterson's arrogance. He could easily picture Denly picking up the phone and calling Gregor immediately, but Peterson couldn't proceed alone and needed an ally.

He knocked three times on the side of the door and heard running footsteps approaching. It opened a crack, revealing the cherubic face of their eldest child, Rebecca. She was eight years old, if Peterson remembered correctly, but it had been what seemed like an age since he had last seen her. It had probably been a year, and in that time she had shot up like a weed. He wondered if she would even recognize him, but his question was soon answered as she swung open the door fully, a wide smile on her face, and she flew into Peterson's arms for a crushing embrace.

"Uncle Jack!" she yelled into his waist, her small voice muffled against the fabric. She was a small child with thin limbs, but her grip was tight, and he found himself laughing despite himself. She was wearing purple tights and a rainbow-colored t-shirt, and her long, blonde hair was pulled back, held in place with a purple scrunchie. He bent down and hugged her, her skin fresh smelling and smooth.

They released, and she took off with a sprint into the house, leaving him kneeling on the exterior front porch. She yelled his name happily, her voice fading as she rounded the corner of the hallway, headed toward the kitchen. He brushed his legs off and slipped inside.

Once inside, he closed the door and locked it behind him. Sarah Denly came around the corner where Rebecca had sped past a few seconds earlier. Rebecca was behind Sarah, pushing her towards Peterson, yelling, "C'mon, c'mon, c'mon!" She was drying her hands on a red-and-green hand towel, looking back at her daughter with an amused expression. She stopped short when she saw Peterson standing in the foyer, and her expression went from surprise to recognition and finally to barely masked fury. She was an attractive woman in her late thirties with curly blonde hair that framed a plump face.

Rebecca latched on to the side of her leg and looked toward Peterson with obvious affection. Sarah reached down and patted her head. "Honey, please go help your brother in the play room." Her voice was sweet and light, but her gaze was fixed on Peterson, and there was not much warmth there.

"But I don't want to play with Ethan," Rebecca protested. Ethan was five, Peterson remembered, and was the spitting image of Charles Denly, merely in a shrunken child form.

Sarah turned to regard her daughter. "Do it," she said, and when Rebecca opened her mouth to say something, she must have noticed the look on her mother's face, because she immediately went silent. Rebecca turned to Peterson, stuck her tongue out, and ran down the hallway, around the left corner, and out of view.

Sarah watched her go, and when she was out of earshot she rounded on Peterson. "What are you doing here?" Her voice was as cold as a winter morning, and she gripped the tea towel in her hand like she was picturing it was someone's neck, his own probably. She waved a hand toward the hallway. "Chuck is almost dead because of you."

Peterson held up his hands in surrender. "I know, and I'm sorry, believe me I truly am. But I had nowhere else to turn. I need help."

She swallowed, trying to bury her anger, and jabbed a finger at his chest. "You get fifteen minutes and then you're out of here, you understand?"

He nodded as if being scolded by a school teacher. Small tears collected at the corner of her eyes and her fury crumbled slightly. "And I don't want you to hurt him. Anymore."

Thirty-Nine

When Peterson entered the living room, he understood what she meant by that last comment. Denly was sitting on the couch, a beer in his right hand. His left arm was completely bandaged from wrist to shoulder, the white cast scrawled with permanent marker drawings that only his kids could have done. His left leg was propped up on a pillow, which had been placed on the ottoman, and like his arm it bore a thick, white cast that completely covered his foot and ended nearly mid-thigh. His face had a network of cuts and contusions, some so large that they were closed with stiches, and his right eye was swollen shut.

Peterson was led into the living room with Sarah pushing him along, and he stopped short when he saw Denly sitting there. He looked like he had been involved in a plane crash, and Peterson was amazed that the hospital had sent him home, amazed really that Denly had survived the crash at all. Peterson checked himself, unsure of how Denly would react once he saw him, but a relieved smile stretched across the injured man's face when he finally noticed him standing in the entry way with his wife.

"Jack!" Denly said, struggling to stand up. Sarah rushed over, moving quicker than Peterson would have thought possible, and gently put a hand on her husband's chest, guiding him back on to the chair. "Okay, okay, okay," he said, holding his hands out in mock surrender. "Jack, sit please," and he motioned Peterson to the chair beside the couch.

When Peterson took the seat, Denly grabbed his hand tightly in his own. "I'm so glad to see you, really." Peterson had never seen Denly so expressive, and he looked up at Sarah for an explanation.

"He's on a lot of drugs right now," she said plainly. And Peterson saw it now, and that partially explained the almost unbridled look of love on the other man's face. His eyes were like black saucers, the pupils so dilated that very little of his eye color could be seen. Peterson patted the man's hand and attempted to remove his own, but it was held fast.

"I've been so worried about you," Denly said. His voice was slurred, and he words ran together to form an continuous line. "Sylvia called me, said you were suspended, and that you had disappeared. You might have killed someone?" The last phrase seemed to Peterson like a dropped bomb, and it took the wind from his lungs.

"You didn't know?" Sara asked, and when she read his confused expression she took the TV remote from the armrest and turned on the regional news. Peterson was not entirely surprised to see Captain Elias Gregor standing in front of a long row of microphones, talking for the camera.

"As I said, we are still in the preliminary stages, but we are searching for Detective Jack Peterson." Looking sombre, Gregor scanned his eyes over the collected crowd of reporters. "I can confirm that Jack Peterson works for the Seattle Police Department and that we do need to talk to him to figure out what happened."

His mouth was downturned, affecting deep sadness, but Peterson could see a predatory hunger in the captain's eyes. Even through the TV Peterson could see the deep scarlet bruise that had formed on Gregor's chin from where he had struck him the day earlier. "If he is spotted, I ask that the public call 911 and make no attempt to approach him. It's difficult to say what state of mind he is in right now, and he could be a danger to himself and others—"

Sarah turned off the TV, throwing the room in silence. Peterson had at least half expected that he would be implicated in the Prihar murder, given all the circumstances that were present, but he never dreamed of this. *Danger to others?* It was ridiculous.

"That man looks like he's out for blood," Sarah offered.

"Well, I did punch him in the jaw, so maybe he's looking to even the score," Peterson said. He pushed himself up and apologized to them both. "I didn't think it was this bad, I'm sorry, I should never have come here." He looked down at Denly, who seemed to be his only friend left in the world. "I'm sorry that I did this to you, Chuck. If I had known, you would get g hurt…" He trailed off as he felt his voice cracking.

Once more Denly grabbed his hand. "Your wife died, man. She was murdered. Of course, you're going to be messed up."

Just then, the phone rang, and Sarah went into the kitchen to answer it. She came out a few minutes later and, keeping her hand over the speaker, said, "He says it's Captain Gregor." She looked between Denly and Peterson, concerned.

Denly grunted and waved for her to hand him the phone.

Peterson stood helplessly as Denly answered and could only listen to one side of the conversation. "Yes, sir. No, not busy at all, just trying to rest." A pause. "Thanks, yeah I hope to get back on my feet soon. Doctors say I might have this cast on for a month, maybe two, and then I can get back up and moving." Another pause, lengthier this time. Denly looked up at Peterson, a half-smile on his face. "Jack? That asshole? No, if he came to me you'd be the first to know. I wouldn't talk to that guy for love or money, believe you me." They talked for a few more minutes, and Denly hung up the phone.

Peterson stared at him, grateful but unable to form the words. Denly handed the phone back to his wife and turned to Peterson. "Now, where were we?"

Forty

Two hours later, Sarah and the kids were in the rec room watching a movie. Despite her earlier threat to kick him out after fifteen minutes, she had warmed up sufficiently enough to invite him to stay for dinner, mostly out of deference to her husband who all but begged for him to stay. Rebecca and Ethan fought over each other for Peterson's attention as the food was served and only stopped when Sarah ordered them to scale it back several notches. She was an excellent cook, and only when the smell of roast chicken found its way to Peterson's nose did he realize how famished he truly was. Laura had been the cook in the family, and ever since her death he had mainly subsisted on frozen foods, take out, and cereal. He couldn't recall the last time he had had an actual home-cooked meal that didn't consist of a reconstituted animal product, and he ate like a prisoner of war.

Afterward, the children said goodnight to Peterson and kissed their father before scampering off to the rec room. Peterson and Denly settled themselves in the den, sitting comfortably before a crackling fire that gave off the pleasant smell of wood smoke. The den appeared to be mainly decorated by Denly, given the number of sports posters and trophies which took space on the wood paneled wall. A large 60-inch TV screen was wall mounted in one corner, and Denly had tuned it to a classical rock station, the level down so low that Peterson could barely make out the song.

The drugs had started to filter out of Denly's system, and he became more coherent and sombre. With it, Peterson could see that the pain was slowly returning as his companion shifted uncomfortably in his large leather recliner, the fabric creaking as it caught on his casts. Peterson offered to get him some more medication, but Denly waved him off.

"I actually want to talk with you and perhaps remember it," he said. "The stuff that they gave me is wild; feeling like I'm on an acid trip half the time."

A silence stretched before them during which neither seemed capable of looking at the other. Peterson absently scratched his leg while Denly ran his hand down the length of his cast while the fireplace crackled and popped. Finally, Denly said, "I really wish you would have told me that you were struggling, Jack. More than that, I feel like I should have figured it out, picked up on it."

"Well, I'm not the best when it comes to sharing," Peterson said.

Denly nodded. "That's true, you are one cagey son of a bitch."

Both men laughed, and Peterson felt some of his tension fading away. He stared at the fireplace as the flames curled against the logs, turning the wood an inky black. "If I ever get out of this with my career intact, I'm going to get some help," he said.

"Good," Denly said. "Very good. How exactly are you planning on getting out of this, and how can I help?"

Peterson inched forward on his seat, eager to discuss something other than his personal problems. "I'm working on a theory, or at least the only thing that makes sense to me."

Denly nodded, an eagerness reflected in his own eyes.

"It's all about timing, I think. Why, of all a sudden, start knocking off everyone related to the Green attack. Why now?"

"Exactly," Denly nodded. "You could have had your revenge years ago."

"Yeah, so I'm thinking that if we want to catch this guy, we have to go to the beginning. Someone is pulling the strings, and I'm tired of being one step behind this guy. I want to get out in front." Peterson explained what he wanted to Denly, and the man looked doubtful.

"I don't know, Jack, it was a long time ago. Do you think they would even be able to do anything with the evidence?"

Peterson shook his head. "I have no idea, but it's worth a shot. Do you know anyone that could help me?"

Denly thought for a moment before nodding. "Hand me that phone," he said. Peterson reached to the side table of the couch where a cordless phone sat in a cradle. He grabbed it and handed it to Denly, who punched in a number. Denly talked for a few moments, explaining what he wanted, and a smile curled at the corner of his mouth. "Great," he said. "And you're sure it's no problem, right? You've watched the news recently?" He nodded again before saying goodbye and hanging up the phone. He smiled again, showing teeth. "Tomorrow morning we start pulling some strings."

Forty-One

Peterson declined their offer to spend the night there. Sarah and Charles met him at the front door, she standing and he sitting uncomfortably in a wheelchair. Peterson had already put his coat and shoes on and was waiting in the doorway, the cool air at his back. "I've already done enough damage coming here and getting you to cover for me, Charles. I don't want to put you in any deeper than you already are." They had given him nearly five hundred dollars in cash and a cell phone that belonged to Sarah.

"You keep in touch, you understand?" Denly ordered, the narcotics slurring the edges of his words again. "I love you man," he added. Sarah rolled her eyes, and Peterson fought the urge to either laugh or cry and shook Denly's hand instead.

"Love you too," he said, giving his good hand a firm pump before letting go and walking out of the house.

Peterson was surprised at this declaration and that he meant it. He had always liked Denly, always appreciated his relaxed manner and ability to look on the bright side of things. But he had never really considered him a friend, beyond work anyhow. Peterson had largely kept to himself, and while on friendly speaking terms with most people, he lacked truly deep relationships. He had nearly killed Denly, and here the man was, giving him money and putting his career on the line for him. Say what you will for cops, but more often than not they will lay down their lives for their partners. He only hoped he could return the favor to Denly one day.

It was getting on nine o'clock, and a damp chill followed Peterson from the Denly house to his truck. He climbed in, fished his screwdriver key out of the glovebox, and started the vehicle, putting it into gear and driving slowly out of the Mount Baker neighborhood.

He thought about going to Juliette's but decided against it and drove to an out-of-the-way motel instead. It was shabby and decrepit, but the aging receptionist who sat smoking a cigarette and said his name was Pete took his cash without a word and handed him a key attached to a large wooden paddle.

It was a one-story accommodation featuring such amenities as a bed and toilet. The walls had a speckled design that had probably been put up in 1950 but now had the added benefit of hiding the various stains and marks that had collected over the years. The TV was an older model and bolted to the dresser while the remote control was secured to the bedside table on a chain.

He took one look at the brown carpet and decided to place his duffel bag on one of the chairs, not trusting the look of the shag. He removed the pistol from his waistband and sat down on the bed, holding the gun in his hand. The bed was surprisingly comfortable, and he closed his eyes for a moment, sitting there, feeling the cold metal of the pistol in his palm. Sighing, he opened the bedside drawer and found it empty, save for a New Testament Bible. Out of curiosity he flipped it and saw the Gideon stamp on the lower right corner. The Bible looked like it had never been opened, and considering that people usually rented rooms like this by the hour, he wasn't entirely surprised.

He couldn't remember the last time he had read from the Bible. Probably back in grade school, he figured. He toyed with the idea of taking it out, but after a moment's consideration he placed the pistol on top of the book and closed the drawer. Still wearing his clothes, he laid down on the bed and stared up at the ceiling.

The heater in the room make a dull ticking sound that mixed in with the highway traffic to create a white noise that he found soothing, and he soon found himself sinking down into the bed until sleep took him. He dreamt of Laura and Juliette, their images commingling disturbingly. He awoke periodically in a cold sweat, kicking off the thin covers he had pulled over himself at some point during the night. In the last dream he had been standing over their old bed, the gun pointed at Laura's chest, and when he pulled the trigger he tasted cordite and gunpowder. Her blood washed over him in a wave and he woke up, drenched with perspiration and clutching his chest. The scars on his forehead and abdomen burned and spots danced over his vision like black balls.

He sat up in bed, swinging his feet over, and pulled his shirt away from his chest, where it stuck to his skin. The room was dark with only the streetlamps from outside filtering in light through the thin curtains. A siren sounded outside, and for a second he thought it was meant for him, but then it faded in the distance.

He checked his watch, finding that it was five a.m., and while he still felt tired he knew that he wouldn't get back to sleep. He stood, peeled the clothing from his body, and took a long, hot shower that did little to wake him up though it made him feel a little more human.

Then he dressed in a clean set of clothes that he got from his duffel bag, pulled the pistol from the nightstand and tucked it back in the bag along with his dirty clothing. He wasn't sure how the rest of the morning would play out and didn't want to be caught with a concealed weapon on his person.

When he was done, it was just after six. The world outside was still dark and quiet. He stepped outside in to a heavy fog that had settled and now hung a few feet off the ground, giving the transport trucks a ghostly shade as they rumbled past, on their way to whatever destination or delivery that awaited them.

The receptionist from the night before, Pete, was gone, replaced by a strung-out brunette who looked like she had been around the block more than a few times and was now worse off because of it. As he passed through the lobby door she turned lazily towards him, looked him up and down, obviously judged him not to be a threat, and turned back to the old TV that sat on the desk. From the sounds of it Peterson thought it was a game show, and the brunette was slumped on her chair, one elbow on the desk while her hand cupped her chin.

"Checking out, hon?" she asked in a gravelly voice.

He stopped short at the counter and slid the keys across the desk, the wooden paddle skipping on the chipped pressboard. She took it with her free hand without looking and skirted it beneath the desk. A faint smell of cigarettes hung in the air, and Peterson judged her to be a three- or four-pack-a-day kinda girl. She looked the part, with facial skin like dried paper and a leathery mouth. "Did you have a pleasant stay?"

"Yeah, you got a real four-star resort here."

She chuckled dryly but didn't respond. *Keep em coming doc, I got a million of them.*

"Can you call me a cab?" he asked.

She swivelled her eyes toward him though nothing else on her body moved. "Pete told me you came in a truck, that big shit wagon out there."

Peterson turned to look through the grimy window where the Millers' Ford was parked. He couldn't risk driving that thing around anymore. He would have to send Bill a thank you note later.

He turned back to the woman. "Not mine. How about that cab?"

The brunette, however reluctantly, called his cab, and thirty minutes later Peterson stood in an alley a block west of Seattle Police headquarters. The area traffic was slowly picking up, and he shielded himself in the relative darkness of the alley, waiting for Denly's contact to let him know it was safe to approach the building. His duffel bag was strapped over his shoulder, and he buried his hands into his pockets and stamped out the cold that was settling on to his skin. From his interior coat pocket he felt a vibration and pulled out the cell phone to find a text message.

Good to go. Come to the back.

He slipped the phone back into his pocket and left the alley. Being part of the downtown district, most of the buildings had exterior security cameras, so he kept his head down, hopeful that his meager disguise would be enough to shield him from a later investigation. The

SPD HQ building, which loomed in the distance, was a cream-colored high-rise with large square windows. He kept off the main streets, taking the alleys, and approached the rear of the building, ignoring the signs that read "Police Personnel Only." He knew that there was a loading dock access on the south side and he headed directly for this area, hopeful that Denly's contact would time it out so that Peterson wouldn't be found loitering outside. He knew that a civilian security team did frequent patrols, and he didn't want to be caught out in the open.

He felt himself relax as the side door past the loading bay opened and Graham Matthews, the forensic member at the original Turner homicide, stepped out and waved him through. "You're a popular guy lately," he said when Peterson slipped through, and Matthews closed the door. He was wearing a pair of blue cargo pants and his brown hair was messy, sleep bags under his eyes as if he had been up at all night.

The hallways were empty, given the early hour, but Peterson knew it wouldn't last. Soon, a host of police and civilian members would be starting their shifts. Matthews knew this as well and without speaking another word let him through the back corridors of the HQ building, which Peterson saw was without security cameras. He was taken to a service elevator, and only when the large steel doors closed did he breathe a sigh of relief. "Thanks for doing this, Graham." He clapped the man on the shoulder who shrugged as if it was no big deal. If Gregor caught wind of this, it could easily mean a code of conduct investigation against Matthews, maybe even criminal charges. "Were you able to get the exhibits?" Peterson asked as the elevator reached the subbasement.

Matthews nodded as they stepped out. The main offices for the forensic section were located on the upper floors, where Peterson knew that the day-to-day paperwork took place. All exhibit examinations took place in the subbasement where the venting systems could kick out all the hazardous chemicals through a shaft in the ceiling. Years back, the ident section complained that the working conditions were depressing, and the city did a review to determine how much it would cost to transfer and retrofit a new lab. When the price tag exceeded six zeros, the ident section was told quite plainly to suck it up and move on.

The walls were a pitted gray concrete, and dull halogen lamps lighted their path as they walked from the elevators, around a left corner, and approached a metal steel door with an electronic keypad mounted on the left side. Matthews punched in a code as he spoke. "It took a bit of phoning around last night, but I was able to get a hold of someone in security there at King's County. I had him ship the exhibits here last night but didn't get much of a chance to look at them. Figured you would want to check them out before I did anything too extreme."

The doors opened with a click and both men stepped through, with Matthews closing the doors behind them. He clicked on a set of lights on the right side of the wall, and the examination room was illuminated by bright fluorescent lamps. The forensic examination section was a square shaped room, thirty by thirty feet, with chrome tables bordering the walls. In one corner there was an ancient computer station flanked by two cyanoacrylate chambers and what looked to Peterson like a DNA drying cabinet, which was primarily used to dry clothing that had been heavily saturated with blood.

A long steel table was set in the center of the room, with a heavy brown cardboard draped over it. On top of this cardboard was a banker's box showing a police file number scrawled on the side with a permanent marker. Written below the file number were the words "Green – Sexual Assault."

They stopped at the table, and Peterson looked into the box. There were eight or nine paper exhibit bags containing items that had been seized during the original assault investigation. He reached down and flipped through the bags, finding what he had expected. The girl's underwear, shirt, and biological exhibits had been collected by the physicians during her medical exam following the rape. At the bottom on the box was an exhibit marked with a police number, date and time, and an officer's initials. In a comments section on the exhibit tag he read the words "Duct tape from victim's mouth."

Peterson picked up the exhibit bag and handed it to Matthews. "What do you think the chances are of getting prints from this?"

Matthews took the bag and placed it on the desk. He rolled over an office chair, and after putting on a pair of latex gloves, sat and used a pocket knife to cut the bag open. He slid out a clear piece of acetate from the bag where a section of duct tape was affixed to the plastic. "Not great," he said after a few moments examination. "Duct tape itself is not the best usually for getting prints." He arched an eyebrow. "What's the point anyway? You know who the bad guys were. Who cares if their prints are on there?"

Peterson said down beside him. "It's not their prints I'm interested in," he said, pointing to the duct tape. "I want to see who else has touched it."

Forty-Two

Matthews led him through the back of the lab where they passed two rooms marked "Dark Room 1" and "Dark Room 2." "Mostly we do our LASER work in there," Matthews explained as he pushed through another set of steel doors. "But here is where the real magic happens." He flicked the lights on to reveal a room no larger than a prison cell. In the center of the room stood a large steel chamber shaped like a torpedo. A series of cables and wires ran from the main cylinder to a computer screen secured on top of a large white pedestal. A second group of pipes and ducts ran from the opposite side of the cylinder and disappeared through a hole that was cut into the concrete. Peterson figured it was the venting system.

A porthole with a thick glass was on the front of the machine, and Peterson leaned forward and saw that a small, steel plate secured by hooks from the top ran down the length of the interior. Two sets of burners and electrical cables on the bottom of the steel chamber showed small scorch and burn marks from repeated uses.

"Looks like an iron lung," Peterson remarked.

"Not far from the truth," Matthews said, patting the outside of the chamber, which gave off a faint pinging sound. "This, my dear friend, is a vacuum metal deposition chamber. It's probably the best bet for looking for prints on your duct tape there."

"Sounds expensive," Peterson replied as he leaned against the far wall.

Matthews laughed. "You don't know the half of it. There's almost three hundred *thousand* dollars' worth of hardware in this puppy." Still wearing his latex gloves, Matthews grabbed a slot-type handle on the outer door and grunted as he tugged it down, swinging the convex door outward with a loud creak. He removed the duct tape from the acetate, explaining as he worked. "The VMDC chamber basically creates a vacuum, hence the name."

Matthews secured the tape on a small hook at the upper edge of the chamber, and it hung there like drying laundry. He turned and went to a small cabinet in the back of the room, removing two plastic petri dishes that fit into the palm of his hand.

Peterson could see through the clear plastic fine, gold- and silver-colored threads. Matthews removed one thread from each dish and held them in his hand. "Gold and zinc are vaporized in the two burners at the base of the chamber, and the metal filings adhere in layers to the fingerprint." He placed the threads in the two burners that Peterson had noticed earlier and closed the door, pulling the handle down. After turning the device on, it made small clicking start-up noises as it went through various system checks. "Works well for older prints," Matthews explained. "So, hopefully I can get something for you."

He waved Peterson over, and they both watched through the small porthole as the system began heating up. Matthews, on the right, was adjusting two black knobs on the side of the chamber, slowly turning the temperature up on the two burners. The gold thread began to bubble on the burner, and then it melted with a hiss, its tiny particles floating in the air in an amber haze. The gold particles settled on the duct tape, painting the item in a gold hue.

Matthews then adjusted another knob, and Peterson watched the process repeated with the zinc. He stared with fascination at the duct tape as silvery fingerprints developed on the outside, almost like magic.

Satisfied with the results, Matthews turned off the burners and pressed a red button to vent the system. After a few moments, there was a loud clunking sound and the vacuum pressure was released, allowing Matthews to open the door, reach in, and remove the duct tape.

He placed the exhibit on a steel examination table and bent down to inspect the tape. Without looking up, he said, "There's about six prints on this, maybe seven." Matthews held the tape close to his eye. "Do you want it run through AFIS?"

AFIS, or the Automated Fingerprint Identification System, was the basic search database for unidentified impressions. If Peterson was right, they wouldn't find their suspect's prints in there. "No," he told Matthews. "I have a different database I want you to search."

Forty-Three

Peterson had Matthews scout ahead of him, waving him on when the coast was clear, and in this way he could steal himself from the subterranean bowels of the forensic lab, to the main floor, and finally to the street beyond. When he had slipped into HQ hours earlier, it was dark. Now, approaching late afternoon, the cloudless sky was a deep cobalt blue. The sun reflected off the damp pavement and stung his eyes painfully, so much so that he had to shield his hand against the glare.

"You okay, Jack?" Matthews asked. They were standing outside the exit door, and Matthews stared at him with open concern.

Peterson rubbed at his eyes with a forefinger and thumb. "Just sensitive to the light, is all." He reached out a hand and gave Matthews a quick shake. "Thank you so much, Graham. And call me if you find anything."

Matthews promised that he would, and Peterson fled from the HQ property as quickly as he dared while remaining inconspicuous. He moved in a southerly direction, weaving through the pedestrian traffic, keeping his head down and hands in his pockets, blending in like any weary traveller. He arrived at the Westlake subway terminal unmolested and wheeled left into the tunnel.

The press of bodies unnerved him, but he pushed it out of his mind as he worked his way to the subway platform. The roaming security guards barely paid him any notice as he boarded the L-train. At this time of day, the transit cops were on the lookout for fare jumpers, and he paid with cash at each of the site terminals. Twenty minutes later, relieved to be out of the enclosed space of the tube,

Peterson was walking up the flight of stairs to Juliette's apartment. He needed a place to hole up for a few hours while Matthews completed the fingerprint search, and he didn't want to risk Denly any more than he already had. He also needed somewhere to think about what he was going to do. Even if he got some results from the fingerprint search, he was still being hunted by the SPD, with Captain Gregor bent on catching him. More than that, he wanted to see Juliette and have a distraction from his problems.

He knocked on the apartment door, looking left and right to find the hallway leading to her apartment empty. A few moments later he heard footsteps and then the deadbolt disengaged. The door opened a few inches, revealing a thick silver security chain. A pair of small brown eyes behind a mop of unruly hair peered out at him.

"Hi, Adam, is your mother home?"

By way of answer Adam closed the door and slid the chain off the latch. The door opened wide for Peterson and he stepped through, closing it behind him and sliding the chain back over the latch, relocking the deadbolt. While he was doing this, Adam, wearing a pair of green jogging pants and a Spiderman t-shirt, stood against the wall watching him, hands clasped behind his back as if evaluating Peterson's progress.

"You were on the news," Adam said.

Peterson adjusted the duffel bag on his shoulder. The 9mm was still inside, loaded and ready to go, and he didn't want to leave the bag lying around for the boy to go through.

"Oh, and what did they say about me?"

"That you're a bad guy and maybe dangerous."

"And what do you think about that?"

Adam shrugged as if the question itself was irrelevant. "Mom's making grilled cheese, you want some?"

Peterson said that he did, and Adam took him into the kitchen where Juliette was standing by the stove, wearing a blue and black apron, and flipping a buttered sandwich in a pan. Her blonde hair was tied back in a bun, a few strands had escaped and lay gently over her forehead. She brushed them away, tucking the hair behind her ear, as he entered the kitchen, standing in the doorway and taking the sight of her in.

She smiled warmly when she saw him standing there. "You're just in time for dinner," she said.

Dinner was exactly what Adam had promised. Grilled cheese sandwiches with chips. Peterson had a beer, while Juliette had a glass of red wine and Adam drank milk. Conversation stayed far away from both Peterson's and Juliette's work. He got the sense that Adam wasn't fully aware of what his mother did for a living, and he felt no need to educate the boy on such things. Peterson learned that Adam did well in school but was bullied relentlessly, and he caught the concern for her son in Juliette's eyes.

After dinner was finished, Adam excused himself and went to the living room. Peterson heard cartoons on the TV as he and Juliette sat across from one another in the kitchen. Now her concerned eyes were on him.

"What will you do?" she asked.

He breathed out slowly and rapped his thumbnail on the side of the coffee mug that he was holding. With his other hand, he rubbed his cheek. "I'm really not sure. Even if I find the person who hired the killer, it still changes nothing. Even I catch the killer, I'm not sure what will happen. There will be an investigation into my actions, maybe I'll even get charged."

She nodded thoughtfully, and they lapsed into silence. Juliette was absently swirling a spoon into her tea when she spoke quietly. "I was thinking of getting into some different work."

He made attempt to hide his surprise, and she laughed at the expression on his face. "Is it because of me or…" He trailed off, unable to finish the thought.

"Not only because of you," she explained. "It's been on my mind for some time now, especially as Adam gets older." She stared in her son's direction, and she looked haunted. "I've lost so many friends." She turned back to Peterson. "I don't want my mistakes to end up costing my life."

He nodded at this. "You need to be here for your son." He took a sip from his coffee and set the mug back on the table. "I know from my own past: if you don't deal with your problems, they can come back and destroy you."

"Do you ever think of how things would have worked out differently if you had made different choices?"

"All the time. Every day. I didn't do my job, and an innocent life was taken. Maybe it was some kind of cosmic retribution." He took a deep breath, feeling the stretch in his lungs, and when he spoke next, his voice sounded haunted to his own ears. "I wish that it had been me that had been killed, not Laura. I deserved to die for my inability to act." As these words left his mouth, something clicked in his mind, a kind of perfect duality that suddenly made complete sense. Juliette was saying something, but he barely heard her and he stared off in the distance. He only became aware of the silence when she had reached across the table and touched his hand.

"Jack, are you okay?"

He swallowed a few times to clear his throat. "No," he said, locking his eyes with hers. "I know who's next." He pushed off the table and grabbed the Smith and Wesson from the duffel bag that he kept by his feet, checking the breech and finding one in the pipe. He tucked the weapon behind his waist and wrote his cell phone on a piece of paper, which he handed to her.

She seemed shocked by this sudden flurry of activity.

"This is my number," he said. "I need to borrow your car."

She went to a drawer and grabbed a set of keys, and he took them from her outstretched hands. Adam, attracted by the sudden activity, was standing in the kitchen doorway watching them.

Peterson kissed Juliette once on the lips and said that he would call her later. He ruffled Adam's hair as he hurried past. "Take care of your mother," he said and closed the door. He hurried down the steps and out in the cold night, finding her car by hitting the door unlock and following the sound of the alarm chime.

Peterson climbed behind the wheel of Juliette's Pathfinder, and his knees hit the dashboard. He started the engine, which emitted a throaty whine as he peeled from the parking spot. Steering with his knee, he phoned Denly at his home and the man answered on the third ring, breathless.

"Sorry," he said. "Sarah took the kids out to see her sister, can't move in this cast." He listened patiently as Peterson explained. "Are you sure?" he said after a brief pause. "I mean, if you're wrong, then you're drawing them right to you."

"I'm not wrong," Peterson said. "Make the call."

Forty-Four

Kincaid was driving a white-panel van that was decked out with the words "Lee's Carpet Cleaning" on the side in wide, blocky letters. He had done a little bit of research and found the company on the lower south side, empty this time of night, and made quick work of the E350 Ford. The thing handled like a boat, but it had been easy enough to hotwire, and he knew that he had another twelve hours before it would be reported stolen. This was the last job, the last one on the list, and by this time tomorrow Seattle would be nothing but another notch on the belt, another set of memories that he would categorise away as a job well done.

He pulled up to the rear entrance of Burberry Meadows retirement home at a quarter to eight, parking in a spot that was reserved for service entrance only. His stolen work vehicle, even if spotted, would attract little attention, and this time of the night the retirement home operated on a skeleton crew. Most of the service staff would probably be watching a holiday movie in the common room on the opposite side of the building, and he would be in and out before they even thought to check their wards.

He had mixed feelings about this last assignment. There were people, many in fact, who deserved to die for some reason or another. He never took on a contract on a whim and did extensive background work to find out as much as he could about his target. By all accounts, Bryce Turner, Arthur Collins, and Chris Solk had been scum, preying on an innocent girl simply for kicks. They had used their power and influence to weasel out of the criminal charge and court proceedings. The secretary, Brant, had been a complete accident, and he had never meant to hurt her. The judge, unfortunately dead by natural causes, and the lawyer Prihar had been complicit in the cover up, and both more than deserved the fate that had ultimately met them. The retired cop, Nielsen, had been all but forced to give up his share of the investigation. Still, Kincaid had a job to do and a reputation to uphold, and he would deal with the moral complications later.

He pulled in between two cars just outside the entrance door, the tires crunching on the ice as he came to a stop. He adjusted his cap, with its logo of the carpet cleaner on the front. Along with the blue overalls, the look was basically complete and would at least pass a minor scrutiny, though he wasn't anticipating even that. He stepped out of the vehicle, careful on the dangerously icy ground, and started to walk to the rear entrance. He had no weapon with him to speak of, though he had a small arsenal in the work van. He planned on killing in whatever way possible; a pillow over a sleeping face would be preferred, though he could employ other methods as well.

As he picked his way across the pavement he stopped, cocking his head to the side as a small sound filtered through the naked trees. A series of sirens, police by the sound, was slowly growing in intensity. He considered the possibility that they were meant for someone else—it was a big city after all, and they probably had dozens of calls they went to that required the activation of their emergency equipment. But he couldn't ignore the sour feeling that was settling in his stomach, and he knew beyond a doubt that they were heading his way.

Kincaid wheeled around to head back to his van, the exit strategy already forming in his mind, when a red SUV punched through the hedges off the road, sending twigs and leaves in a thousand directions, driving madly over the lawn, heading straight for him.

The wheel of the Pathfinder shuddered in Peterson's grip, and when he slammed through the hedges, the vehicle became airborne for a moment, sending him pitching toward the roof, only to be stopped by the seatbelt that he had pulled tightly over his chest. With a loud groan of protest, the SVU slammed down on the semi-frozen field. He gave the chances of the axle snapping in two equal odds, but amazingly it held as he punched the accelerator down and snapped back on target.

From the roadway he had spotted the square, white-panel van pull up to the service entrance and park. It had been difficult to spot the driver from the distance, sheltered by the tinted windows, but Peterson doubted that carpet cleaners worked such hours.

When the man stepped from the interior into the glow of the street lights, he knew who it was. The height and build were on point, but it was more in the way the guy walked. Peterson had sensed it at the lawyer's office, the man's predatory nature, but had been too dense to act. He wouldn't make the same mistake again.

He thought of holding back, letting the killer get inside the building, and helping the responding units box him in. But at the last moment before entering the retirement home the killer had stopped, listened for a moment, and then turned about to go back to his truck. Through his own windows Peterson heard approaching sirens and cursed Gregor for his stupidity. You come in hot to a bar fight, full lights and sirens, and scare the idiots away. You go in silently when you want to catch the guy in the act.

There were at least three exits from the retirement home, all of which would potentially allow the murderer to slip through the net, making it back to a larger artery where he could get lost in the city traffic. The killer hesitated but a moment as Peterson drove headlong through the field toward him. The man ran back into the white van and peeled in reverse, throwing the vehicle into drive just as Peterson painfully jounced over the curb and back on to the pavement. With a spinning of tires, the van fishtailed for a moment before fleeing from the parking spot, Peterson now in hot pursuit.

They curled around the service road at speeds that were never meant for such a small laneway, and Peterson felt the tires of the Pathfinder skid on the slick pavement. He doubted highly that Juliette had winter tires on the SUV, and they handled like onion skins. The vehicle ahead of him fared little better, and Peterson gritted his teeth in satisfaction as the van slid to the side, the tire walls bouncing against the curb. As soon as the marked units arrived, Peterson planned on backing off and letting them take over, but for now he needed to keep on the fugitive.

The van managed to make it out of the service road, hitting the side streets doing forty miles per hour, and Peterson pushed his vehicle onwards, keeping the pressure on the van ahead. The vehicle turned left, Peterson painfully aware that it was leading away from the sirens and from backup, and took off toward the main streets, which would eventually lead to the freeway and highway exits. Traffic was almost nonexistent in this part of town but would be heavier in other areas, making pursuit not only more difficult but also more dangerous for civilians.

The killer drove confidently, weaving past parked cars deftly, and Peterson kept both hands on the wheel, white-knuckled trying to keep up. The Pathfinder shimmied and whined with the effort, and he wondered how long the vehicle could hold up with this intensity. They were quickly coming to a three-way stop, a T-intersection that led in an east-west direction, and Peterson tapped his brakes, trying to anticipate what the killer would do, turn right or left. Instead of slowing down the van pulled away, increasing speed as it approached the intersection. The van blew through the stop sign at highspeed, hitting the far curb, threading between two parallel parked cars. The van launched in the air, twisting slightly with the driver's side arcing toward the sky, before dropping like a stone to the sound of crunching metal and churned earth.

Peterson was so stunned that he nearly forgot his own speed as the T-junction snapped into focus before him. He fought the urge to hammer on the brake, and taking his foot off the gas he tapped at it, feeling the vehicle shudder and slide as it fought the momentum. It twisted to the side before lurching into place, twisting again as it caught more ice under the worn tires. With clenched teeth and his jaw set in a grimace, he willed the SUV to slow. Amazingly it began to respond, and he was able to stop a few feet from the parked cars on the far side of the street.

He slammed the vehicle in park, leaving it stopped askew on the street and was on the ground in moments, gun drawn as he approached the far edge of the curb. The intersection led to a gully, a steep decline at the base of which was a deep ditch. Here the van lay on its side, the driver's door pointing to the starry sky. The front end was smoking, partially covered in long grasses. In the distance, an eight-foot fence separated the field from the beginnings of an industrial area that was dark and quiet. The sound of the approaching sirens was increasing in intensity, backup only minutes away.

Steeling himself, Peterson stepped on the half-frozen grass, patchy with icy snow. He partly slid, partly walked down the embankment, feeling exposed but keeping his pistol in the low ready, heart hammering in his chest as he approached the van. When he was five feet away he took a deep breath and gave a loud police challenge, his voice strong and clear in the chill night.

There was no response, and he waited a beat before closing the distance between himself and the van, approaching the rear doors. He took another deep breath, which puffed in front of him in a fog. He pulled open the rear door, clearing the interior with his pistol. Cleaning supplies were strewn about the interior cabin, papers and chemicals lying haphazardly on the passenger side. But other than that, the interior was empty. The killer was gone.

Forty-Five

Backup, which included three squad cars, arrived two minutes later. Peterson was lucky in that one of the patrol members knew him and could get the other units to drop their guns before plugging him full of holes.

Peterson's relief was short lived, however, as an unmarked car showed up fifteen minutes later, and out stepped Sylvia Partridge and Captain Elias Gregor. Peterson had been speaking to two of the uniforms when the vehicle had pulled up from the east, and Gregor gave him a long look from across the street before walking down to the van and inspecting the scene from there. Partridge had approached him immediately, surprising him with a strong hug.

One of the uniform members he had been talking to raised an eyebrow, and Peterson mirrored his expression.

He moved on without a word, leaving him and Partridge alone. He put a hand up, tapping her back lightly with the tips of his fingers, and she released him. As she moved back her eyes were glassy, and she coughed into her hand.

"I'm so glad to see you, Jack." She punched him on the shoulder, not gentle at all, and it left his muscle tingling and sore. "What the hell is wrong with you, you stupid idiot," she said. "I've been looking everywhere for you."

"I know, I saw the news." He looked down in the direction of Gregor, who was bent low, inspecting the contents of the van. Peterson had tried following the killer's trail, but it had gone cold. The long grass had been pushed aside some, leading toward the high chain link fence on the far side. Likely the man had fled in that direction, probably toward a vehicle that he had stashed earlier. Gregor turned in Peterson's direction, and even at this distance his scowl was clearly visible.

Peterson turned back to Partridge. "Has the flavor of the day changed?" he asked her. "I thought I would be in cuffs by now."

She shook her head and jammed her hands into the light tweed jacket she was wearing. "Gregor jumped the gun on that one. By the time we finished the interviews, it was clear that there were two guys there and the shooter wasn't you." She flicked her head toward Gregor. "He's already been talked to by the brass. Told to pull it back some."

"How did he react to that little nugget?"

Sylvia chuckled. "Oh, he was pretty incensed. By the time we got your call about Nielsen, he had shifted his focus away from you. How did you figure it out?"

"He's the only one left who dropped the ball on the Green investigation. It finally made sense to me that he was the last thread to be tied up. What about Nielsen, have we got someone with him? I could see the killer coming back to finish him off."

"Yeah, we have a detail with him now. He'll have to go through four cops to get to Nielsen now." Peterson was about to tell her that stronger precautions should be taken when Partridge leaned in and spoke quietly. "Don't look now, but you got company coming."

Finished with his inspection, Captain Gregor was storming in his direction, the scowl still firmly set in place. "You're lucky I don't put you in lockup right now," he said as he pulled in close. He waved a hand toward the van in the ditch. "You let the killer get away."

"The killer let the killer get away," Peterson said, angry now. "He had this planned out, just like everything. You don't get to be a guy like this and not be aware of every angle. And don't forget, I called it in." In the distance Peterson could hear the chirping of the K9 unit as it tried to establish a track through the grasses. He asked Gregor, "What about Canine? Did they find anything?"

Gregor breathed out, the anger at Peterson momentarily displaced. "They lost it beyond the field there. There's a parking lot with fresh tire tracks. He probably hopped into a car from there." He turned back to Peterson and jabbed a finger toward him, the bruise from where Peterson had struck him the day before red and pulsating like a warning beacon. "That doesn't forgive the fact you disobeyed a direct order and that you struck a commanding officer. I told you to step off the investigation, and you kept going."

"I'm just a concerned citizen doing my due diligence, I can't be blamed if I was in the right places at the right times."

Gregor looked as if his top might blow, and he rounded on Peterson to deliver another tirade but then a ringing in his front pocket diverted his attention. "What?" he demanded before immediately turning acquiescent. "Oh, yes sir, sorry sir," Gregor stammered before moving away to talk with what probably was some NCO with a higher pay grade than his own. Even the big fish had bigger fish coming at them, Peterson thought as he turned back to Partridge. She had an amused look on her face and seemed to be studying him.

"What is it?" Peterson asked.

She kinked her head in the direction Gregor had ghosted away. "You two are like those fighting chickens, beaking at each other."

Peterson pushed her gently on the shoulder, which rocked her off balance. "Ah, stuff it," he said playfully. They both stared at the wreckage below as the various police units flitted to different jobs. He could see the vague silhouette of the K9 unit in the distance, beyond the chain link fence, moving like a shadow through the tall grasses. A forensics unit was dealing with the van below, dusting for prints. Traffic Section had a GPS Total Station mounted on the blacktop like a totem pole, while general duty members stood on guard, watching for any threats that might endanger their brothers and sisters. So many people with a common goal, bound together by duty and purpose. It struck Peterson suddenly that he had no desire to let this go, this purpose, this meaning.

From his left Partridge spoke, her shoulder brushing up against his. "So, what now?"

Peterson didn't speak for a time, but when he did his voice was quiet. "We wait."

Forty-Six

Kincaid wasn't the waiting type. Before the van had hit the ground, he had already formulated a plan, his mind working furiously, planning one step after the other. He braced himself for the impact, and the soft dewy earth absorbed most of the energy. The crash was jarring, but he had already moved out of the driver's seat before the van came to a rest. He was out the driver's window before it came to a stop and climbed the fence and had reached the other side before he heard the cop's vehicle stop on the upper section of the roadway.

Kincaid knew was the cop Peterson. He realized the moment the Pathfinder crashed through the hedges and bore down upon him. Had it not been for the inevitability of police backup, Kincaid would have engaged the cop right there and then, taken care of him, and then finished the job with the retired cop in the home. But plans change, and one must adapt or die.

It takes time for a police roadblock to be established, and Kincaid was already long gone before the thought even entered their minds. He ditched his clothing while fleeing the scene, throwing it out the window, and took a random route away from the main location. Entirely free from pursuit, he allowed his mind to drift, to plan. All was still not lost, even with the final target under police protection. For he had inside information about Peterson that could always be twisted to his advantage. It was a question of leverage and how best to apply it.

Forensics learned nothing, the van was clean. The police dog lost the trail at the parking lot, and the tire tracks were a sure indication that the killer had fled in a stashed vehicle. An BOLO, or Be On the Lookout Of, was put out, but the information was scant, save for a white male with brown hair, of which Seattle had about a hundred thousand.

Peterson stayed at the scene for another hour, talking with Partridge. He was still on medical suspension and would need to remove himself from the investigation entirely, but he had succeeded in saving Nielsen which gave him a degree of closure on the whole affair. But he still felt wistful and sad as he climbed back into the Pathfinder and drove away from the scene, the red and blue lights of the perimeter security fading in the distance as the miles between them increased.

It was just after ten when he finally left and he went straight to Juliette's, confident that she would still be awake. He parked on the street, locked the car doors, and walked to the apartment entrance, using the gold-colored key on the vehicle key ring to unlock the main door and slip inside.

When he reached the fourth-floor landing, he took out another brass key and held it to the lock to her door, preparing to put it in. He stopped short when he noticed that the door was open an inch, a large boot print on the below the handle from where it had been kicked. His breath caught in his throat, and a dull ache settled in his chest. He checked left and right out of habit and pulled his Smith and Wesson from his rear waistband, bringing it up in a two-handed c-clamp grip. He used his left elbow to nudge the door open and cautiously peered inside.

The security chain was hanging off the frame, part of the door still connected to the brass plate, and all the signs of a struggle were there. A lamp overturned in the living room, a chair knocked over, a small spot of blood on the floor, which was inky black in the moonlight. Juliette, or Adam, had responded to the knock on the door, opened it with the chain attached, and all hell broke loose from there.

Peterson did a rapid search through the apartment, finding it empty as he expected. He ended up in the kitchen and sat heavily on a chair, setting his pistol on the table. He didn't bother turning on any lights, and he sat in darkness, knowing what he had to do but dreading it all the same. With fumbling fingers, he pulled his cell phone out of his pocket and dialed Juliette's number. There was a moment as it was ringing where he toyed with the hope that Juliette and Adam had gotten away, were holed up somewhere safe, simply waiting for him to call.

His hope fell when a deep voice answered the call. "Detective Peterson," the killer said. "It's about time."

Forty-Seven

Peterson took a steadying breath before he answered, but his voice sounded shaky to him all the same. "Where are they?"

"*Tut, tut,*" the voice on the other end answered. It was deep and confident, without a hint of nervousness. Similar to the short conversation he had with the killer at the lawyer's office they could have easily been discussing movies or the weather. "All things in good time, detective. You know I normally don't go down this route, I prefer not to involve innocents, but you forced my hand on this one."

"Let me speak to them," Peterson demanded. "At least give me that."

There was a pause on the phone for a few beats before the killer came back on. "That sounds reasonable. Stand by." There was a rustling sound, like cloth dragged over the receiver, and Juliette's panic stricken voice came on.

"Jack!" she yelled into the phone, crying.

"It's okay, Juliette," he said. "I'm going to get you out of there, ever—"

She stepped through his words, terror fueling her onward. "He has us at—"

There was a smacking sound, flesh on flesh, and Juliette cried out in pain. Peterson clutched the phone, yelling her name, but there was the sound of more crying before it was cut out entirely.

The killer came back on the line, sounding slightly out of breath. "Sorry about that. She was trying to ruin the surprise."

"You son of a bitch, if you hurt them—"

"You'll what? I'm the one calling the shots here, detective, so mind your manners. Play this right, and things will be fine. You and your little whore can go on living your little dream life, have some kids maybe. Perhaps this time you can stop this one from being killed, but don't get confused about who's running the show."

Peterson didn't respond, and dead silence filled the air.

"Good," the killer continued. "Now you have something I want, and I have something you want. Both of us can benefit if we cooperate with one another. I don't want to hurt your little woman or her son, but don't think I won't kill them if I must. I'll put a bullet in each of their heads and won't blink an eye about it. If you call your friends, if you screw around, they'll be dead in a heartbeat, trust me."

"What do you want?"

"To finish my job, of course. I was hired to do some house cleaning, and I really want to finish. You bring me the old man, you get your people back, simple Simon."

"He's in police custody, under guard, how am I supposed to do that?"

"You're a smart guy, *Jack*. Figure it out. You got two hours, plenty of time. Got a pen handy?" Peterson fumbled for a pen in the kitchen, found one near the fridge, and sat back down. The killer rattled off another phone number, probably a burner cell that couldn't be traced. "Call that number at two a.m. I'll tell you where to meet me. Remember, you messed around and the blood will be on your hands. And there will be plenty of blood."

The killer made as if to hang up but Peterson broke in, "Wait. Who hired you?"

The killer laughed. "I have no idea, detective. All I know is the cash was good. Now, no more chit chat," he said. "You got some work to do." And the line went dead.

Two hours later Peterson was back in the Pathfinder, parked outside of Juliette's apartment, with the engine running and the heat blowing. The temperature had dropped again, and small flakes of puffy white snow felt from the sky, peppering the windshield. Taking a calming breath, he called the number that the killer provided, and it was answered on the first ring.

"So, how did we make out?" the killer asked.

"I got him," Peterson responded. "Where do you want to meet?" The figure in the passenger seat shifted, nervousness radiating off them in waves.

"Ah, great. And you'll come alone?"

"Yes," Peterson responded. "Just Nielsen and me. Now where?"

"That's an easy one, detective," the killer said. "Just come home."

Forty-Eight

His house looked completely normal when he pulled the Pathfinder into the driveway. The windows were dark, no movement inside, exactly how he left it. But a malignancy, more acute than had been present before, when it had simply been bad memories residing there, seemed to pulsate outward from the windows, like a tell-tale heart.

There were no other vehicles in the driveway, nothing else out of place to suggest where the killer had stashed his vehicle or how he had arrived at the property. But there was a feeling of wrongness as Peterson shifted the SUV into park. He had no doubt that the killer was there, hopefully with Juliette and Adam. Hopefully with both were still alive.

He took one last look up at the house through the windshield and went to open the door. He paused and reached out to his passenger, who had a plaid blanket draped over their bony legs. The leg twitched under Peterson's touch, like a frightened rabbit.

"It's going to be okay," Peterson said. "I'm going to get you through this," he promised, before stepping out of the vehicle and closing the door.

When he had left Juliette's apartment snow had began to fall. Now it had increased to the point where the flakes stung his eyes and slapped against his skin, small pinpricks of ice that seemed to fall from the sky sideways. If he made it through this he would once again wake to a white morning; already the snow had begun to collect on the sides of the house in small drifts.

Heart hammering against his chest he approached the front door, testing the handle to find it unlocked. He turned back to the figure in the passenger seat, who watched him through a window that had already begun to fog over, nodded once, and slipped inside. Peterson closed the door behind him, trying to will his racing heart back to a normal rate, and checked his surroundings. It appeared quiet, just as he had left it hours before. He slowly slipped the 9mm handgun from his pocket, rocked back the slide, saw brass firmly seated in the pipe, and put the weapon in the low ready.

He worked quickly on the lower level, stepping lightly on his instep, checking each room, and finding them empty. He didn't bother with the lights since he knew the layout of his own home and felt that in this situation the darkness was to his advantage. Peterson moved through the kitchen, pausing at the foot of the steps, and peered up. All the rest of the house had been empty, so there was only one other place they could be. There were perhaps eight or nine steps, and at the top he could see a small pooling of light, just enough to penetrate the darkness. Peterson swallowed, remembering the last time he had attempted to climb those steps.

Breathing in and out, throat raspy and vision swimming, he went one step at a time, pausing on the middle riser as small pinpricks of darkness danced across his eyes, and he thought he might pass out right there. He placed his left palm against the wall to steady himself, his right hand holding a pistol that now felt like it weighed a ton. He waited until things cleared, until his mind settled back into some semblance of control, and then he climbed the rest of the stairway, feeling winded and out of breath by the time he made it to the top stair.

There was a long hallway that stretched before him, unchanged from the last time he had looked upon it. In early March he had followed Laura up those stairs, about to settle into the normal routine of getting ready for bed. She had been only three months pregnant at that time, barely showing, and he had checked out her butt as she got to the top, commented on it. She had laughed and tried to smack him on the shoulder, missed, and he had collected her in a fierce but playful embrace. Three hours later she was dead, and he too was well on his way there.

Now both side bedroom doors were opened but the master bedroom door at the end of the hall was closed, a small sliver of light sneaking from the bottom gap. He felt his upper limbs go slack, and he battled to get them upright again, bringing the gun up to shoulder height and pointing it toward the door. Slowly, cautiously, he crept forward, checking the side bedrooms as he passed: empty.

He paused before the master bedroom door, hand inches from the handle, breathing heavily and deeply, vision narrowed from stress, hearing acute, all systems firing in tandem, ready for what was beyond the door. He thought he could hear a muffled cry, but his own heartbeat was loud in his ears, a terrible *whooshing* that overrode everything else.

In a swift movement, he cranked on the door handle, kicking the door wide so hard that it slammed on the other side of the wall and swept his gun left and right, ready to engage the killer. He wasn't there, but in the center of the room, each secured to a chair with duct tape, were Adam and Juliette, struggling against their bonds, fear blazing in their eyes. He stepped forward into the room to go to them, but then a cool ring of metal was placed against his left temple as he stepped through the threshold, forward gun sights digging into his skin, and he heard the hammer being drawn back, and then the a familiar voice.

"So glad you could finally join us, detective."

Forty-Nine

Peterson stopped, rage and fear and terror commingling in a dizzying flood of senses. Juliette began to sob; the sound being muffled from the duct tape over her mouth. Adam sat stock still, trembling like a leaf, fingernails dug into the side of the heavy wooden chair that he was taped to. The room was different than what he remembered, empty, no furniture. The bed and carpet had all been thrown away, the carpet replaced with a low pile, grey shag that matched the rest of the interior. In delicate terms, he had been told that the carpet and underlay had been completely saturated with blood, both his own and Laura's, and was unsalvageable. The renovations had all occurred while he remained in the long-term rehab center. Now the details flooded in and out of his mind in a millisecond, processed away as he focused on more immediate concerns. Like the pistol that was jammed into the skin of his temple and the professional killer behind it.

"Your gun," the man said. Peterson still had the Smith and Wesson in the low ready, a two-handed grip with his forearms resting on his upper thighs. "Drop the mag with your right thumb, do it now."

Peterson did as he instructed, the magazine with fourteen rounds falling to the carpet with a thump.

"Okay," the killer resumed. "Holster up."

Peterson grunted to himself. The man was clearly knowledgeable on his guns, knew enough that this model of Smith and Wesson couldn't fire with the magazine ejected. Peterson could reload at any point, but he knew that the killer would plug him full of holes before he even got the chance to take the piece of out his pocket.

Feeling defeated, Peterson slid the pistol in his front waistband, the weight and solidness comforting even if it was nothing much more than a glorified paperweight, and turned to face the man.

"Your phone too," he said to Peterson. "I don't want anyone listening in to our little *tête-à-tête*."

Peterson took out his cell phone out, dropped it noiselessly to the carpet, and turned to the killer.

The killer looked much as he did before, square chin, strong face, intense blue eyes. He had a black Desert Eagle in his right hand, the pistol huge and menacing in the low light that spilled from the attached bathroom on the right side of the room.

Beyond the pistol, Peterson counted at least three other weapons on the man. A silver-plated MP5, a compact submachine gun capable of spitting out multiple rounds in short bursts, hung loosely from a fabric rig around the man's wide shoulders. Another pistol, smaller than the Eagle, was strapped to the man's left thigh. And a huge knife peeked out from a boot holster on the right side. He was dressed head to toe in black military grade gear, thick cargo pants, and a long-sleeved shirt. Judging by the bulk of the vest that he wore Peterson figured it for bullet proof armor, likely with ballistic panels in the forward and back pockets to guard against rifle rounds. The man looked ready for war and eager to start it, judging by the hunger in his eyes.

"I saw you pull up," he said. "Is that Nielsen in the passenger seat there?" Peterson nodded but said nothing. "Well, bring him up," he said cordially, waving his free hang in a come along gesture.

Peterson shook his head. "He's infirm, needs a wheelchair. I barely got him in the car before I was caught."

Keeping an eye on Peterson, the killer stepped back toward the curtains, pulling them aside and peering down quickly. From this vantage point he could see Nielsen through the front windshield, probably shivering and cold under the thick, plaid blanket that Peterson had thrown over him. From the window the killer could see far in either direction, any type of police backup would have been noticed in an instant. He pulled the curtains back and leaned up against the windowsill. "Well, adapt and overcome, right? At least you were able to get this far." The killer looked bulky with the military grade clothing he was wearing, but he moved easily in a way that Peterson found disquieting on an unknown level, an awareness that the man before him was an apex predator and wouldn't hesitate to kill him, Adam, or Juliette.

He must have read the disgust in Peterson's eyes because the corner of his mouth curled into a small smile. "You must think me a monster, don't you, detective?" He pushed himself off the window ledge and stood behind Adam and Juliette.

"I think anyone that kills for money has a serious mental disorder," Peterson responded.

"Says the pot calling the kettle black. Don't lecture me on having head space issues. Fact is, once I got out of the service, I had all these talents and not much to do with them. It's not as if I could go bagging groceries, after all. I started doing some work for the government and found that it was more…" he paused, looking for the word, "profitable to go into private retail. And, well, here we are."

"You talk of death as if you're preforming some kind of public service. You're no different from any of the psycho killers out there, you just happen to get paid for your jollies."

If the man was insulted by Peterson's tone, he didn't show it. He merely shook his head and pressed on. "Tell me, detective, do you ever think of killing the man that took your wife?"

Peterson took a deep pull of air in and blew it out slowly. No sense lying to the man. "Every day. Every damn day. But there's a difference between thinking about it and actually doing something about it. It's not my call, and it's not up to me whether he lives or dies."

"Oh, so now you take the moral high ground. You talk as if some kind of higher power is involved. Well, tell me, *Jack,* where was God when your wife was bleeding out in this room? Huh? Where was he during any of this?" The killer pressed his pistol against the back of Adam's head so hard that the boy's skull was forced forward.

Juliette struggled against the tape holding her wrists down, her face a twisted mask of rage and fear. The killer paid her no attention and tightened his finger on the trigger. Leaned forward and brought his mouth close to Adam's ear. "Do you think God would step in and stop me from pulling this trigger?"

A steady stream of tears fell down the boy's face, sliding over the duct tape, and dripping off his chin.

Peterson felt his jaw tighten. "No, God probably wouldn't do anything at all to stop you. But you better damn make sure that you turn that gun on me right after, because if you pull that trigger I'm coming for you."

The killer laughed, lowered the pistol, and stood up straight. "There you go, that's the spirit." He checked the watch on his wrist, sliding the pistol into a shoulder rig and swinging the MP5 off the harness. He held the submachine gun in a two-handed grip, offset from Peterson but ready to engage at a moments notice. "Time to go, detective. Places to go, people to see."

Peterson nodded and made to walk out of the bedroom, but he heard the click of the MP5's safety being released. He looked back at the killer who was giving him a serious glance. "I applaud your efforts, detective. Separate me from the hostages." He removed a knife from his pocket and threw it toward Peterson, who caught it one handed. "Untie them, Jack. We're all going for a walk."

Fifty

Kincaid stepped back as the detective used the pocket knife to cut off the tape. The knife he handed him was small, only about four inches, and the blade was blunt enough to cut tape and not much else. Still, the man was unpredictable, and the fire and rage in his eyes was enough to make Kincaid wary. He wanted some distance between himself and Peterson in case he needed to open up with the MP5.

He had posted himself by the window as the detective pulled up, the large bay windows allowing for a nearly complete 180-degree view of the surrounding streets. No other police cars, no backup, no eye in the sky that he could immediately discern. Just Peterson and the old man, alone in a beat up and rusted out Pathfinder.

After Peterson cut the woman and child loose, he had them stand in the doorway, and he pointed the MP5 to each of them in turn. Peterson's eyes narrowed and he thought the woman and kid would pass out on the spot. Nothing like looking down the barrel of a gun to really ramp up the sphincter factor.

Kincaid gave them curt, quick instructions. "We're going to walk out of here. You'll stay ahead of me in a straight line. You move to run, you move to fight me, and I'll cut you down." No anger in his voice, just an understanding of the circumstances. He asked each of them if they understood, and they responded in individual ways. The detective said yes. The woman and child merely nodded in the meek, frightened way of the uninitiated. Yes sir, no sir, two bags full sir.

With instructions given and apparently understood, he ordered them to walk forward and they headed down the stairs. When they reached the front door, he had them pause, gave them further instructions. "When you open the door, walk outside two feet and then stop. Do you understand?"

They nodded their assent, and Kincaid told Peterson to open the door. A flurry of snow and blowing wind spilled through the opening as the door swung outward, a blast of cold air that made Kincaid involuntarily shiver. If the weather continued to turn, his flight out of here would probably be delayed, which would create, while not unacceptable, annoying complications. After taking care of Nielsen, he planned on finishing off the detective and his little family. The police would be too busy mopping up their blood and brains to worry about his exit plan. But still, the travel delays would at the very least be an aggravation.

As instructed, the trio paused a few feet outside the door, the woman and child to the detective's right and left sides, and Kincaid watched as he hugged them close, trying to shield them from the pressing cold. Ignoring them momentarily he craned his head left and right, looking down the street that ran east and west, wary for any movement, but he saw none, though in the howling wind and snow it was difficult to make out much of anything that wasn't five feet in front of him.

Satisfied, he ordered them to move again, and they turned right, walking slowly toward the passenger side of the Pathfinder where Kincaid could just make out the frail form of Nielsen through the frosted glass, bony shoulders shivering, a wide-brimmed fedora pulled low down his face. Kincaid's finger tensed on the trigger as they slowly closed the distance in a unit.

When they stepped outside the front door, Peterson felt himself pushed back by the stinging wind, and over his shoulder he could see the killer looking left and right, checking for threats. Juliette was on his left side, Adam on his right, and he pulled the pair close, heads inches apart. Both were trembling violently, whether from fear or cold or a combination of both he couldn't say. He gave them a quick set of instructions that the killer couldn't hear over the squealing storm that seemed to press on all sides.

"Just be ready," he told them.

Peterson felt more than saw the submachine pointed at the back of their heads, and an uncomfortable itch seemed to crawl up the base of his spine and settle at the back of neck, a niggling sensation that refused to go away. By the time the Pathfinder came in view, he could hardly control the twitch that was streaking through him, and he took deep breaths to control his own sense of mounting terror. The next few seconds would be critical, and he knew that there was a very real possibility, nearly a certainty, that his plan, which now seemed foolish at best, would prove to be his downfall. But he continued, his path set before him, and held fast to the people that were on each side of him, holding their hands tight in his own, trying to appear calm and confident, if only for their sakes.

The vehicle was almost a shapeless form when they crept upon it, and Nielsen's outline was hardly visible through the fog that had settled on the windows. The figure twitched, head swivelling toward them, and Peterson tensed.

Kincaid saw Nielsen's head turn toward them, and he was about to tell Peterson to step aside when the figure behind the window moved with such quickness that he was momentarily stunned.

The detective pulled the woman and the child to the ground as a flash of gunmetal appeared from behind the window, and there was a deafening boom as a 12-gauge shotgun blew out the glass. Out of pure reflex Kincaid dived to the side while simultaneously bringing the MP5 around, finger depressing the trigger. His own weapon raked the side of the vehicle, spraying bullets from the rear passenger to the front, as one of the shotgun pellets tore into his shoulder, blowing him backward.

A female voice in the vehicle cried out in sudden pain. Kincaid hit the ground hard, spun from the impact of the shotgun round, the MP5 flying from his grasp, and felt the world spinning in pain and fury. In the distance sirens pounded, and he became dimly aware of the trap that had been sprung on him.

Another shotgun round pummeled the ground beside him, kicking up snow and dirt that sprayed his face, and heedless of the mission, he scrabbled to his knees and took off at a sprint away from the house.

Peterson had pulled Juliette and Adam to the ground with him, throwing his body overtop as the gunfire erupted around them. Juliette was crying, screaming, holding on to Adam who seemed to have gone silent, and amidst the rattle of the MP5 and the massive booming of the shotgun he became aware of the police sirens closing in.

The shotgun peeled a second time and then all seemed to go silent save for the sirens that grew in pitch. By the time Peterson looked behind him the killer was gone, the snow stained dark red from where he must have gotten hit from the shotgun. He told Juliette and Adam to stay down, and he got to his feet. He ran toward the Pathfinder, which was pockmarked with several rounds, extending from the rear passenger side to the front, the passenger door punched with at least three large, oblong holes. He tore the door open and was relieved to see that the figure still moved inside, one hand clutching the 12-gauge Mossberg shotgun, the other hand held to her side where dark sticky blood poured through interlaced fingers.

"Shit," Sylvia Partridge said through gritted teeth. She looked at Peterson with a glazed over expression. "This hurts like a bitch."

The wound in her side bled fiercely, and Peterson couldn't be sure if anything vital had been hit, but she was conscious and breathing, and that would have to do. To this point, Peterson's plan had worked, the killer had been fooled by Partridge, who had the similar dimensions as the retired police officer, but he had hoped the first shotgun round would have blown his head off. Partridge had either shot wide or the killer had been able to move out of the way. Either way, Sylvia was in a bad spot, and the killer, while injured, was getting away.

Peterson called Juliette over, giving her quick wound instructions: keep pressure on the wound, keep her conscious. She listened in a daze but put her hand where Peterson told her to, looked up at him with round frightened eyes as he picked up her son and put him in the backseat, getting him out of the cold. The boy didn't protest or show any signs of emotion and seemed to be in shock. Peterson couldn't blame him.

He went back to the passenger side, and Partridge tracked him with her eyes. He looked toward the east where the sirens were almost upon them. *Where the hell are they?*

"Don't go," Partridge said in a weak voice, reaching out and grabbing his hand with hers. Her skin was cool to the touch. The blood was being drawn away from the extremities to her vital organs. Not a good sign.

"I have to," he told her, squeezing her hand once and then releasing it. He grabbed the shotgun out of her other hand, and she released it without a struggle. He slid back the action, confirmed there was a round in the chamber, 00 buck. Slid the action back in place and lowered the shotgun to his side.

"Take care of her," he said to Juliette, and he turned from them both and looked in the direction that the killer had fled. Little could be seen through the whipping flurry, but he could see a small sign of tracks, indistinct footwear covered with flecks of red from the killer's blood. Taking a deep breath, he plunged forward.

Fifty-One

Following the scant tracks blindly through the snow Peterson became lost quickly. Already the footwear impressions were being filled in, slowly brushed away by the relentless impact, and he merely tried to concentrate on the blood, which looked black against the whiteness of the snow. He lost sense of time and place, keeping his head close to the ground, bent at the waist, squinting in the darkness. Over hedges, over fences and through yards, around houses, he pressed on, feeling his own breath coming ragged from the effort. The sounds of the sirens faded as he moved onward, and he hoped that an ambulance had been ordered for Partridge. Hoped that she wasn't already dead.

With jeans and a thin coat, the cold worked quickly through him. Within minutes he felt the chill seep in through the clothing. His skin tingled, and the shotgun felt like a block of ice in his hands. The world became a swirling mass of ice and snow.

He only became aware that he had moved on to the lake when he nearly slipped on the ice, and the black sheet of glass became visible through the snow. How far had he walked in? Five feet. Twenty? He couldn't say. On the bank the ice was thick, but closer in the center it was thinner than tissue paper. Peterson checked left and right, the snow stinging his eyes, realizing with a muted sense of despair that he had lost track of the killer. There were no footwear patterns to see, and the small droplets of blood were covered up by the falling snow.

Sensing movement to his right, Peterson brought the shotgun up to bring it on target, then felt a terrible crash as the killer shouldered into him, lifting him up off the ice and slamming him back down as the thin structure cracked under his weight. Peterson was thin, lighter than he had ever been, and the killer was strong, muscular. It felt like he had just gotten hit by a brick wall, his breath knocked out of him, and the shotgun slipped out of his grasp, skidding across the ice four feet away from him.

Peterson struggled to his knees, placing his hands out on the cool smooth surface of the ice, and he saw out of the corner of his eye the killer closing the distance. A sharp pain exploded in his ribs as the man kicked him in the side, and he fell on his back, holding both hands to his ribcage, which felt like it had been broken. He let one hand go, and his hand reached for the pistol in his waistband. He had an extra clip in his pocket, if he could reload—

A loud click snapped as the hammer of the Desert Eagle was drawn back. Peterson shifted his gaze, finding that the killer was standing over him, the barrel of the 44 magnum like a giant black eye against the snow swept sky.

"Don't," the killer said, gun hand still and unwavering. He stood a few feet from Peterson, feet shoulder width apart, bladed for grip on the ice. In his right hand he held the pistol trained on Peterson's forehead, his left arm hung loosely at his side, blood loss and the damage from the shotgun rendering the limb useless. His eyes were alive, and if Peterson didn't know any better he would say that the man was enjoying himself. As if to confirm this assumption the killer smiled at him, teeth stark white in the darkness. "Damn, detective, I misjudged you." The man had to yell over the wind, and still Peterson could hardly hear him. "I mean, I thought you would just roll over and play dead, but you got real heart, real spunk." He cocked his head to the side. "It's almost a shame that I have to kill you."

Peterson was unable to draw his eyes away from the barrel pointed at his forehead, ready to spray his brains all over the snow. It would probably be the K9 unit that would find his corpse, covered with snow and frozen on the ice. Or maybe they wouldn't find him in time, and he would fall beneath the ice, lost in the dark water until the expanding gases of his decomposing body brought him bobbing up to the surface. He felt frozen with fear, unable to move, hardly able to breathe, transported back to a time when a similar-looking handgun had been pointed at his forehead. He had been lucky with that one, the round hadn't fragmented, and he had remained alive. He didn't think lightning would strike twice in this instance.

"You *are* really messed in the head, aren't you?" the killer commented. The weapon remained locked in place, but the killer's eyes rested on Peterson. "I mean, look at you. You're trembling like a bloody leaf. You want to die, don't you?" The pair remained locked in place for what seemed like an eternity, and then the killer walked slowly around Peterson, weapon never moving, until he came to the shotgun. He kicked it toward Peterson, where it skidded across the ice and stopped within his grasp.

"Go ahead," the man said. "I want you to pick it up."

Confused, Peterson waited a moment before slowly reaching the gun. The killer made no move to stop him, merely kept the pistol in place. With painfully cold fingers he grabbed at the shotgun and, still on his back, rested it against his chest, the barrel pointed vaguely in the direction of the killer.

"Point it at me," the killer said. "I'm curious."

Peterson swallowed and made to raise the weapon, but his limbs felt heavy, wooden, and his eyes were locked on the barrel of the handgun, ready and waiting to blow him into darkness. An aching sob reached deep in his chest and slowly escaped through his mouth, the sound lost in the wind. He wanted nothing more than to raise the shotgun and end this madness but found that his arms refused to cooperate. It moved an inch, two, and then the shotgun collapsed back on his chest.

The killer laughed deep in his chest, a violent, wrenching sound. "You can't even do it," he said. He shook his head slowly, and a small smile curled on his lip. "You know what, detective? I'm going to do you a courtesy." The pistol dipped towards Peterson's chest, towards his heart, and he could see even in the darkness the killer's finger tightening on the trigger. "I'm going to put you out of your misery. And once you're gone I'll turn my attention on the old man, finish what I started."

In his own hands Peterson gripped the shotgun, pointed slightly away from the killer at a downward angle. With the handgun no longer pointed at his forehead, Peterson felt the weight shift off his mind slightly. He didn't trust his arms to work, but his finger worked just fine. He pulled the trigger of the Mossberg.

It kicked in his hand like a mule, and his hand was pulled back painfully, but half of the 00 buck rounds struck the killer in the ankle, blowing apart the limb in a shattering flurry of bone, blood, and clothing. The other half of the ordnance smashed into the ice beside the killer like a jackhammer. The sound of breaking ice was like rifle shots in the night, cracking and peeling through the howling wind. Even as the man fell to the side, his own gun forgotten and dropped on the snow, the ice around him was snapping, shifting, and he groped for the damaged ankle, shrieking with pain and fury. As the ice gave way, the killer smashed his jaw on to a ragged shard that had shifted up. It caught him in the throat, and Peterson saw a deep gash form underneath his jawline, gaping and angry.

The hairline fractures of the ice spread toward Peterson like white ribbons, and he scrambled back, using his heels to dig into the ice and snow and skate supine while watching the killer struggle. The man was up to his neck in the water, splashing with his good arm to try and catch some kind of purchase, but the blood loss and cold were making quick work.

"Help me, Jesus, help me," he yelled, though his eyes were unfocused and fixed beyond Peterson, the pupils dilated with fear.

Peterson turned on to his stomach, inching forward, driven by an irrational need to help this man who moments earlier had meant to kill him. He reached out and their fingers touched, the killer's hand inches away. Peterson scrambled forward, and when he got within two feet the ice underneath him cracked, and he was pulled forward towards the water, his right arm sinking underneath the blackness up to this elbow. He pushed backward again as newly formed cracks fractured toward him.

Peterson had no choice but to simply watch the scene that was unfolding before him.

The killer's movements were less frantic now, slowed and dulled, and his skin was ghostly pale in the darkness. His fingernails scraped at the ice as it swallowed him down, inch by inevitable inch, until the hand disappeared entirely in the murky water. An eerie stillness settled in the night, broken only by the howling wind and the pulsing of the wayward snow.

Fifty-Two

Peterson headed away from the large hole that the killer had slipped through. It seemed the safest bet, though he had no clue if he was moving toward deeper waters or back to the shore. His limbs and fingers felt frozen, the skin so hard to the touch that he thought if he hit it the wrong way it might shatter entirely. It was only when the vague shapes of houses came into view that he knew he was heading in the right direction. He picked the closest one and made a beeline toward it, keeping his legs and feet wide, mindful now of the cracking and snapping of the ice beneath him, as if the killer was but too small of a meal and the water demanded more flesh.

As he approached the house other shapes became visible in the squall, indistinct outlines of men and women who moved with an officious air, searching and intent. Not wanting to get shot, he called out in the darkness, and they began heading in his direction.

Three of them approached him, two men and one woman, dressed in thick inclement weather that the SPD members typically carried in the trunks of their patrol cars, reflective rain proof pants and heavy parkas. All three of them had their guns trained on Peterson, their bodies coiled and tensed, ready for action. The muted red and blues of their patrol cars flashed deep in the gloom, reflecting off the snow in steady pulses.

"Detective Peterson, is that you?" the woman called to him.

"Yes," he yelled. "Don't shoot me."

They relaxed, if only marginally, when the distance was closed, and they held their pistols down and away, still prepared to come up on target but unlikely to blow a hole through his back if one of them happened to slip on some ice. The female officer, Berkeley, holstered up when they were a few feet apart, her male partners scanning the surroundings, still wary for any potential threats.

Berkeley was in her late thirties, a thick muscular woman, her extra clothing adding to this effect. She had a black toque on with the SPD logo emblazoned on the front, and her brown hair spilled out the side, flecked with white from the falling snow.

"Are you okay, sir?" she asked.

He wanted to say no, he was far from being all right, but he told her he was fine instead. Now was not the time for a drawn-out conversation, he merely wanted to get warm and dry, in that order. He did ask her if they got to Partridge, and Berkeley nodded. "Yeah, the medics are taking her to the ER now. She was stable. We got them looking at the kid and woman too, though I think they're just shook up, shock mostly." She hooked a head back from where Peterson had come from. "What about the shooter, did you get him?"

Peterson thought for a moment, looking in the direction where the killer's body was probably scraping against the lake floor. He told them the story in the most basic of terms, and by the time he had finished all three members had holstered up, their body positions relaxed, and Berkeley watched him with open concern.

"Are you okay, sir?" she asked again.

He was unable to bring himself to look at her and continued to stare over the frozen lake. Very quietly, he said, "I don't think so."

Fifty-Three

Berkeley offered to escort Peterson back to his house, but he had refused, and before he was halfway he wished he had taken her up on her offer. In the open lights of the street lamps he caught sight of himself; his clothing was covered in blood and torn, and he walked with a pronounced limp. His ribs ached from where the killer had kicked him, and his limbs felt encased in ice. At least twice he was forcibly stopped by the squadron of police on scene, the second time by a K9 member who must have been a linebacker in his previous life. His dog looked like a cross between a horse and an elephant, and it strained at the leash to get to him, jaws snapping air as the animal struggled. Ironically, it was the appearance by Captain Gregor that convinced the handler that Peterson was on the level. The dog wasn't so easily swayed, and it looked back at him with open hunger as it was led away, saliva dripping from its mouth in foamy strings.

"What the hell is this shit show," Gregor demanded, rounding on Peterson like the dog had a few moments earlier. Peterson half expected Gregor to begin frothing at the mouth and latch on to his ankle. Feeling bone tired, Peterson leaned up against a car parked on the side of the curb and closed his eyes as Gregor launched into his tirade. Peterson heard a lot of words being thrown at him, most of them having to do with his ass being in a sling, but he barely heard them, and they washed over his mind without leaving any kind of wake.

He only became aware that Gregor was all through when a silence stretched in the street. He opened his eyes, and the man was standing in front of him, red faced, both hands on his hips. "Well, what do you have to say for yourself?"

With a grunt of effort Peterson pushed himself off the car. Two blocks down he could see his house, surrounded with police tape and flooded with activity. Wearily he turned his eyes back to Gregor. "We got the killer," he said, hooking his thumb over his shoulder.

"What the hell are you talking about? *We* didn't do anything. *You* went off half-cocked with half my department. I turn around for a second and you and Partridge and six of my members had disappeared." He grabbed a fistful of Peterson's shirt, and for a second he thought Gregor was going to clock him. "I'm not touching this one with a ten-foot pool."

Peterson put his face close to Gregor's, smelled the man's breath and his fear. "You sure about that, cap? How's the brass going to feel when a member who was medically suspended went off on a rogue mission and managed to stop a multiple murderer? How they going to react when they find out you had nothing to do with it?"

"It'll all be pinned on you," he said, looking very cautious now.

"Or, it could be pinned on you. Think about it, you made up this daring plan on the spot. Pulled it off with almost no collateral damage. Sylvia got hit, but she'll survive, probably get a damn medal. You brought this guy down. You'll be a bloody hero."

Gregor released Peterson's shirt and stepped a few feet back from him. His eyes were hooded and wary. "Why would you say such a thing?"

"Self-preservation," Peterson responded. "Eventually I'm going to come back to work, and I don't want you stomping on my career in the meantime. Second, I pulled Denly and Partridge in with me, and I don't want anything negative to come down on them. I'm prepared to give you the glory, Gregor. No muss, no fuss."

Both men stood facing each other, breaths coming in silver puffs that slowly floated to the night sky. The snow was coming down in lazy flakes, the intensity waning, and Peterson could see the twinkling lights of the night stars ahead. Finally, Gregor pointed a finger toward Peterson's chest. "If you're yanking my crank on this one, Jack, you're a dead man."

Peterson held up two fingers. "Scout's honor," he said, and he pushed past Gregor. He just wanted to go home.

Juliette and Adam were in the back of an ambulance when he walked up, parked kitty-corner to his house. The medic outside told him that there were both suffering from shock but would probably be fine. They would be taken to the hospital for precaution only but would likely be released later in the morning. He poked his head around the rear doors of the ambulance and peered inside. Both were sitting on the side bed, Adam with his feet tucked under his body and his head resting on his mother's shoulder. His eyes were closed, and Peterson figured he was asleep. Juliette stared straight ahead, eyes wide and darting like a spooked rabbit, and she clutched her son a little tighter when she took in Peterson's form.

Without a word, he climbed into the back and sat across from her, put his hands in his lap, and gave her a half smile that wasn't returned. She not so much looked at him but through him, and Peterson found it disquieting. Who knows what kind of mental games the killer had played with them while they were in his custody. He wasn't so sure that he wanted to know.

"How you holding up?" he asked, and he saw that her breathing was tight and tense, as if her self control was hanging on by a very thin thread. She made to speak, but closed her mouth again, her lips forming a tight line across her face. She looked to have aged about ten years, and she had dark bags under her eyes that gave her a sunken appearance. When he reached to touch her knee, she pulled away violently, her knee striking the side of the ambulance wall. Adam stirred in her arms but didn't wake up.

She looked upon Peterson fiercely, and he found himself drawing back. "That monster almost killed us, Jack. He almost killed my baby. And the only reason he came after us was because of you."

"I know," he said. "And I'm sorry, I never thought that would happen."

Juliette held her son tighter and her face hardened. "Why do people always get hurt around you? Why do you always come out of it unscathed?"

He opened his mouth to respond, but someone coughed in the back of the ambulance. He looked to see a EMT standing there, looking uncomfortable. He said, "Sorry, sir, I need to, uh, take the lady and her son to the hospital."

Peterson nodded and stepped out of the ambulance, watched as the EMT climbed in the back and closed the door. Juliette never looked at him, just stared straight ahead and held her son close.

Fifty-Four

He watched the ambulance drive away until it turned a corner and was out of sight. He sighed once, looked back up at his house. The usual teem of activity ebbed and flowed, scene security standing around looking bored, upper brass polishing themselves, getting ready for the interviews that were soon to follow. A pair of forensic officers had their flashlights trained on the bullet holes on the Pathfinder, a third one was swabbing some of Sylvia's blood. He wondered if, when the reporters arrived, any would remember this having been a crime scene just a few months earlier. Who really remembers anything unless it directly affects them anyway?

He received no protests from the scene security officers when he asked them if he could go inside, and he went past them as if parting the Red Sea. There were a couple of members standing around the kitchen looking slightly embarrassed when Peterson nodded to them, but they said nothing as he walked past. Peterson hesitated slightly at the foot of the stairs, took a deep breath, and climbed up, reaching the top landing feeling hardly out of breath and only a slight chill on his skin to indicate that he was sweating.

There was a fourth forensic officer in the bedroom, taking photographs with a huge digital camera. He was a slight man, Asian, with spiky black hair that shot in odd angles. He was about to say something to Peterson as he approached, but shut his mouth quickly when he noticed who Peterson was.

"It's okay," Peterson said, stopping at the threshold of the door. "I'm not coming in. Don't want to contaminate what you're doing here." He pointed to the carpet where he had dropped his phone. "I was just wondering if I could that." He wanted to call Denly and update him on Sylvia's condition.

The tech considered Peterson's request and then nodded, walking over and retrieving his phone. When he handed it to Peterson he said, "Here you go, detective. I'm uh, sorry about your wife and all."

Peterson nodded, a lump forming in his throat. "Yeah, me too," he said. He thanked the officer and turned around, pausing at the top to open his cell phone. He saw that there was a missed call and a message left from Graham Matthews, and he brought the phone up to his ear to listen to the message.

"Hey, Jack, it's Graham. Sorry for calling you so late, but you said to call whenever I got a result. It wasn't easy, they don't have an electronic database here and I had to go through the prints by hand. Anyway, if you got a pen handy I'll give you the name of the person I identified to the prints on the duct tape."

Graham gave him the name, and Peterson found that he didn't need a pen at all. He closed the phone and put it back in his pocket, feeling much more tired than before.

Fifty-Five

"I'm afraid that date is not going to work for me," the defence lawyer said, flipping through a screen on his iPhone. Peterson had walked into the trial already in progress, but it was winding down. He got the sense that there were some issues being hammered out and that both parties were making a new date to continue the trial.

It had been a day and a half since the events at his house, and he had spent most of it doing background checks and trying to establish a connection to the name that Matthews had provided him. This had proved difficult as he was still on a medical suspension and had to conduct business through Prince and Matthews as conduits.

"That would work for me," the prosecution said, as he wrote a date down on his calendar. The courtroom was mostly empty, this being the last trial of the day, and the only persons in attendance were the crown, defence, court house staff, the accused, and one or two witnesses and rubberneckers. Eventually, the matter was settled and the court clerk ordered everyone to rise and the grey hair judged walked off the bench and through a set of double doors in the back. Once he was gone, Peterson sat back down on the hard-wooden bench in the back, watching as the various players collected their belongings and left. Soon he was alone with the court house staff, which included the court clerk and the stenographer.

The stenographer noticed Peterson sitting in the back and smiled at him, waving a hand in his direction. He nodded himself and stood up, walking to the front of the courtroom while the stenographer sat at her desk, making a few final notes on her typecast machine.

"Hello, Jessica," he said as he stopped in front of her desk.

"Detective Peterson," she said in response. "I didn't expect to see you so soon." She gave him a wry smile as she shut her computer down. "Do you need me to find another file for you?"

"No, but I did want to thank you for your help." This morning Jessica was wearing a long, brown skirt that reached to her ankles and a bulky white cardigan that was buttoned to her neck. Her thick-framed glasses were perched on the top of her head. "And I've been thinking about what you said, about justice." She gave him a curious glance but said nothing. "My wife was killed by someone I thought was a friend, someone I trusted. He was caught and punished and will probably never get out of jail. But sometimes I wish for more. Why should he live while my wife is dead?"

She nodded, crossed her arms over her chest. "It's not fair."

"No," he agreed, and he sat back on the edge of the table, put his hands on his knees. "Tell me, when did you decide to kill them, *Isabella*?"

They had moved to the front set of pews and sat beside each other, Peterson on the outside, Isabella Green to his right. Their knees were touching, but she didn't seem to mind. When he called her by her name, her real name, she had said nothing, showed no emotion, and had merely nodded, as if was an inevitability that she had expected, had prepared for. She had offered no resistance when Peterson invited her to sit with him on the pew that was so often occupied by victim and accused alike, and Peterson wondered where the pair of them fit into the grand scheme of things. Each of them was sinner and saint, each of them with a dark and haunted past.

"I had originally suspected that it was someone from the courthouse, I just wasn't quite sure who," Peterson said. Isabella sat with her back stiff, staring straight ahead, hands clasped in her lap as if in prayer. "It was the only way someone could access the case file, get rid of the documents. More than that, there was the issue of timing. A few weeks after Bryce Turner's charges were dismissed, he was killed. I figured that it would have to have been someone who had been present at the trial."

Isabella said, "Nothing had changed. He was still the same pig, skirting the system, absolving himself of any responsibility."

"So, you reached out and hired a killer?"

She turned to face him, eyes alive with anger. "Yes. They needed to pay."

"What about Katrina Brant? Detective Nielsen? Them too?"

"I never wanted her to get hurt, that was an accident. But Nielsen is just as guilty as they are. You may be a good cop, Detective Peterson, but he stood by and did nothing. Now he'll live out the rest of his miserable life in comfort."

Peterson shook his head slowly. "Not that long, I'm afraid. We were able to get to him before your killer, but he's got advanced cancer. Bone. Doctors give him maybe two months at the most, probably less." He stood up and inched from the pew, putting his hands in his coat pockets and looked down at her.

She resumed her faraway stare, looking beyond the judge's seat and through the wall. "I went to the river where you crashed your car," he said. "Why fake your own death?"

She chewed her bottom lip before answering, looked up at him. "I got tired of the way people were looking at me, like I was this broken doll. I wanted a fresh start, to become someone else. And it had worked until Turner came in the courtroom. He saw me, you know? And he didn't even know who I was. He had forgotten all about me, they all did."

Peterson heard movement from the doors and looked to see Officer Berkeley poking her head in. He nodded at her and the door closed, muffled voices beyond the entryway. "Not everyone," Peterson said, and he turned back at the door as it opened fully, and Berkeley led a dishevelled man through. He was dressed in the exact same clothes that Peterson had seen before, dirty and drab outerwear that crinkled as he walked. Michael Green looked fearfully around the courthouse, to Peterson, and back to Berkeley. Probably the only time he had been in places like this was when he had been charged for some crime of vagrancy or another, and he likely half expected he was going to be thrown in jail.

By the time Green turned back to Peterson, Isabella had twisted in her seat and was watching the homeless man approach.

Green's eyes settled on his daughter, and he took a step back as if struck, and Berkeley put out an arm to stabilize him. "Isabella?" he croaked, and on unsteady feet he walked towards her, dreamlike, and gently pushed Peterson aside as he entered the pew. He sunk to his knees in front of her, reaching out a shaking hand and placing it tentatively on her leg, testing her for substantiality.

His fingers clawed and clutched at her skirt, and he sunk his head on to her lap and began to sob, his back heaving with the effort. Isabella sat stock still, hands above her father's head, inches above his hair. Her lower lip began trembling, tears collecting in her eyes, and then she placed her hands on her father's head, bent over, and held him tightly. Her own cries were soft, muted, and the pair held on to each other as their shared pain rolled through them.

Peterson watched for a moment and stepped back to join Berkeley at the back of the courthouse. She nodded to him as he stood beside her. She cleared her throat and asked quietly, "How long should we give them?"

Peterson looked back to reunited father and daughter, separated by so much pain and anguish, and about to be separated again, perhaps forever. After this, Isabella would be arrested and charged with a litany of crimes, including murder and conspiracy to commit murder. Chances were she would never see the outside of a prison ever again.

He said, "Give them as much time as they need," and he patted Berkeley on the shoulder and pushed through the courthouse doors, the sounds of Michael Green's sobs echoing through the empty corridors.

Fifty-Six

Five days later Peterson stood on his front lawn, sweating while working at removing the "For Sale" sign on his front lawn. Most of the snow had receded, the little remnants left found only in shadowed sections, hiding from the bright orange afternoon sun that blazed overhead. The crime scene techs had finished up with his house on the third day, and he had stayed with Denly during the interim, during which time he had alternated watching football and hockey with Charlie and playing with his kids in the snow. Denly had looked on through the kitchen window, still wheelchair-bound for the next couple of weeks. Partridge was still being kept in the hospital, in stable condition, and was expected to make a full recovery.

Peterson stepped back a moment to wipe the sweat off his brow, using the back of his gloved hand to mop up the sheen that had collected on his forehead. As he shrugged off his jacket, he heard a car pulling up to the curb, and he turned to see Archie Prince putting a brown Ford Crown Victoria into park, lumbering out of the driver's seat.

Peterson waved a hand at him as the man walked up to him. Prince was wearing a pair of flat leather shoes and he stopped where the sidewalk met the lawn, hesitant to step onto the sodden grass. Peterson hung his jacket on the sign and met Prince at the edge of the pavement, shaking his naked hand with his own gloved one.

"Damn hot day," Prince said, releasing Peterson's hand. Prince was wearing a set of faded blue jeans that looked too big for him, a throwback to his heavier days, and a light brown rain jacket that crinkled as he moved.

"Damn nice day," Peterson countered. "Nice not to be wet for once."

"It'll start raining soon, just a little break in the weather."

Peterson nodded. Soon they'd be entering the true rainy season, through January to February, and it could well be days and weeks before they'd see the sun again. "I'd thought you'd like to know that they pulled buddy from the lake," Prince said.

Peterson nodded, looking out to the Green Lake which rippled like an emerald jewel in the distance. With the warmer weather, the ice had slowly receded, and he had seen the divers and dredgers out, searching for the killer's body in the dark water. Earlier in the week he had watched as a mobile body removal service had collected a body bag from the shore and had driven towards the county morgue. Life could resume on the lake, at least in that respect, though it would probably be some time before people started swimming there again, even after the water warmed up.

"They got an ID from his fingerprints," Prince continued. "Some military guy that was discharged a few years back. Seems like he enjoyed the action a little too much, made some of the head shrinkers a little jumpy."

"Didn't stop him from continuing on."

"Do what you're good at, I guess," Prince commented. He nodded toward the "For Sale" sign. Peterson had succeeded in removing the main part and was now trying to dig the post out of the frozen ground. "What's up with that? I thought you were selling."

Peterson shook his head. "Nah, nobody's biting anyway, bad time to sell." He placed his hands in his pockets and sighed. "Besides, I got some things inside I need to take care of, and I got time for projects now. Might as well make the most of it."

"Your suspension. How's that looking?"

"Day at a time," he said. "I have an appointment with a shrink at the end of the week, start talking some things through, I guess."

Prince nodded and seemed eager to change the topic. A not-too-kind smile settled on his face. "Hey, you hear that your pal Gregor's getting a promotion?"

"I thought I heard something about that," Peterson said. "Some political liaison thing? Getting posted to HQ in a few months?"

"That's it, yeah. Apparently, the brass was so impressed with how he handled this cluster that they felt obliged to give him another star on his cap."

"Imagine that," Peterson said, smiling. "I guess when I get back I won't have to deal with him at WestOps."

Prince chuckled. "Yeah, imagine that. What happened with that lady that was here?"

"Juliette?" Peterson shifted slightly, looked off into the distance. "She took off. Her and her son went up north, home, I guess."

"That's too bad," Prince commented. "I interviewed her for this whole deal. Seems like a nice lady."

"She is that," Peterson agreed. Prince shook Peterson's hand, wished him good luck, and lumbered back to his car. He opened the door but stopped short of getting in. "Hey, you call Harriet yet?" he yelled from across the way.

Peterson hooked his head towards his work on the "For Sale" sign. "It's on my list," he called. "As soon as I finish this." Prince nodded, satisfied, and climbed back into his car. It rumbled to life, and Prince waved at him as he drove off. Peterson watched him go until his car was out of sight and turned to look out of the horizon. The sky was a clear, intense blue, but in the far distance he could see grey clouds forming above the mountains. In another few hours it would bring rain and maybe even worse. But for now, the sun shone brightly, and it felt warm on his face. For now, that was just fine.

Made in the USA
Columbia, SC
26 August 2017